W9-BMN-688

Death at Blenheim Palace

ROBIN PAIGE

BERKLEY PRIME CRIME BOOKS, NEW YORK

THE BERKLEY PUBLISHING GROUP
Published by the Penguin Group
Penguin Group (USA) Inc.
375 Hudson Street, New York, New York 10014, USA
Penguin Group (Canada), 90 Eglinton Avenue East, Suite 700, Toronto, Ontario M4P 2Y3, Canada
(a division of Pearson Penguin Canada Inc.)
Penguin Books Ltd., 80 Strand, London WC2R 0RL, England
Penguin Books Ireland, 25 St. Stephen's Green, Dublin 2, Ireland (a division of Penguin Books Ltd.)
Penguin Group (Australia), 250 Camberwell Road, Camberwell, Victoria 3124, Australia
(a division of Pearson Australia Group Pty. Ltd.)
Penguin Books India Pvt. Ltd., 11 Community Centre, Panchsheel Park, New Delhi—110 017, India
Penguin Group (NZ), Cnr. Airborne and Rosedale Roads, Albany, Auckland 1310, New Zealand
(a division of Pearson New Zealand Ltd.)
Penguin Books (South Africa) (Pty.) Ltd., 24 Sturdee Avenue, Rosebank, Johannesburg 2196,
South Africa

Penguin Books Ltd., Registered Offices: 80 Strand, London WC2R 0RL, England

This is a work of fiction. Names, characters, places, and incidents either are the product of the authors'
imagination or are used fictitiously, and any resemblance to actual persons, living or dead, business es-
tablishments, events, or locales is entirely coincidental. The publisher does not have any control over
and does not assume any responsibility for author or third-party websites or their content.

DEATH AT BLENHEIM PALACE

A Berkley Prime Crime Book / published by arrangement with the authors

PRINTING HISTORY
Berkley Prime Crime hardcover edition / February 2005
Berkley Prime Crime mass-market edition / February 2006

Copyright © 2005 by Susan Wittig Albert and Bill Albert.
Cover illustration by Teresa Fasolino.
Cover design by Annette Fiore.

ISBN: 0-425-20237-2

BERKLEY® PRIME CRIME
Berkley Prime Crime Books are published by The Berkley Publishing Group,
a division of Penguin Group (USA) Inc.,
375 Hudson Street, New York, New York 10014.
The name BERKLEY PRIME CRIME and the BERKLEY PRIME CRIME design
are trademarks belonging to Penguin Group (USA) Inc.

PRINTED IN THE UNITED STATES OF AMERICA

10 9 8 7 6 5 4 3 2 1

CAST OF CHARACTERS
* Indicates historical persons

Blenheim Palace: Residents and Visitors

*Charles Richard John Spencer-Churchill (Sunny), the ninth Duke of Marlborough and master of Blenheim Palace

*Consuelo Vanderbilt Spencer-Churchill, the twelfth Duchess of Marlborough and mistress of Blenheim Palace

Charles, Lord Sheridan, Baron Somersworth and amateur forensic detective

Lady Kathryn Ardleigh Sheridan, aka Beryl Bardwell, author of a number of popular novels

*Winston Leonard Spencer-Churchill, son of Randolph and Jennie Churchill, first cousin to the Duke, and Member of Parliament

*Gladys Deacon, unconventional American beauty who dazzled European society in the early 1900s, the Duke's lover

Lord Henry Northcote (Botsy), Miss Deacon's suitor

Blenheim Staff

Mr. Stevens, butler

Alfred, footman

Mrs. Raleigh, housekeeper

Kitty, Ruth, Bess, housemaids

Mr. Meloy, estate agent

Badger, fishery manager

Woodstock Residents and Visitors

Bulls-eye

Dawkins

Ashmolean Museum Staff

John Buttersworth, Curator of Classical Antiquities

*T. E. Lawrence (Ned), museum volunteer, amateur antiquarian, later the legendary Lawrence of Arabia

We shape our dwellings,
and afterwards our dwellings shape us.

—Sir Winston Churchill

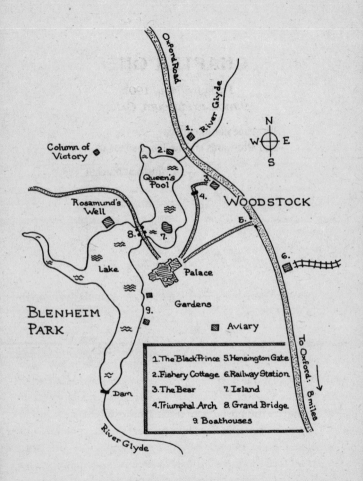

CHAPTER ONE

⊷═◅⊶

The Ashmolean Museum, the oldest public museum in Britain, houses the University of Oxford's unrivaled collection of art and antiquities from Europe, the Middle East, and Asia.

The Ashmolean Museum
Arthur MacGregor

"Oh, sir!" the boy cried excitedly, as John Buttersworth stepped into the conservation laboratory in the basement of the Ashmolean. "The shipment from Crete has arrived at last! Shall we open it, sir?"

Buttersworth regarded the large wooden crate in the middle of the floor. He did not mind the administrative routine of his post as Curator of Classical Collections, and he particularly enjoyed the business of setting up exhibits, such as the display of items from the Knossos excavation, scheduled to open next week. But the happiest moments in his life came when he could indulge his heart's true passion: holding and fondling the objects themselves, each one with its own beauty, its own history, its own secret story. Ah, yes, the shipment from Crete. He rubbed his hands together.

"Well, then, my boy," he exclaimed. "By all means, let's have a go at it!"

Ned Lawrence fetched a long screwdriver and a hammer so ancient that it might have been mislaid from a Roman collection, and eagerly attacked the crate. Buttersworth stood to one side, admiring the deft way the boy handled the tools. Robust and sturdy, young Lawrence had the maturity and discipline of someone much older, and he stood out from all the other Oxford lads who hung about the museum, professing an interest in antiquities and begging to go on the local digs. He was a great favorite among the staff, all of whom felt that, as an archaeologist, he had the stuff in him to go far.

In a few moments, Ned had the lid up and off. Inside, packed in clean straw, were a number of smaller crates, with a large envelope on top. Buttersworth opened the envelope, removed a typed inventory, and began to compare the numbers with those stamped on the small crates that Ned lifted out and stacked to one side. There were nearly a dozen of them.

Buttersworth took off his gold-rimmed spectacles and polished them on his pocket-handkerchief. "Let's start with this one," he said, nodding at the top crate. "It should contain a five-inch Roman green glass pitcher."

Ned placed the small crate on the bench and applied the hammer and screwdriver until the top came loose. Buttersworth pushed the straw aside and carefully lifted out a small blown-glass pitcher. Turning it in his hands, he gave an involuntary sigh of purely sensual pleasure. The piece was exquisite, the shape round and voluptuous, the design delicate and skillfully executed. Originally, the glass had been a translucent green, but after nearly two millennia in an alkaline soil, it had taken on a metallic irridescence. The surface was a dancing rainbow of yellows, reds, and blues.

Ned seemed to be holding his breath, his eyes fixed on the pitcher. For a moment, neither spoke as Buttersworth held it up and turned it slowly, so that it caught and reflected the light.

"It's perfect," Ned said at last, reverentially. "Who owned it, I wonder—and what happened to him?" He paused, wrinkling his forehead. "No, it would have belonged to a woman, wouldn't it? I wonder how she got it. What did she think of it? Did she admire it because it was so beautiful? Or was it just something to hold—what? Wine? Water?"

Buttersworth smiled. This was what he liked most about young Lawrence: his desire, rare in one so young, to know the unknowable, to ask questions and imagine answers. If he were really determined to become an archaeologist, this desire of his was essential, for the quest for answers was what drove men of Buttersworth's profession. The need to know the who, what, how, and why of these ancient objects—some with their own intrinsic aesthetic value, others plain and insignificant-looking, still others monstrous and ugly, yet beautiful in their ugliness. The need to understand, to unearth, to investigate, to analyze, and, above all, to appreciate, to *feel*.

Buttersworth beamed at his protégé. "Good questions, lad. But there is another also to be answered." He set the pitcher safely on the shelf and stepped back. "The real question is how such a fragile object managed to survive all the forces that have been set against it throughout the centuries. And not just natural forces, either. There have been vandals in every age, and Philistines who wouldn't recognize the value of a piece like this beyond the price it would bring." He rubbed his hands again. "Now, let us see what other treasures we have been sent."

They had just completed the inventory when a bell rang, signaling that Buttersworth was wanted in the reception area. Still engrossed with the objects, Buttersworth sent Ned off to find out what was needed. Some moments later, he was back. He closed the door behind him and spoke in a low voice.

"There's a lady in the hallway, sir. She refuses to wait upstairs. She insists on speaking to you privately."

Intent on a rose-colored glass ampulla from the first century, Buttersworth spoke absently. "A lady, eh? What does she want?"

Ned frowned. "Wouldn't give her name or state her business. She might be a patron, but——" He shrugged.

Buttersworth put down the perfume bottle with an inward sigh. Maintaining cordial relations with wealthy benefactresses was one of his duties, but certainly not his favorite. He was much better with objects—the older the better, of course—than with people, and he was never at his best with women, who often wanted to complain about something or other, usually something inconsequential.

"Well, I suppose I must," he said, resigned. "Show her in, Ned. And I should like you to go upstairs and ask Mr. Gilkes for the catalogue of Roman glass in storage. There are one or two objects I want to compare."

With a show of exaggerated formality, Ned opened the door and bowed the lady in. She was modestly dressed in a dark walking suit, dark gloves, and a blue straw hat with an unassuming silk bow. Her face was swathed in a dark blue veil, but through its folds, Buttersworth could see that it was quite striking. The nose, especially—classic, very like the nose on a piece of ancient Greek statuary. And the eyes, blue and set wide apart. He did not know her—had he ever seen her, he would surely not have forgotten that stunning Grecian profile—and from her unpretentious dress, he judged that she was not one of the museum's patronesses, those elegant ladies who swept in with an air of ostentatious wealth and offered him their hands as if they owned the place.

She did not offer her hand. "You are John Buttersworth?" Her voice was low, pleasant, cultured. A lady's secretary, perhaps.

"I am." Buttersworth cleared his throat. "How may I be of service, madam?"

"I understand that you are the Ashmolean's expert on classical antiquities."

Buttersworth inclined his head. "I have that honor."

"Very well, then. My employer has asked me to bring these items to you. She would like your opinion of their value." The veiled woman produced a brown leather pouch from her purse and placed it on the table.

Their value? Buttersworth was momentarily amused. The Ashmolean was not a pawnshop. But the woman might be acting as an agent for a potential donor. There would certainly be no harm in having a look. He loosened the drawstring and emptied five small objects onto the table, each one tidily wrapped in tissue paper. He chose one, undid the tissue, and held in his hand the effigy of a large beetle, covered with a turquoise glaze.

Surprised, he reached into his pocket for his jeweler's loupe, pushed his spectacles onto his forehead, and put the loupe in his left eye. Squinting, he examined the beetle's underside, which was engraved with intaglio hieroglyphics.

The piece was a seal, the hieroglyphics mirror images of the impressions they would make in wax or clay. An Egyptian scarab, Eighteenth Dynasty, he thought. *A pretty piece of faience, of the sort that often turned up in the Cairo bazaars.*

"Mmm," he said.

The woman said nothing.

The second item proved to be a small polished stone of a smoky color, with three rectangular faces, the ends cut as triangles. The rectangles were covered with intaglio designs. Buttersworth's pulse quickened. It was a Minoan prism seal from Crete, Bronze Age, perhaps fifteenth century B.C. It was rare, quite rare, and very beautiful.

With growing excitement, he unwrapped the remaining three pieces and held them in the palm of his hand. They had the polished sheen of semiprecious gems, and each bore intaglio engravings. He recognized them as Hellenistic seal-stones, the red cornelian, the green olivine, the blue chalcedony. Fine pieces, very fine indeed, and Buttersworth felt an intense stirring of desire, of the sort that some men felt for beautiful women. He should certainly be pleased—more than that, he should be *thrilled*—to have them in the Ashmolean's collection.

He repocketed his jeweler's loupe, replaced his spectacles, and managed to refocus his attention from the specimens to the woman—now, with more than a little curiosity. These stones did not have the look of a casual collection. Their appearance in a group suggested that the person who assembled them had possessed a well-trained eye, the patience of an experienced collector, and rather a lot of money.

Buttersworth felt a flutter of unease. He had learned to be careful when it came to business of this sort. One of his jobs was to protect the museum from any threat of scandal, a task that he had recently to undertake. "How did you say your mistress came by these?" he asked tentatively.

"I did not say." If the woman found the question offensive, she did not reveal it. Behind her veil, her expression was unperturbed.

"Do you know if she has similar pieces?"

She gave a slight smile. "Perhaps," she said, in a tone of ambiguous promise. "I cannot be sure, but I think it likely."

So there *were* others! Buttersworth almost stammered in his eagerness: "And . . . and it is her intention to . . . to sell them?"

But of course one had to be careful, oh, yes, indeed, very careful. The museum had all too many critics these days. One had to be absolutely certain that any acquisition was appropriately documented and came without even a whisper of illegitimacy. Even as he reminded himself of this, however, Buttersworth was mentally reviewing the possible sources of funds by which the Ashmolean might acquire these pieces, and the others—oh, yes, the others, certainly—before they vanished into the greedy hands of a private collector, as had the Marlborough Gemstones some thirty years before. The Ashmolean had wanted desperately to acquire that marvelous collection when the seventh duke sold them, but had unfortunately lacked the funds. Christie's had knocked them down to thirty-five thousand guineas.

At the thought of the Marlborough Gemstones, Buttersworth's fluttering uneasiness began to take on a more solid form, and he frowned. Was it possible that these gemstones were—

He reached for the Minoan prism seal to have another look, but the woman was already rewrapping the pieces and replacing them carefully in the leather pouch.

"I cannot speak to my employer's future intentions," she said. "But I assume from your look of interest that these items are of some value. I was asked to inquire how much they are worth."

"I am unable to say exactly," Buttersworth replied warily. "The individual items would be worth more as part of a collection, the value of which of course depends upon its breadth and scope. However, you may tell your employer that if she wishes to dispose of them, the museum might be willing to make an offer."

Might be willing? John Buttersworth almost betrayed himself with a guilty chuckle. He would give his eyeteeth to have those seal-stones.

"Thank you." The woman put the pouch into her purse. "I shall report your interest to the Duchess. That is, to my employer." She bit her lip in sudden vexation at the slip of tongue that gave too much away. Coloring, obviously flustered, she raised her chin. "Good day, sir."

Buttersworth stared at the closed door. The Duchess. The woman could only have been speaking of the Duchess of Marlborough, whose residence, Blenheim Palace, was not above seven miles away. And then a thought struck him, a thought of such enormity that it fairly took his breath away. Perhaps the entire collection of Marlborough Gemstones had not been auctioned, as was thought! Perhaps there were others. Perhaps—

He frowned. But why should it be the Duchess of Marlborough who was making this inquiry, when the gems— if these were indeed part of the original collection—had belonged to the family of the Duke? And how would the Duke respond if he were to discover at some later date that the Duchess, unauthorized, had sold his family heirlooms?

Given what he knew about the Duke's efforts to reestablish the Marlborough treasures after the reprehensible spoliations of his father and grandfather, he doubted if the response would be favorable.

Upon reflection, John Buttersworth began to feel that the Ashmolean might not be so anxious, after all, to possess those classical gems.

CHAPTER TWO

Friday, 8 May
Blenheim Palace

Some respectable looking young women, in the service of middle-class and fashionable families, are connected with burglars and have been recommended to their places through their influence.

London Labour and the London Poor (1861)
Henry Mayhew

Kitty had finally learnt to make her way about the great house without getting lost.

When she first came into service at Blenheim some three months before, she could go about only in the company of one of the other housemaids, and she was frequently turned around. The Duke's house—the palace, everybody called it, which in Kitty's opinion it certainly was, being an awfully grand place, filled with enormous paintings and all sorts of ornaments on the walls and shelves—was a confusing labyrinth of corridors and rooms, and rooms inside of rooms. She so often found herself turned around when she went out of one and into another that it was like riding on a merry-go-round, and when you got off, you were dizzy and had not an idea in your silly head where you were.

Kitty, of course, was not new to service, although she did not intend to make it her life's work. She had been employed in several great houses—not very long in any, to be sure, but long enough to get a good character and not call attention to her departure—and Blenheim Palace was like most of the others, except in one important regard. It was seriously understaffed. Even Mrs. Raleigh, the head housekeeper, had admitted the difficulty, when Kitty, during her interview, expressed some surprise that there were only ten housemaids. Ten!

"Why, at Welbeck Abbey," she had said, nodding at the letter of character signed by the Duchess of Portland's housekeeper, "we had fourteen housemaids, and the house was ever so much smaller than . . . *this.*" The words *this monstrosity* had been on the tip of her tongue, but she thought it better to keep her opinion to herself. Still and all, why anybody should actually want to live in such a place was beyond her imagining.

"The family is small," Mrs. Raleigh said in a conciliatory tone, "just the Duke and Duchess and their two little boys. And of course we always bring in help from the village when we have a large number of guests." She brushed back an escaped wisp of sparse, graying hair. Quite an elderly, frail-looking woman she was, Kitty thought, to have charge of such a large house, especially without the staff to keep it proper.

Mrs. Raleigh was continuing in a sniffy tone. "All the housemaids gladly share the work. I feel sure that you will not find your duties exceedingly arduous."

Kitty suppressed a laugh. She knew exactly what "gladly share the work" meant, and what the duties would be, especially with only ten pairs of hands—ten!—to share the labor. She knew, too, that it was getting much harder to find experienced housemaids these days, what with girls wanting to work in factories, or running off to the cities to make something of themselves. She had no fear that her application would be rejected, even though she had asked for the top wage: twenty-two pounds a year, to be paid monthly.

She was right. She was hired on the spot, and she pretended not to notice Mrs. Raleigh's vast sigh of relief when she said that she was available to begin her duties the next day.

Like the other country houses in which Kitty had been employed, Blenheim had its own order of duties. If she wanted to get along in her work, the first thing she had to do was to learn the house's schedule, its rules, who was responsible for what, and where people were supposed to be at any given time. It also helped, of course, to know who really had the authority, which was not always as immediately obvious as it might seem from the Order of Duties posted in the housemaids' sitting room.

The first candle of the day was lit at six A.M. in Housemaids Heights, the southeast tower where the housemaids, kitchen maids, laundresses, and stillroom maids slept, two together in small rooms as bare as cells in a nunnery. Kitty shared her cell with Ruth, a tidy, earnest young woman whose family lived in nearby Woodstock, with whom she had quickly struck up a friendship. It was particularly useful, Kitty had found, to have a friend who was well-acquainted with the local village.

Combed and pinned and aproned, the ten housemaids made their way downstairs for two hours of morning chores—opening draperies, sweeping carpets with wet tea leaves to absorb the dust, dusting furniture, polishing brasses,

lighting fires in bedrooms and dressing rooms and seeing that
the coal-scuttles were properly filled, and carrying brass jugs
of hot water to ladies and gentlemen—all this before assem-
bling for breakfast in the servants' hall, where the daily dish
of above-stairs gossip was served up together with hot tea,
cold meat pie, and a great deal of teasing and practical jokery
among the porters and hall boys and pages and odd men (the
men who did all the odd jobs). The six footmen took their
breakfasts and other meals in the butler's pantry, so Kitty did
not often see Alfred, the chap who had been at Carleton
House and Welbeck Abbey with her. Which was just as well,
she told herself, for she regretted having encouraged his
attentions—not because she hadn't enjoyed them, but because one shouldn't mix business and pleasure. And also
because having once encouraged him, she couldn't seem to
discourage him. Now he was writing notes to her, foolish little love notes, which was dangerous. In some households, it
could mean that both of them would be sacked.

In general, the Blenheim servants seemed to be a disor-
derly lot, much less disciplined, Kitty thought, than their
counterparts at the other houses where she had served. Most
seemed to know a great deal more than they ought about
what was going on above stairs, where on houseparty weekends, the guests played musical beds with as much gay
abandon as the servants below-stairs played musical chairs.

Kitty did not mind the gossip and bawdy jokes, but she
did think that the lack of discipline among the servants
showed how the house was managed. It was a straw in the
wind, so to say, which she was (all taken in all) not sorry to
see. It had been her experience that when the uppers—the
butler, housekeeper, and cook—tolerated rowdy behavior
among the lowers, they were less attentive in other matters, as

well. This seemed borne out by the rumors she'd heard, such as the kitchen maids' illicit trade in beef and bread, some of which flew out the back door and down to the village faster than it could be served up at table. And the coachmen were said to enjoy a profitable connivance with regard to their livery, scheming with the tailor to substitute their old livery for the new suits the Duchess ordered for them and pocketing the difference. Lax a little, lose a lot, Kitty's old gram used to say, and here at Blenheim, Gram looked like being right.

The rest of Kitty's day was as full as its first few hours. At nine, the household gathered for prayers in the chapel, and afterward the housemaids hurried off to the bedchambers of family and guests, where they spent the morning making beds, hanging up clothing, dusting, and emptying wash basins and chamber pots. In the afternoon, they were sent in pairs to dust the Great Hall, the Long Library, and the drawing rooms. After tea, the upstairs work resumed, as they carried more cans and jugs of hot water, laid things out for the ladies' and gentlemen's before-dinner baths—soap and sponge bowls, towels and mats—and made up the bedroom fires. Then the baths had to be emptied, and the beds turned down, and then there was supper at nine. And finally, just before the family and guests retired, the maids were back in the rooms, making up the bedroom fires and putting warming pans in the beds, for the rooms were cold as the grave. In Housemaids Heights, it might be two or three A.M. before Kitty could snuff out her candle and pull the blanket over her head, to catch four hours of sleep before the next day began.

Bed hadn't come quite so late tonight, since there were no guests in the house. But Kitty's long day was not quite over.

Trying to quell her mounting excitement, she lay beside Ruth until the other young woman began to snore. Then she got out of bed, pinned up her reddish-blond hair, pulled on her clothing and her shoes, and closed the door stealthily behind her. Lighting a candle, she crept down the tower's narrow stairs all the way to the bottom, where the outside door was left off the latch for the servants' late comings and goings—another example of the laxness of the house.

Outdoors, Kitty extinguished her candle and tucked it behind a potted plant, where she could retrieve it on her return. The summer night was softly lit by stars and a pale sliver of moon, and a low mist rose from the wet grass. At first, she was not exactly sure which path to take, for the directions she had been given seemed confusing, and she had not yet been in this part of the grounds. And there was an owl quavering a low, ominous *whoo-hoo-hoo* somewhere in the trees along the lake—a sure portent of death, Gram used to say.

But Kitty had never let Gram's superstitious nonsense frighten her, and she put the thought out of her mind. After a few moments of uncertainty, she found herself on the path to the boathouse, and went forward with greater confidence. She had done this sort of thing before, of course, at other houses: getting up in the middle of the night, making her way silently down the back stairs, meeting her accomplice, taking the items, and delivering them into the waiting hands. It was all part of the job.

But tonight was different. Tonight, her accomplice—that silly, romantic boy who persisted in writing love notes to her—was safe in his bed, asleep, and what she was doing was not part of the job. Tonight's adventure was wholly her own, and she would pocket the profit herself. Tonight was *her* night, and the thought filled her with an excitement that was heightened by the sense that she was taking a rather large risk.

But of course it was a risk, Kitty reminded herself. Life itself was a risk, a game, a big gamble from beginning to end, and you didn't gain a farthing unless you were willing to take a chance. Well, she was willing. What's more, she wasn't afraid . . . not very much, that is. If her lips were cold and her hands were trembling, she told herself, it was with anticipation, not fear.

She reached the boathouse, found the skiff, and clambered in. Picking up the oars, she began to row. As she leaned into the rhythms of rowing, she and the boat moved over the water as silently as a cloud shadow across the moon, all the way across the lake to the grassy slope beneath Rosamund's Well, a magical spring that had flowed unceasingly for centuries. The spring's waters, Ruth had told her, had wonderfully transforming powers. If you dipped your hand into them and wished, your wish was bound to come true, no matter how wild and silly it was. That was what had happened to Fair Rosamund centuries and centuries ago, Ruth said. Rosamund was just a plain, ordinary girl—a scullery maid in a Woodstock house, people said—until she dipped her hand in the spring and wished to be loved by a king. Not long after, her wish came true. King Henry fell passionately in love with her and would have married her, if he hadn't happened to have a queen already, who was as jealous and mean as anything. But he built her a beautiful house on the hill above the spring, and himself a splendid palace not far away, and whenever he could get away from the queen, he'd come and make love to Rosamund.

Well, Kitty thought, when she finished transacting her

business tonight, she'd dip her hand in that spring, too, and wish that some handsome man with lots of money and power, a duke or a prince or somebody like that, would fall in love with her and get down on his knees and beg her to marry him. But she wouldn't have to depend on magic to have money in her pocket, or wait for some fairy godmother to wave a wand and free her from service. She was about to make *that* happen herself!

As Kitty beached the boat and went toward the spring, she thought with an almost giddy delight that it would not be long before her dreams came true. After tonight, she would have the means to leave the drudgery and hard work behind, to buy jewelry and pretty clothes and hire a ladies' maid who would fix her hair. And she would live in London in a fine house and go to the theater whenever she felt like it. After tonight, nothing would be the same, ever again. Tonight was the end of her old life and the beginning of something brand new and different.

Kitty thought she saw a glimmer of light among the shadowy trees above the well, where Rosamund's house had once stood. He was there waiting for her, she thought with an indrawn breath, and she stepped forward eagerly. And then, just as she reached the spring, there was a shadow behind her, and the soft sound of a footfall. Surprised, she turned, and saw the glint of something shining in the moonlight.

Kitty was half-right. Tonight, her old life would end, but the future she had imagined would not come to pass.

CHAPTER THREE

Wednesday, 13 May
The Ashmolean Museum

❖═◎═❖

There was a brisk traffic in stolen antiquities around the turn of the century, as a number of wealthy industrialists attempted to use the patina of antique treasures to burnish their newly acquired wealth and bolster their sense of belonging to the aristocracy.

The Social Transformation of England: 1837–1914
Albert Williams

Lord Charles Sheridan stood at the door of the Ashmolean's Knossos exhibit, just off the main gallery, and looked around the room, shaking his head in disbelief. It was overwhelming, this immense collection of pottery, stone, and metal artifacts, all of it dug up on the island of Crete, where Arthur Evans, the Ashmolean's chief curator, had recently uncovered a remarkable Minoan palace. It looked as if, Charles thought, the entire contents of the palace were being crated up and transported, bit by bit, to England.

Charles admired Evans's archaeological work and hoped that the new site would open the way toward a better understanding of a hitherto unknown civilization, whose princes had once thought themselves the lords of the earth. But this wholesale exportation of artifacts— Well, some critics argued that it was little more than thievery, just another example of the British Empire's habit of pilfering the priceless treasures of other cultures, and on the whole, Charles had to agree with them. If the precious antiquities could be safeguarded against the attacks of time and human greed, Crete's ancient treasures had better be left in Crete, rather than put on display in an English museum.

If Charles had thought about it, he would also have had to admit that this was rather an odd point of view for a British peer. He was, after all, the fifth Baron Somersworth, patrician owner of a sprawling family estate and country house in Norfolk and holder of a hereditary family seat in the House of Lords. He should have been entirely committed to maintaining and preserving, at all costs, the long and proud traditions of his landowning family and governing class. He should have been wholeheartedly and unreservedly delighted to see the British Empire extending its influence to the far corners of the globe and acquiring the treasures of ancient civilizations to burnish its own.

But these were not traditions from which Charles took any comfort. He had the feeling, as Joseph Chamberlain had remarked in the House of Commons, that the center of power was shifting, the old order giving way to a new, founded on democratic rather than aristocratic principles. In time, he suspected, the landed aristocracy of England would find itself entirely anachronistic, every bit as extinct and forgotten as the unremembered kings and queens of ancient Minoa, and exactly as dead and dusty as the dinosaurs.

"Sheridan!" a voice exclaimed. "So glad to see you! And what do you think of our little exhibit, eh? Quite a sight, is it not?"

Charles turned. The man striding energetically toward him, hand extended, was John Buttersworth, the Ashmolean's Curator of Classical Antiquities.

"Little exhibit?" Charles managed a chuckle. "I must say, Buttersworth, you and the museum have outdone yourselves this time."

"Indeed." Buttersworth beamed. "And there's more to come, Sheridan, much, much more. The number of artifacts Evans is uncovering is simply astounding, and each of them is a treasure in its own right." His smile became broader, the light glinting off his gold-rimmed spectacles. "And it's all to be shipped right here, every bit of it. A real feather in the Ashmolean's cap, if I may be permitted to say so. The museum shall be acknowledged throughout the world as the chief repository of the glories of Minoan Crete."

"I'm sure," Charles said dryly. There was no point in confiding his feelings about the exhibit to Buttersworth, who could neither understand nor share them. Instead, he raised the question that had been his real purpose for coming to the Ashmolean.

"I haven't been upstairs to look," he said, "but I take it that the Warrington Hoard has been restored to its proper place."

"Indeed it has," Buttersworth said warmly. "I must admit that we would have been lost without your assistance, Sheridan. To work through the usual channels would have been to risk scandal, and that was out of the question. I was utterly at my wits' end when you came to tell me that you'd got word of the Hoard."

By "the usual channels," of course, Buttersworth was speaking of the Oxford police. Charles understood the museum's reluctance to involve them in the theft of a major holding, such as the Warrington Hoard. While local constabularies were adequate to the tasks of suppressing street crime and preserving order, they lacked the tools and finesse required to perform complex investigations. And once the police were brought into a case, all hope of confidentiality flew out the window.

This was a special problem where adverse publicity—"scandal," as Buttersworth put it—might cause just as much damage as the theft itself. The museum's reputation would have been irretrievably ruined if the public had got wind of the theft of the Warrington Hoard, causing prospective donors to think twice before they trusted the Ashmolean with their precious collections. If the museum couldn't safeguard the Hoard, how could it protect other acquisitions?

The Hoard—a dozen major pieces of fine jewelry and tableware, perhaps the most exciting cache of Celtic gold and silverwork ever unearthed in England. It had been one of the Ashmolean's most popular exhibits until some six months before, when the museum had abruptly closed it—for cleaning and conservation, officials said. The truth was that the Hoard had been stolen. Suspicion had fallen on a recently hired char woman, who, it appeared, possessed a remarkable talent as a screwsman (or in this case, a screwswoman) and had made copies of all the necessary keys. Charles Sheridan, known to his friends and associates as an amateur sleuth of some reputation, had been instrumental in the Hoard's recovery. He felt he could hardly claim any credit in the business, however, since his involvement had been entirely fortuitous.

It was an interesting story. Mr. Rupert Dreighson of Castlegate Hall, some fifteen miles from Oxford, had retired from a profitable career as the owner of a string of drapers' shops in Liverpool and Manchester and, now that he could afford such things, had become an enthusiastic collector of Celtic antiquities. In his passionate search for treasures to add to his collection, Mr. Dreighson had suggested to antiquities dealers that if a hoard should happen to turn up, he would be willing to pay a handsome price for it. Of course, everyone knew that such a transaction would have to take place on the wrong side of the law, for one who dug up a cache of gold and silver objects was required to turn over everything to the Crown. But these days there were a great many collectors who possessed more money than scruples, and the legalities were frequently disregarded.

In the event, Mr. Dreighson was delighted when an unknown lady—a well-bred woman of quiet demeanor and modest dress—called upon him at Castlegate Hall one day and offered to sell him an antique golden earring, with the suggestion that if he were interested, several similar pieces might be available, the price to be negotiated. The earring's workmanship being quite extraordinary and Dreighson, being confident that it was without a doubt the real thing, handed over the money without demur, expressing an enthusiastic interest in the remainder of the collection.

Within a few days, he received a letter describing the pieces in detail and quoting a price for the whole. While the amount was high enough to raise Dreighson's eyebrows, he was not the sort of man to quibble when it came to something he wanted as badly as he wanted this. Arrangements were made, the required amount was deposited, in cash, in the designated London bank, and the collection—a dozen pieces of great beauty and rarity—was safely settled in Dreighson's capacious private vault.

And there it might have safely remained, if Rupert

Dreighson had not been a braggart. He could not resist the temptation of showing off his newly acquired treasures to a friend from London, who had come for a weekend's fishing to Castlegate Hall. A few days later, the friend happened to bump into Lord Charles Sheridan, and casually mentioned that a chap in Oxfordshire had privately got his hands on something rather remarkable, which—dash it all—had not come up for auction so others might've had a go at it. Charles, who had heard a whisper of rumor about the Warrington Hoard going missing, made a discreet inquiry at the Ashmolean, and Buttersworth was forced to admit the theft.

The next bit of business proved surprisingly easy. Under the guise of having a gold Celtic bracelet to sell, Charles arranged an introduction to Mr. Dreighson and talked his way into the Castlegate vault. Then, armed with the Ashmolean's catalog and documentary photographs of the Warrington Hoard, he confronted Dreighson, who gave him a cock-and-bull story about buying the lot from a pair of navvies who had turned it up while digging a drain in a field in Essex. But the story soon fell apart and the truth about the clandestine purchase emerged.

Dreighson, of course, claimed that he had not had an idea in the world that the pieces were stolen property, that he had purchased them fair and square, and that they were his. But a visit from the museum's solicitor persuaded him of the wisdom of returning the items in exchange for the addition of his name to the patron's list—a distinction that would polish Mr. Dreighson's prestige quite brightly indeed, and allow him to shine like a star among all the other retired drapers in the kingdom.

The Ashmolean, of course, was overjoyed at having regained the Hoard without having to admit publically that it had been lost. But Charles did not share in the general pleasure, for while the stolen property had been returned, the thieves were still at large. As was to be expected, inquiries at the bank turned up nothing; the account had been opened under the unrevealing name of George Smith and closed immediately upon the withdrawal of the money. The postal address also yielded no clues. What troubled Charles most was the apprehension that this theft might be just one of several. He had recently heard, for instance, of a theft at the Duke of Portland's establishment in Nottinghamshire, which could only have been carried out by a ring of clever thieves, some of them working as servants.

"By the way," Charles said, looking around, "I haven't seen Ned Lawrence today—your young helper. Does he still come to the museum?"

Charles had met young Lawrence during his dealings over the Hoard and had been impressed with the boy's knowledge of the local archaeological sites and his passion for exploring. Since Charles planned to be near Oxford for a few days—he and Kate, his wife, were staying with the Marlboroughs at Blenheim—he thought he might drive the Panhard to Chipping Norton for a look at the Rollright Stones, a Neolithic stone circle which, in Charles's view, held every bit as much interest as the more famous Stonehenge. Young Lawrence might like to come along.

"Ned?" Buttersworth asked. "Oh, yes, I wouldn't part with the boy—although I'd be glad to lend him to you, if there's something you want him to do." He smiled. "He'd be delighted to lend you a hand, you know, if you had another investigation. He was enormously impressed with the way you handled that business with Dreighson."

Charles chuckled. "I know. He offered to come on as my assistant—without pay. Watson to my Holmes, he said. Very keen."

"That's Ned," Buttersworth said, amused. "Like most boys his age, he loves adventure. Too much Stevenson, I'm afraid. He'd sail off to Treasure Island in a minute. However, he's far above other boys in his competence and his range of interests." He smiled. "Why, he reads the newspaper's police reports as religiously as he reads his lessons." His smile faded. "Something of a sad story, though, and rather a mystery. His family, that is."

"Oh?" Charles asked.

"His father is an Irish gentleman of some consequence named—" He stopped, shifting his weight from one foot to another. "On second thought, perhaps Ned would rather tell you himself, if the opportunity arises. Were you thinking of taking him out with you?"

"I was," Charles said, "if he can be spared. My wife and I are staying with the Marlboroughs, so I'll be in the area for a few days."

Buttersworth seemed to hesitate. "With the Marlboroughs, you say. At Blenheim, I take it."

Charles nodded. "I'd like Ned to see the Rollright Stones, if he's not been there already. I want to encourage his interest in archaeology—although I suppose he'll be disappointed to hear that I don't have a case he can help investigate."

"Oh, by all means, take him with you," Buttersworth said. Behind his glasses, his eyes became more intent. "But speaking of cases—"

"There's not been another theft, I hope," Charles said warily.

Buttersworth fluttered a hand. "Oh, no. At least, not here at the museum, I'm glad to say. It's only that—" He broke off, obviously troubled. "But perhaps I shouldn't mention it. It is only speculation, after all. My suspicions, if that's what they are, are probably quite unfounded."

Charles waited, feeling that there was more here than the man wanted to say—more, perhaps, than he wanted to hear.

"On the other hand," Buttersworth went on after a moment, "since you are staying with the Marlboroughs, perhaps I ought to—" He looked in both directions up and down the hall, then lowered his voice. "I was visited by a rather remarkable woman on Friday, you see." He paused.

"Remarkable in what way?" Charles asked.

"Well, her appearance, for one thing. Her nose, quite classical, exactly like that of Sappho, whose bust we have in our collection." Buttersworth seemed to reflect on this phenomenon for a moment.

"And this remarkable woman—" Charles prompted.

Buttersworth started. "Ah, yes. Well, she claimed to represent her employer. Wanted my opinion on several antique pieces."

Charles smiled. "I shouldn't think such a request would be all that unusual, in your line of work."

"It was not the request, it was the items themselves. One was a rather ordinary scarab seal—people are always fetching those things home from holiday in Egypt. But she also had a Minoan prism seal and three very fine Greek seal stones, and she suggested that there were more."

Charles tipped his head to one side, remembering Dreighson's story—when the truth had finally been forced out of the man—of being visited by a woman who had sold him an earring. "I see," he said. "I suppose you thought of the Dreighson affair."

"I did," Buttersworth said ruefully. "But I was also reminded of the Marlborough collection. The Marlborough Gemstones." He paused. "I suppose you know of them."

"Ah, yes," Charles said reflectively. "A large assemblage of very fine gemstones—more than seven hundred, as I recall—gathered at enormous expense by the fourth duke. And sold by the seventh duke, who needed the money to keep the palace going." He smiled crookedly. "Alas, they went for just thirty-five thousand guineas, although they were said to have been worth twice that."

Buttersworth cleared his throat. "But there's something else, you see," he said, distinctly uneasy. "The woman who brought the stones—she let it slip that she had been sent by the Duchess."

"The Duchess?" Charles repeated with a chuckle. "Come now, Buttersworth. You can't be serious."

"I know," Buttersworth said gloomily. "Well, of course it could only be the Duchess of Marlborough. And I wondered, you see . . . Of course, it was just a thought, but I couldn't help asking myself whether some of the gemstones might have escaped the auction block, after all, and were now being offered for sale, clandestinely. Although I must say," he added quickly, "that it does seem rather strange. The Duchess was Consuelo Vanderbilt before she married the Duke, as you know. The Marlboroughs' pockets are said to be empty, but I doubt that a Vanderbilt would need money. Or, if she did, that she would stoop to sell the Duke's family jewels."

Buttersworth's story, Charles thought, was highly unsettling, and not because the Duchess would be involved in anything underhanded. "There may be a scheme afoot that doesn't involve the Marlboroughs," he said, thinking of the Dreighson affair. "A plot of which the Duke and Duchess know nothing."

"It's possible," Buttersworth agreed. He gave Charles an anxious look. "You'll keep it in mind while you're there?"

"I shall," Charles said. "I shall indeed."

CHAPTER FOUR

I felt awed, ant-like, apprehensive, as I gazed at Blenheim's huge baroque mass, its fearful symmetry, its threatening roof-scape of ferocious lions and plunging swords, its trumpeting central portico and tremendous, trailing wings. . . . This is a dragon of a house which once breathed fire and was turned to stone by some terrible curse.

Blenheim: Biography of a Palace
Miriam Fowler

Kate Sheridan, carrying a string bag containing her purchases, walked past Woodstock's town hall, past The Bear, past St. Mary Magdalene's church, and along a row of rose-covered Georgian houses and pretty shops. At the last shop, she turned left, crossed a grassy quadrangle, stepped through an imposing stone arch, and paused to admire the sweeping view that lay before her—the finest in all England, it was widely reckoned.

Before her lay a quiet lake girdled with mature beechwoods and soft green meadows, its glittering surface reflecting the shadows of moving clouds and the darker, heavier shadow of a massive stone-arch bridge. To the left of the lake

rose the walls and towers of Blenheim, and Kate thought
with a shiver that, even softened by distance, it seemed cold
and fierce and forbidding, more like a prison than a palace. To
the right, through the trees, she could see the tall stone Column of Victory, monument to John Churchill's decisive de-
feat of the French at the Austrian village of Blenheim two
hundred years before. A grateful Queen Anne had awarded
the nation's hero a dukedom and crowned the honor with the
grant of the eighteen hundred–acre royal manor of Woodstock, promising to build on it, at government expense, "the
Castle of Blenheim."

Never mind that the park and woodland, the site of Henry
I's famous hunting lodge and Henry II's royal palace, had
fallen into a sad decline, seldom used, derelict and neglected.
And never mind that certain cynics in the court hinted that
the Queen had merely taken the opportunity to off-load a sur-
plus royal estate that had become a royal embarrassment.
Most agreed that it was a magnificent gift, worthy of a victo-
rious general and a munificent queen.

But things hadn't sorted out as the triumphant Churchill,
now known as the Duke of Marlborough, might have wished.
Having paid out nearly a quarter of a million pounds for
Blenheim's construction, the Queen repented of her promise,
snapped shut the royal purse, and died, leaving to Marlborough and his heirs the pain of finishing the palace out of their
personal pockets, which, unfortunately, were not very deep.

The task had been difficult and prolonged, but eventually
the grand house had been completed, and eight succeeding
dukes had carved out the landscape that now held Kate's
admiring gaze. The famous landscape architect, Capability
Brown, had dammed the River Glyme to create the lake
and artfully planted beeches and oaks around it, creating the

illusion of the long-vanished medieval forest that had once surrounded the King's favorite hunting lodge. And on the lake's far shore, beyond the bridge, a clump of trees marked the oldest, most historic, and most romantic site of all: Fair Rosamund's Well, that mysterious spring about which Kate had heard so many stories. In fact, Rosamund's Well was the reason she had come to Blenheim, to see for herself the setting of one of the most tantalizing romances in English history.

By this time, Kate had reached the elm-lined avenue that led from Hensington Road to the East Gate of the palace. She had just turned onto the lane when, behind her, she heard the chugging of a motor and the peremptory tootle of an airhorn, and turned to see her husband Charles piloting their Panhard along the graveled road. He slowed the motorcar to a stop, pushed his goggles up on his forehead, and leaned over to open the door with a smile.

"Climb in, Kate."

"Happily," Kate said, gathering her skirts and stepping up into the motorcar. She leaned over and kissed her husband on the cheek, not caring that his brown beard and moustache were gray and gritty with road dust. "I'm glad to see you, dear. Did you motor straight down from London?"

The House of Lords were sitting, and Charles had been in the City for several weeks. Kate (who hated London) had been at Bishop's Keep, their Essex home, and had taken the train to Woodstock on Monday, at the invitation of the Duchess of Marlborough, to join several other guests. Now that Charles had arrived, the party was complete.

"Not directly," Charles said in reply to her question. "I stopped at the Ashmolean on the way. I'm glad to report that the Warrington Hoard is back in its place." He changed gears, let up the clutch, and the Panhard chugged forward. "What are you doing out here all by yourself, Kate?"

"I've been to Woodstock," Kate replied, "where I discovered a bookstore full of fascinating old books." She held up her bag of purchases. "I found one about Fair Rosamund and Eleanor of Aquitaine and another about the history of Woodstock Park. And the owner—an odd little old man, really—has promised to find several other books he thinks might be hidden away in dusty corners."

"That's my Kate." Charles chuckled. "She's invited to visit the grandest house in the kingdom and what does she do? Takes herself off in search of books."

Kate knew that her bookstore expedition was no surprise to Charles. Under the pseudonym of Beryl Bardwell, she had become a successful author while she still lived in her native New York City, composing penny dreadfuls for sensation-seeking readers. And after her arrival in England some nine years before, she (and Beryl, of course, whom she had come to regard as an invisible but indivisible part of herself) had enjoyed a gratifying success as a popular writer. The most recent book, a ghost story set at Glamis Castle in Scotland and echoing with the mysterious strains of the song "Where is the lad who was born to be king?" had been published only a few months before.*

For the subject of their next novel, Kate and Beryl had settled upon Rosamund Clifford, mistress of Henry II, known to the world as "Fair Rosamund." When Kate mentioned the

---

*The story of Kate's and Charles's adventures in Scotland, while Kate was doing research for her book and Charles was carrying out a Royal assignment, may be read in *Death at Glamis Castle*.

idea to Jennie Churchill (now Mrs. George Cornwallis-West), Jennie had suggested that she visit the site of Rosamund's Well and King Henry's palace, located on the Churchill family estate, Blenheim. Obligingly, Jennie had written to Consuelo, the Duchess of Marlborough. Not long after, Kate received a warm letter from the Duchess—whom she had met when they worked together to raise money for the American hospital ship *Maine* during the Boer War—inviting her to come to Blenheim and stay for as long as she liked. And since Charles and Winston Churchill were friends, and Winston (first cousin to the Duke) was also to be a guest at Blenheim, Charles had been invited as well.

Over the noise of the motor, Charles said, "I hope you've not been bored here, Kate. Has Winston been amusing you? And Miss Deacon? She's said to be a highly entertaining young lady."

"Winston?" Kate returned the chuckle. "I've scarcely seen him, except at meals. He's locked himself away to work on his father's biography."

"Ah, yes," Charles said dryly. "He sent me several chapters of the manuscript last week. Rather a job of whitewashing, I thought."

"And as for Miss Deacon," Kate continued in a meaningful tone, "she and the Duke went off to admire some new plantings in the Italian Garden. The Duchess," she added, "retired to her rooms with a headache."

"Uh-oh," Charles said. He gave her a serious look. "But I thought Winston was hoping that Miss Deacon might—"

"I believe it is rather Lord Northcote, the other guest, who has hopes—great expectations, rather. You know Botsy Northcote, I believe." Kate smiled thinly. "However, the Duke seems to take precedence over Botsy."

"Ah, Kate," Charles said, with an affectionately teasing laugh. "Your first ducal houseparty, and you have landed in a hotbed of romantic intrigue."

Kate frowned, feeling troubled. "Don't treat it so lightly, Charles. I'm not a prude, by any means, and I have no idea whether there's anything serious going on between Gladys Deacon and the Duke. But it's making the Duchess utterly miserable. And there doesn't seem to be a thing she can do about it."

Charles glanced at her. "She's confided in you? Well, I don't suppose I should be surprised. You're both Americans, after all."

"No, she hasn't confided in me. She may be an American, but she's a Vanderbilt. She's too conscious of her position and too reserved to break her silence on the matter, and of course, I wouldn't presume to intrude." Kate paused, then added sadly, "But she can't conceal how she feels. And now is an especially difficult time for her—because of the Royal houseparty, I mean."

"Royal houseparty?" Charles asked in surprise.

"The first weekend in August," Kate replied. She made a little face. "The King and Queen and two dozen of their closest friends—with all of their servants, of course. Perhaps it should be called a Royal circus."

Charles was wearing a look of horrified surprise. "But not us, I hope. Oh, God, Kate, don't tell me that—"

"No, not us," Kate said firmly. "The Duchess was kind enough to extend a personal invitation, but I declined. I told her we had a prior engagement in Scotland that weekend, and couldn't possibly break it."

"In Scotland? But I don't remember—"

"That's all right, Charles," Kate said with a little laugh. "I blush to say that I lied to the Duchess. I have no more desire to attend a Royal houseparty than you do." And that was all there was time to say because they were approaching the East Gate.

Kate looked up at the immense stone palace, its fierce, cruel weight looming above her like an overhanging cliff, and gave an involuntary shiver. Blenheim was not, could never be, a pleasant place. It suddenly seemed to her, in a moment of wonderment, that the house had no soul, and she opened her mouth to say so to Charles.

But Charles was waving cheerfully at the liveried porter, and then they were driving through the stone arch and into the East Court. They left the motorcar to an attendant, who rang the bell at the door to the Marlboroughs' private quarters. As a footman ushered them in, Kate heard a loud gong resounding hollowly through the hallways.

They had arrived just in time to dress for tea.

CHAPTER FIVE

Consuelo Vanderbilt Marlborough was awakened by the echoing sound of the dressing gong. Feeling drained and dispirited in spite of her afternoon nap, she swung her feet off the high bed and wrapped her arms around herself. It might be summer out-of-doors, she thought bleakly, but the sunshine had little chance of warming this wretched mausoleum of a house. Blenheim was supposed to be centrally heated—a convenience purchased, together with electric lighting and repairs to the palace's lead roofs, with the eleventh duchess's dowry—but the rooms were always cold.

"Would Your Grace prefer the blue or the lilac?" Rosalie

asked, holding up two gauzy tea gowns. Her maid, who was stern and reproachful, had been selected by her mother-in-law, Lady Blandford. Consuelo couldn't shake the uncomfortable thought that Rosalie might be more loyal to the Duke's mother, or to the Duke, than to herself—that she might even be a spy.

"Your Grace?" Rosalie repeated severely. "The blue or the lilac?"

"I'll have neither." Consuelo shivered. "I should like something *warm*." She glanced up. At the foot of her bed, on the opposite wall, there was a marble mantlepiece that looked exactly like a tomb. On it, in large black letters, the seventh duke had carved three words: DUST, ASHES, NOTHING. She woke up to that desolate admonition every morning, went to sleep with it every night, and heard it echoing in her dreams. It seemed to represent her life.

Fifteen minutes later, Consuelo was dressed in a blue velvet gown with a high cream-colored valencian lace collar embroidered with cut crystal and silver beads, and was seated at her dressing table, fastening her diamond bracelet while Rosalie silently arranged her hair.

Without much enthusiasm, Consuelo studied her reflection in the gilt-framed mirror. She knew that she was said to be a beauty, although of course, the newspapers had to print things like that, since she was a Vanderbilt by birth and a Marlborough by marriage, and such women were always supposed to be beautiful, no matter what they really looked like. She was tall—at five-foot-nine, she overtopped her husband by a full three inches—and willowy, with an elegant posture, the result of having worn a steel brace as a girl. Her deep-set brown eyes and arched brows were her best features, as well as her graceful neck and flawless white shoulders. But her jaw was decidedly firm, her capable hands were the size of a working man's, and her nose—

Oh, that ridiculous retroussé nose, with its silly tip-tilt, which entirely spoilt her face! Consuelo made a self-deprecating grimace as she thought how her mother had blamed her nose when the Duke seemed disinclined to have her, in spite of her tempting Vanderbilt dowry.

"It's your nose, I'm sure of it," Alva Vanderbilt had wailed, after three weeks of wondering whether the Duke—Sunny, as he was incongruously called—had decided not to propose after all. "He must be afraid that your children will inherit it."

But Marlborough had either discounted the importance of Consuelo's nose or weighed it against her father's fortune, for after three long weeks of ducal shilly-shallying, he had at last proposed, to the great delight of Mrs. Vanderbilt, who immediately set out to create the grandest wedding that had ever been seen in North America.

The offer of the Duke's hand had brought Consuelo no happiness, however, for she loved someone else—dear, sweet Winty Rutherfurd, who had begged her to throw over everything else and elope with him. She had tried to tell her mother that she could never love Marlborough, who had not even had the grace to pretend that he loved *her*, but it was of no use. Mrs. Vanderbilt was absolutely dead set on the marriage: "An English *duke!* My dear child, what a coup! You should be eternally grateful to me for arranging it." Consuelo had finally bowed to the inevitable.

The extravagant wedding was followed by the obligatory Mediterranean honeymoon, and in the course of time, Consuelo had obligingly presented her husband with an heir and then a spare, neither of whom were disfigured by their mother's nose. This attention to duty had pleased the

Duke's grandmother, the old Duchess, who on their first meeting had told her that it was her responsibility to have a son, "because it would be intolerable to have that little upstart Winston become Duke."

At the thought of Winston, Consuelo smiled, for he had become one of her closest friends, perhaps because his brashness was very American (after all, his mother Jennie *was* an American) and very unlike the stuffy Marlboroughs and their stiff friends. She wished she could talk to him about her present troubles, but they involved the Duke and she always hated to put Winston in a corner when it came to the family. But perhaps—

Her thoughts were interrupted by a light tap on the door, which burst open before she had a chance to call out. A young woman danced into the room.

"Oh, Connie, *vous voilà!*" she cried, with a toss of her beautiful head. "I have been searching all over for you! I have something exciting to tell you!"

"Thank you, Rosalie," Consuelo said, dismissing her maid. She turned from the mirror, smiling fondly. "Gladys, my dear. How pretty you look."

No matter how angry she might be at Marlborough for the reckless way he was behaving with the girl, Consuelo found it hard to be angry at Gladys herself, who was as innocent as a child in such matters. Innocent and free, Consuelo thought with a sudden pang of envy—free to be lively and winsome and pursue her dreams as willfully as she pleased, privileges that she herself had never enjoyed.

Gladys threw herself on the bed with a theatrical flutter of white chiffon. "Oh, I am too, too weary, dear Connie, simply *trop fatigué*. The Duke insisted that we tramp around and around the garden, pausing to sit only a little." She raised her arms above her head, showing off delicate white hands like little birds. "Did you know, *ma cherie,* that Marlborough has commissioned a Venus fountain? And it is to be in *my* likeness! Isn't that a deliciously enchanting idea? Oh, that wonderful Duke of yours—he does all in his power to entertain!"

Consuelo's lips tightened. She thought of the silent Sunny—what an irony there was in that family nickname!—who, when they had no guests, ate his dinner with neither a word nor a glance, let alone any thought of entertainment. But her husband's churlishness toward her was scarcely Gladys's fault, any more than it was Gladys's fault that Marlborough was so obviously smitten—although Consuelo could wish that her young American friend might use just a little more discretion. Twenty-two was a bit old to play at being a flirtatious young girl, and Gladys's giddiness might get her into trouble—as it very nearly had when the Crown Prince of Germany had fallen in love with her the year before, and insisted on exchanging his mother's communion ring for Glady's bracelet. The ring, of course, had been returned at the Kaiser's command, but the indiscreet flirtation had nearly created an ugly international incident.

Consuelo glanced up to see her young friend watching her in the mirror, her luminous, wide-apart eyes the color of sapphires, a sphinxlike look on that beautiful face with its lovely straight, fine nose that Consuelo, despite her best intentions, could only envy. She had overheard a pair of housemaids whispering that the girl had persuaded a doctor at the Institut de Beauté to inject paraffin wax into the bridge of her nose, to form a classical line from forehead to tip. It was likely true, Consuelo thought, having herself noticed something of a difference in Glady's profile, as well as a slight puffiness between the eyes. But it had been a ridiculous and dangerous thing to do—and quite unnecessary, for Gladys had been perfect just as she was.

To be fair, Consuelo could understand why her husband was infatuated with the girl, whose slender, boyish figure and enchantingly mercurial temperament gave her the air of a provocative young god. She herself had loved Gladys from the moment they met, although not, she supposed with her usual caustically self-deprecating humor, in quite the same way as did Marlborough.

Or Lord Northcote, for that matter—Botsy, everyone called him, who had turned up at Blenheim the previous week, in pursuit of Gladys. Botsy was simply mad for the girl, and had even told Consuelo that they were engaged. At first, Consuelo had welcomed the news with relief, thinking that Gladys's marriage would put Marlborough off the chase. But when she had asked Gladys about it, the girl had only smiled her lovely, mysterious smile and refused to say whether it was true. Unfortunately, Botsy only seemed to add to the general tension, and Consuelo found herself wishing that the fellow—he was really rather silly, she thought, and not much of a match for Gladys—would go away again.

Consuelo picked up her engraved silver mirror, turned to inspect the arrangement of her hair at the back of her neck, and smiled at the girl. "I'm glad the Duke has amused you, my dear." The gong sounded again, signalling teatime, echoing like a hollow, damning voice through the empty corridors of the immense house. She put down the mirror with a sigh. "Shall we go down to tea?"

As if they had any choice, she thought with dull resignation, following Gladys out of the room. For when the Blenheim gong sounded, everyone obeyed, like it or not.

CHAPTER SIX

My dear . . .

I hesitate how to begin. "Sunny" though melodious sounds childish; "Marlborough" is very formal; "Duke" impossible between relations; and I don't suppose you answer to either "Charles" or "Richard." If I must reflect, let it be Sunny. But you must perceive in all this a strong case for the abolition of the House of Lords and all titles. . . .

Winston Churchill
to his cousin, the Duke of Marlborough
1898

Hearing the distant dressing gong, Winston put down his pen, took out his pocket watch, and glanced at it. Tea in half an hour—he had just time to change.

He leaned back in his chair and surveyed the pleasant room in which he was working, just off the arcade beneath the Long Library. The shelves contained his research material—books and documents he had carried down from the Muniments Room—as well as eight plaster busts, of no particular artistic merit, of the eight previous dukes of Marlborough. The table contained the stack of manuscript pages he had written so far in his *Life of Lord Randolph Churchill*.

The work was good, indubitably so, he thought with a comfortable pleasure. When it appeared in print, it would finally silence his father's critics (of which there were still a surprising number, given that Lord Randolph had been dead for eight years). And it would please the Duke, his father's nephew, which was not a trivial outcome. While Winston was confident that he had the grit and the muscle to fight his own fight, having the Duke of Marlborough in his corner was an asset that not many junior members of the House of Commons could claim.

As if summoned by Winston's imagination, the door opened without a tap or an announcement, and His Grace slipped inside, moving with his customary stealth. Charles Richard John Spencer-Churchill had been called Sunny as a child, not for his disposition but for his title as Earl of Sunderland. The undersized child had grown into a small man, with dark hair parted at one side and smoothed back from his forehead, a melancholy aristocratic face, a petulant mouth under a thin, turned-down moustache, and the prominent eyes of the Churchills—"bullfrog eyes," Winston's mother Jennie had called them. The Duke's narrow shoulders seemed bowed under the burden of Blenheim's past and future, which he had assumed when his father died a decade before.

It was a weighty burden, Winston knew, for the seven-acre house and twenty-five hundred–acre parkland easily swallowed a hundred thousand pounds a year in mere up-keep, never mind improvements (like bathrooms) or major repairs (like the roof). Winston himself was a romantic at heart and would never think of marrying for money, but he understood the dilemma his cousin had faced—that *he* would have faced, if things had gone a different way and Winston

Spencer-Churchill had become the ninth Duke. Sunny was obligated to maintain Blenheim, and he'd had no choice but to go in search of a dollar duchess: an American heiress with her own money.

And Consuelo Vanderbilt had come with a magnificent purse: $2,500,000 in railroad stock and $100,000 in annual dividends for both Consuelo and the Duke, although of course everything came to the Duke. The annual payments had been enough to repair the roof, gild and refurbish the drab rooms of state, and replace the books, tapestries, and paintings auctioned off by Sunny's father and grandfather. Winston, whose strong family pride had been wounded by Blenheim's seedy appearance, could only applaud the uses to which the Duke had put the Duchess's money.

"Ah, Winston," Sunny said, in his almost inaudible drawl. "Hard at the writing still, are you?"

"Just stopping for tea," Winston said. He paused, then added, in a guardedly neutral tone, "I trust that you enjoyed your walk with Miss Deacon?"

Winston disapproved strongly of his cousin's relationship with the young American woman. Gladys Deacon might have the gamine winsomeness of an innocently mischievous child, but in Winston's opinion, she was dangerous. She was duplicitous, deliberately provocative, and entirely out for Gladys. And what was worse, in Winston's opinion, both Sunny and Consuelo seemed blind to her true nature—a fact which made Gladys even more dangerous.

Even so, Winston was ambivalent, for he could not deny that Gladys was dazzling—even more attractive than Pamela Plowden, whom he had hoped to marry someday. But his political ambitions had quite naturally occupied all his time and attention for the past several years, and the impatient Pamela had given up and flounced off to marry Bulwer-Lytton. And of course, no rational man who aimed at higher office (Winston himself had some exceedingly high aspirations) could afford to be involved with someone like Gladys. She was lovely, yes, indeed, but she was unwise and undisciplined and could never be trusted to avoid the pitfalls that frequently opened at the feet of political wives.

So it was with some smugness that Winston congratulated himself on having the wisdom and foresight not to fall in love with Miss Deacon. He also congratulated himself on being able to see through her, which was more than the Duke could do, or Botsy. Botsy—Lord Henry Northcote—was making a monkey of himself over the girl. Winston had even heard that Botsy had asked her some weeks ago to marry him, when they were both guests at a houseparty weekend. Of course, one couldn't trust rumor, but it was also said that he'd given her a valuable diamond necklace that had belonged to his paternal grandmother. Winston doubted if the Duke knew this, and he did not mean to be the one to tell him.

Sunny shifted uncomfortably, but when he replied to Winston's question, his voice as carefully neutral as his cousin's. "Yes, thank you. Gladys and I had a most pleasant walk. The gardens are coming along nicely. Still a great deal of work to be done, of course." His tone warmed. "I've commissioned Waldo Story to do a Venus fountain, which is to stand in the exact center of the Italian Garden. Miss Deacon has generously agreed to allow the sculptor to use her likeness."

Winston regarded his cousin. Having refurbished the interior of the palace, the Duke had turned his attention to the vast Blenheim landscape. He lined the Great Avenue with elm trees, replaced the grass in the three-acre Great

Court with stone pavings, and built a parapet, a stone wall, and iron gates along the north front to keep out the curious. Now he was working on the gardens outside the east wing, where he had laid out an intricate arabesque in dwarf box hedge, with orange trees in tubs and flowers in jars. Consuelo did not appreciate this fastidious formality, but it intimately revealed, Winston thought, the Duke's turn of mind. The perfect palace was to be displayed within the perfect setting, and Marlborough, both the owner of this incredible jewel and its jeweler, could never stop polishing and perfecting it. And now this statue of Venus.

The idea of Gladys Deacon's stone likeness planted in the center of the Duke's garden brought Winston a deep disquiet. For Sunny, Blenheim was much more than a family obligation, it was an obsession—and, like his obsession with Gladys, dangerous, for in his passionate indulgence, he totally ignored his wife. Both Blenheim and Gladys, Winston very much feared, had the potential of destroying the Marlborough marriage.

And that would be a great pity. Consuelo had admirably performed the first duty of a duchess, having given the Duke not just one son, but two. She was a conscientious mother and a superb hostess as well, and Blenheim would not be the same without her. While Winston didn't like to think of the matter in terms of money, one had to be realistic. If Consuelo left, she took with her nearly a quarter of a million dollars a year. The Duke did not seem to realize it, but losing his wife would be a terrible blow, both to the family pride and to the family purse.

Winston and his cousin had always enjoyed a cordial friendship, in part, perhaps, because they rarely spoke of personal feelings. Politics, the Royals, family history, the latest novels of Henry James, the plays of Ibsen and Stevens, Marconi's triumphs, the reforms of the Webbs and the Fabians—the two men had a world of things to discuss, but personal relationships were never on the table. Gladys, however, was becoming too serious a threat to simply let the business slide. Winston feit he must say something.

He cleared his throat. "My dear Sunny," he said awkwardly, "I wonder if we might have a confidential word—man to man, I mean."

The Duke dropped his eyes and ducked his head as he always did when he felt uncomfortable. "About what?"

Winston moved a book a quarter of an inch to the right. "About Miss Deacon."

There was a long silence. The phalanx of plaster dukes, like a Greek chorus, peered down, dumb and empty-eyed, at two very different descendents of John Churchill. Winston was a physical man, robustly, energetically self-assertive, while Sunny, pallid and polite, maintained an aloof disdain. Winston's father had left him nothing but debts, and he had to depend on his pen and his wits to fill his pockets. Sunny's father had left him an estate and a title; he had traded the title for his wife's American fortune, and now his pockets were full. Winston lived a restless, hard-fought life in the world at large; nothing came easily to him, nothing seemed guaranteed, whether it was besting a political opponent or conquering a childhood stammer. Sunny, on the other hand, confined himself to Blenheim, where everything came easily to him, where everything was guaranteed—except happiness.

But while they might be very different, what bound these two Churchills together was their passionate love of Blenheim and their common determination to once again raise the Marlborough standard to its previous heights of respect and admiration. That was why Winston was smoothing over the rough places in his father's life, and why the Duke was landscaping the palace. And that was why Sunny must be made to understand, Winston thought, that Gladys Deacon threatened all of them—not just Consuelo, or Sunny, but the entire family.

Sunny, however, was not to be confronted. He raised his hooded eyes and met Winston's challenging look with the famous Marlborough blank stare.

"I believe I heard the gong for tea," he said. "I think we had better change. We do not want to be late."

CHAPTER SEVEN

A plague upon it when thieves cannot be true to one another.

King Henry IV, Part I
William Shakespeare

It was early Wednesday evening as Alfred hurried through
the small gate beside the River Glyme where it flowed under the Park wall. In fact, the hour was so early that Bulls-eye
might not yet have put in an appearance at the pub. But Alfred had no choice—it was now or not at all. And by this
time, he was feeling desperate.

Alfred's destination, the pub called the Black Prince, was
located just across Manor Road, a much-traveled coach-road
which ran from London to Oxford and Woodstock, then
northward to Chipping Norton and Stratford-upon-Avon.
Alfred darted across the road, busy with the usual clattering
traffic of carts and drays, and pushed through the crowd of
hooting children and barking dogs which was trailing a
noisy motorcar. He paused at the door of the Prince, pulling
down his cap to hide his powdered hair and allowing his
eyes to grow accustomed to the dimness.

The Prince was certainly not one of Woodstock's poshest pubs. The ceiling was low and smoke-stained, shoals of filthy sawdust drifted across the stone floor, and the company was rowdy and quarrelsome. But the place was dark as a pit, even in broad daylight, and the din of the crowd blanketed private conversation, which made it a right-enough place to meet somebody if you didn't want to be noticed or overheard. Over the weeks he'd been in service at Blenheim, Alfred had spent a leisurely evening or two here, in the company of one or another of the other footmen.

But tonight Alfred was in a hurry. It was his half-day off, officially, but Manning had hurt his hand and Alfred was made to serve at tea. He would have to serve at dinner, too, which meant that he had to get this business done and get back before old Stevens missed him. The butler wasn't hard on the footmen, but he was particular about seeing that everyone kept to the duty roster. With relief, he spotted Bulls-eye at his usual table in a far dark corner, hunched over a mug and a pitcher of ale. He pushed his way through the crowd toward him.

At the table, Bulls-eye lifted his head and regarded Alfred with a frown. "Wot're ye doin' 'ere?" he demanded, over a roar of laughter at the bar. If he was surprised, he didn't betray it, only looked annoyed. "There's a rule 'bout meetings, y'know. Less we're seen together, the better fer all concerned."

"I had to come," Alfred said breathlessly. "Something's gone wrong."

"Gone wrong, 'as it?" Bulls-eye kicked out a chair and Alfred seated himself. "Wot's gone wrong?"

At the bar, there was a loud clink of glasses and another roar of laughter. "It's the girl," Alfred said, trying to be off-hand. He cast an uneasy glance over his shoulder, hoping that none of the other servants were here. He couldn't be charged with doing anything wrong, of course. It *was* his half-day off, even if he'd had to stand in for Manning. He had every bit as much right to be here as the next man. Still and all, Bulls-eye's remark had reminded him that this wasn't an ordinary meeting, and he felt apprehensive.

"The girl?" Bulls-eye scowled. "She's keeping up 'er end, ain't she?" He paused, seemed to collect himself, and picked up the pitcher. "If ye want a glass, get one from the bar."

Alfred shook his head. He couldn't serve at dinner smelling like a brewery. "I don't know whether she is or not," he said. "I haven't seen her since Friday, and that's a fact."

"Since Friday?" Bulls-eye's forehead puckered. He was a short man, stout and thick-chested, with heavy shoulders, beefy hands, and thick, bushy black hair that stuck out in all directions. "An' today's Wednesday. I shouldn't think ye'd be likely t'see 'er all that much." He frowned at Alfred. "Doan't work in the same places, d'ye? Doan't take yer meals together, d'ye?" He paused, lowering his brows. "Anybody at the house askin' questions 'bout 'er?"

"Questions?" Alfred repeated uneasily. "Not that I've heard."

Bulls-eye's comments were to the point, however, because under ordinary circumstances and in most of the big houses, a footman would cross a housemaid's path only occasionally. At Blenheim, the housemaids ate with the lower servants in the servants' hall, while the six footmen took their meals together in the butler's pantry. During the working day, the footmen waited on the family and guests in the drawing rooms and Saloon and rarely found their way into the private quarters, while the housemaids mostly worked in the upstairs bedrooms, with only short stints in rota for dusting and carpets downstairs.

However, Blenheim wasn't the first place Alfred and Kitty had worked together, and they had become friends. Much more than friends, at least as far as Alfred was concerned. Kitty wasn't any prettier than other girls, but she had a lovely head of abundant hair the color of strawberries in the sun. And she was crafty and resourceful and enterprising and used her wits in a way that Alfred—for all his other good qualities—knew that he didn't. She always had a sharp eye out for the main chance. She could see possibilities for independent enterprise when Alfred himself would simply do what he was told. At Welbeck Abbey, their second assignment together, Kitty had suggested that they might find it to their mutual advantage to join forces, not just to get the job done, but to make sure that there'd be a little something extra in it for themselves at the end. Alfred, a simpler soul, had agreed, and they had come out of it very much to the good and nobody the wiser.

And after Welbeck, there had been those two nights in London—Alfred's heart burned inside him to think about it—two long, delicious nights, filled with exotic and unimaginable pleasures, for Kitty, undressed and uncorsetted, was a creature of wildly abandoned charms, and she had bestowed all of them, with an uninhibited generosity, upon Alfred, who'd never in his life thought to receive such gifts.

In return for these treasures, Alfred had fallen fiercely, frantically in love with Kitty, and thought—hoped, rather, for she kept her feelings veiled and never gave him so much as a hint—that she might come to love him, if not now, then soon. If all went well with this job, he had begun to think that it was time to leave off what they were doing and take their earnings and set themselves up in Brighton, where his cousin owned a pub just off the Pier and would be glad to take Alfred as a partner. Kitty could stay at home and raise their children—the dear little Alfreds and Kittys who would come along—and they would all be blissfully happy together.

Which was why Alfred had managed to keep an eye out for Kitty in more than the usual way, and why he had written to her, and why he was unhappily aware that Friday was the last day she had been in her regular place. But he kept all this to himself, saying only, with a careless little shrug, that the girl hadn't been at morning prayers or in her rota in the drawing room and he was just wondering if perhaps she'd made some sort of contact with Bulls-eye, and if so, whether there had been a change in plans.

"No change in plans," growled Bulls-eye darkly. He leaned forward, his eyes narrowed. "You and the girl—friends, are ye? Been talkin' t'ye, has she? Sharin' 'er secrets, like?"

Alfred stiffened, not liking the other's accusing attitude. "Why shouldn't we be friends?" he asked defensively. "Why shouldn't we talk, or share secrets?" Bulls-eye seemed to be watching him with a different interest now, and he began to wonder uneasily if it was considered unwise to be involved with one's confederates. He added, more carefully, "Of course, we have to share secrets, don't we? Working together as we do, each of us has to know what the other knows. Believe me, we'll make good use of it when the time comes."

Bulls-eye regarded him narrowly, as if he were trying to make up his mind about something. Alfred waited for the lecture he feared was forthcoming.

But Bulls-eye said only, "Ye'd do well, young fellow, t'concentrate yer mind on the business at 'and. I trust ye've been noticing the ways in and out and wot doors're locked and when and by 'oo. I trust ye'll not come up short on the day."

"Of course not," Alfred said indignantly. "I simply wondered if something had happened and Kitty'd been pulled out of the game. I—"

"If anybody's pulled, ye'll know it," Bulls-eye said in a definitive tone. "Now, you go back and do yer business and keep yer mouth shut. Oh, an' keep yer eye out for a new hire who'll 'ave yer instructions." It had been the Syndicate's habit, Alfred knew, to use a local boy or young man to carry messages. Boys could go from the palace to the village and back again, without suspicion. "An' doan't come round 'ere lookin' fer me," he added sternly. "It's dang'rous business, an' it's bad practice. Not t' say against the rules."

Alfred nodded. From the tone of Bulls-eye's voice, he knew he'd got all he was going to get. None the wiser about Kitty, and with a dreadfully heavy heart, he got up and left.

CHAPTER EIGHT

Gladys Deacon was a beautiful girl endowed with a brilliant intellect. Possessed of exceptional powers of conversation, she could enlarge on any subject in an interesting and amusing manner. I was soon subjugated by the charm of her companionship and we began a friendship which only ended years later.

The Glitter and the Gold
Consuelo Vanderbilt Balsam

Seated at the round dining table which was always used when there were only a few guests, Winston bestowed an approving glance at his fish soufflé—pale gold, dressed with a frill of parsley and decorated with prawns. For him, dinners at Blenheim were the most enjoyable part of the day, for the French chef in the Marlborough kitchen was outstanding, the wines in the Marlborough cellar were the best that Vanderbilt money could buy, and the Saloon—the state dining room, used when the Marlboroughs entertained—was a glorious room, with its red marble dadoes and *trompe l'oeil* wall frescoes rising some thirty feet to a frieze of military scenes and then another ten feet to the frescoed ceiling.

The effect was martial, and although some felt it overwhelming, Winston always found it inspiring.

The first Duke, Winston's own forebear, was indisputably one of the nation's greatest military heroes. Winston felt that he himself had made no little contribution to the family's reputation by offering his own efforts in that regard, including his participation in the splendid cavalry charge at Omdurman in the Sudan and his daring escape from the Boers during the war in South Africa, and he would count himself fortunate if fate gave him other opportunities to bring military glory to the Churchill name.

The Marlboroughs were always the consummate host and hostess, but Winston enjoyed the other guests as well: Kate Sheridan, with her easy, unpretentious American charm, so like that of his own American mother; and Charles Sheridan, with his wide range of intellectual and scientific interests and his willingness to talk liberal politics and the need for social reform. He even rather liked Botsy Northcote, a tall, good-looking fellow with a military moustache. Botsy was a lively conversationalist with a wide acquaintance of people and ideas, when he was not off his head with love and despair—as he seemed to be now, no doubt because Miss Deacon was not paying him the kind of attention he deserved, in view of the fact that she was wearing the diamond necklace he had given her. And of course, there was Consuelo, gracious and elegant, whose first care was to make her guests comfortable and happy and see that each one had everything his or her heart could desire.

But therein lay a dilemma, for Miss Deacon was the heart's desire of at least two men at the table—the Duke and his friend Botsy. Tonight, seated across from Botsy and between Winston and Marlborough, she was wearing a low-cut silk gown of an unusual shade of burnished gold that highlighted her red-gold hair and displayed a perfect curve of breast and shoulder, as well as that splendid diamond necklace. Perhaps it was the danger she posed to Blenheim and the Marlboroughs that made it difficult for Winston to keep his eyes off her, or perhaps it was her outrageously flirtatious glance, her exotic conversation (one could never predict what she might say next), or even the heightened color of her cheeks and lips. She certainly seemed to be flirting with him—although he suspected that she was only doing so to make Botsy even more jealous than he already was, poor chap.

Making men jealous seemed to run in the Deacon family. Winston knew, of course, that Gladys's father had shot and killed his wife's lover. Everyone knew, and Gladys herself seemed to take a mischievous delight in the scandal.

"Simply imagine my feelings!" she had whispered to him at teatime. "I was there when it happened, Winston, although I was only twelve at the time." She opened her beautiful eyes wide. "My mother in hysterics, my father with the gun, still smoking, in his hand. I saw it all!"

Winston could never be sure whether Gladys was telling the truth, for she dramatized everything. But the murder itself was all too real. Gladys's mother was a great beauty, notorious for a string of adulterous relationships that drove her husband so mad with jealousy that he had fatally shot one of her French lovers. Alexandre Dumas had called Deacon an assassin, and the Paris newspapers were outraged at the notion that an American would kill a Frenchman who was merely engaged in the national pastime. Deacon went to prison and later died in an insane asylum. The scandal, which reverberated throughout Europe and America, inevitably tainted Gladys and her sisters. There were many in England who still regarded her as the daughter of a mad murderer and a woman who trapped unsuspecting men with her deadly beauty and wit.

At that moment, Winston saw Sunny put a finger on Gladys's wrist—a light touch and quickly withdrawn, but accompanied by a glance that spoke openly of intimacy and intrigue, even a kind of possessiveness. Winston felt himself flush.

This sort of public display is taking things much too far, he thought, the apprehension pumping through him. What can Sunny be thinking?

Winston was not the only guest who had noticed the Duke's possessive gesture, as he realized when he glanced up and saw Botsy Northcote's eyes narrow, his mouth tighten, and his handsome face go purple. So far, Botsy had managed to control himself, but he was not a man who handled his temper or his alcohol well, and he had already drunk several glasses of wine.

Winston gave an internal sigh. They would be lucky if they got through the evening without an explosion of some sort. He cast a surreptitious glance at Consuelo, who was seated to his left, to see if she had noticed the Duke's hand on Gladys's wrist, or Botsy's reaction to it. But the Duchess was chatting gaily with Sheridan, and seemed to take no notice of what was happening on the other side of the table. For that, at least, Winston was thankful. Perhaps it was time he had a talk with Consuelo about the situation and warned her against taking any ill-considered action. In one way or another, they all lived their lives in the public eye, and none of them could afford any sort of scandal.

And then Winston was distracted by Gladys, who bestowed an enchanting smile on him and asked him whether he had ever visited Rosamund's Well, on the other side of the lake.

"Of course," he said. "Used to go there often when I was a boy. Not much to see, though. Just a spring flowing out of a stone wall and into a square, shallow pool. Whatever else was there—Rosamund's Bower, the famous labyrinth—they've all disappeared."

"Oh, that's too bad," Gladys exclaimed with a wistful air. She appealed to the Duke. "Don't you think, Your Grace, that it would be divinely romantic to build a rustic retreat there, like the house that Henry built for Rosamund? Or perhaps a sort of Gothic ruin, surrounded by a labyrinth, where people could go and pretend to be Rosamund and King Henry, and fall madly in love." It happened that no one else was speaking at the moment, and her light words seemed to fall like bits of broken crystal in the silence.

"A folly, you mean?" Northcote asked with ironic emphasis. He leaned forward. "Not a romance with a happy end," he added in a warning tone, his words slurring just slightly. "Rosamund and Henry didn't get away with it, y'know."

Gladys's laugh tinkled up and down a full octave. "Why, of course!" she exclaimed, with a delicate shiver. "Didn't Eleanor murder poor, sweet Rosamund, to keep Henry for herself? Poison, I've always heard. But Eleanor ended her life in prison, poor thing, repenting the whole while." She seemed to glance toward Consuelo, then leaned toward the Duke and put her hand on his sleeve. "Oh, Sunny, I've just thought of the most glorious idea! Let's all row across the lake tonight after dinner and spy out a place to build the Marlborough Folly. Doesn't that sound like marvelous fun?"

The Marlborough Folly? Winston thought darkly. The Marlborough Folly was on exhibit before their eyes, at this very table. And God only knew where it would take them. Into disaster, if it went on the way it was going now.

"A folly might be rather nice," the Duke said with an indulgent smile at Gladys. "In fact, I think that my grandfather had the same idea, and went so far as to commission an architect to draw up plans. But I think we should not go at night, Miss Deacon. If one is planning to build something, it is only prudent to scout out the site by daylight."

Gladys pushed out her lower lip. "Oh, pooh," she said in exaggerated disappointment. "And I was trying so hard to coax a little bit of nocturnal fun out of everyone. It's so dull here."

Northcote was watching her with a devouring look. "You and I could go, Gladys. We're not required to be prudent, of course, since we're not doing the building. We can scout out several sites and report our recommendations to His Grace."

Carelessly, Gladys tossed her head. "Oh, thank you, Botsy. You're terribly sweet, but I think the Duke is right. We can all go tomorrow, and take a picnic lunch." She leaned forward, past Winston, and spoke to the Duchess. "What do you think, Consuelo, dear? Wouldn't that be great fun?"

The corners of the Duchess's mouth turned up slightly. But there was no smile in her eyes and her voice was strained as she said, "Why, yes, of course, Gladys. What a delightful plan."

Charles Sheridan had not been so deeply engaged in his conversation with the Duchess that he failed to observe Marlborough's possessive touch on Miss Deacon's wrist, Winston's uncomfortable expression, and the flush that rose quickly in Botsy Northcote's face. Charles did not usually take much notice of the romantic affairs of his acquaintances, but this business was too obvious.

And hazardous, too, he thought. Quite apart from the morality of things, Miss Deacon struck him as a reckless young woman who scorned concealment and preferred open indiscretions. And from the bewitching glances she was casting in Winston's direction, Charles suspected that she was capable of making serious trouble, not only between the Duke and the Duchess, but between Winston and the Duke. And then there was Botsy Northcote, with his flammable temper and combustible jealousies. Botsy had been known to make rather a fool of himself on occasion, especially when he had been drinking.

Charles could see, of course, what interested Marlborough and Northcote and seemed to fascinate Winston. Gladys Deacon was dazzling, both in appearance and in manner, although she was nervous and high-strung to an unusual degree and there was a certain forced and brittle quality in her gaiety. But Marlborough was obviously mesmerized by her, and his caressing touch on her wrist hinted at a physical intimacy between them. Charles was not an expert in such matters—he had never loved a woman before he loved Kate—but he guessed from the look on Northcote's face that he was no less besotted than the Duke, and was intoxicated, to boot.

Charles turned his head a little to his left and caught his wife's glance. Kate smiled at him in a way that never failed to warm his heart and make him feel that however inclined others might be to make romantic fools of themselves, their love for one another was unshakable. Exquisite in a green gown that set off the modest emeralds at her throat and ears, she was still the most beautiful woman in the world to him. Just now, Kate was leaning forward to say something to

Sunny about the history of Blenheim Park, momentarily distracting him from the girl—intentionally, Charles thought. She, too, had seen the Duke's hand on Miss Deacon's wrist.

"And you, Lord Charles?" the Duchess asked, and Charles turned with a start, realizing that he had been neglecting his hostess. "What do you think of Miss Deacon's plan for taking a picnic to Rosamund's Well tomorrow, with the idea of planning a folly there?"

"A picnic would be fun," Charles agreed, "although I'm afraid I have no opinion about the wisdom of follies." He had been thinking of driving to Oxford to see if he could find Ned Lawrence, Buttersworth's helper, and take him off to see the Rollright Stones, but that could wait.

"The wisdom of follies," the Duchess said, tossing her head with a laugh. Diamonds sparkled in her dark hair and in the bodice of her ivory satin gown, and Charles thought that she had an inborn, stylish elegance that Miss Deacon could never hope to achieve. Consuelo could be only four or five years older than the girl, but she carried herself with a dignified grace and cultured stateliness that added years to her age.

But even though the Duchess was smiling, Charles saw that her glance rested on her husband and Gladys Deacon, who seemed once again oblivious to the others at the table. The corners of her lips tightened and Charles thought that her eyes held the deepest sadness he had ever seen.

Or was it only sadness? Charles remembered what Buttersworth had told him about the gemstones that might have come from the famous Marlborough collection, about the appearance of the woman with Sappho's nose, about the mention of the Duchess's name. Well, the woman could not have been Consuelo herself, for her nose could never be said to be classical. That was an honor that would have to go to someone like Miss Deacon. But it was possible that the Duchess had decided on some strategem to embarrass her husband, or to exact some sort of revenge for his behavior. Or perhaps— incomprehensible as it might seem, since the Duchess was a Vanderbilt—she needed money, and fearing to pawn her personal jewels and refusing to ask her husband, had chosen something she thought might be sold without raising questions.

Charles sat back and allowed the footman to remove the remains of his fish soufflé and empty wine glass. Whatever the business at the museum, he could not help feeling sorry for the Duchess, who was so obviously unhappy. But at the same moment, he heard Kate laugh, and felt himself buoyed by an enormous lightness of spirit. Thank God he did not have such troubles as the Duke and Northcote were in for, if they continued to fling themselves like a pair of mindless moths at Miss Deacon's seductive flame. Thank God for Kate, for her great good humor, her good sense, and her steadfast love. He wouldn't trade her for all the duchesses in the world.

At that moment, Kate leaned forward. "Charles," she said, "did you happen to see a newspaper when you were in Oxford today? I wonder if you have any news of the American motorist who is attempting to drive across the continent." The story was being followed by the British press, which seemed to be as astonished by the idea that some lunatic might make the attempt as by the possibility that he might actually succeed.

"Horatio Nelson Jackson and his bulldog, Bud." Winston put in with a laugh. "What a wild, woolly adventure, and so out-and-out American! Almost as brash as Roosevelt's scheme to dig a canal across the Isthmus of Panama."

He sobered. "Although of course Roosevelt has exactly the right idea. If he has a canal, he won't need two navies, one on the east coast and one on the west."

"The canal, the motor car trip—it's all the same idea, when you stop to think about it," Charles replied. "A linkage between east and west. Except that Horatio Nelson Jackson—what a wonderful name!—is doing it on his own. The ultimate personal effort."

"The ultimate folly, if you ask me," Marlborough said, pulling his thin eyebrows together. "What idiot would want to drive a motor car where there aren't any roads? And if Jackson wanted to get across the country, why didn't the fool simply go by train?"

"Where's your sense of adventure, Sunny?" asked Miss Deacon playfully. "I think it sounds like divine fun, and frightfully dangerous." She shivered deliciously. "Why, the man might be captured by Indians, or murdered by robbers!"

"As a matter of fact," Charles said, "I read that Jackson drove safely into Omaha, Nebraska, on Sunday. Must have been quite a celebration. But he still has a long way to go— some thirteen hundred miles."

"Yes, but if he's got as far as Omaha," Kate said, "he's more than halfway there. And he's over the Rocky Mountains, which must have been the worst part. It's all downhill from there, so to speak."

"I'd give anything to be in New York when he arrives," Consuelo said, her eyes sparkling. "Wouldn't you, Kate? Such an amazing feat—I'm sure the whole city will turn out. There'll be a parade on Fifth Avenue, and bands and bunting and flags flying everywhere, just like the Fourth of July. Glorious!"

"You Americans," Marlborough said scornfully. "Always so childish. Any silly excuse for a parade."

Consuelo, obviously wounded, lowered her eyes. Charles thought the remark offensively patronizing, and did not even smile, but Miss Deacon laughed and Northcote and Winston joined in.

And with that, dessert was served.

CHAPTER NINE

Thursday, 14 May

Rosamond the fayre daughter of Walter lord Clifford, concubine to Henry II (poisoned by queen Elianor as some thought) dyed at Woodstocke where king Henry had made for her a house of wonderfull working, so that no man or woman might come to her, but he that was instructed by the king, or such as were right secret with him touching the matter. This house by some was named Labyrinthus . . . which was wrought like unto a knot in a garden, called a maze. . . .

Stowe's *Annals,* ed. 1631

Walking was one of Kate's passions. When she was at home at Bishop's keep, the estate she had inherited from her Ardleigh aunts, she went out for a tramp through the lanes and footpaths almost every day, wearing sensible boots and an ankle-length walking skirt and carrying field glasses and a stout walking stick. She'd brought her walking gear to Blenheim and hoped to go out often, if only to escape from the uninhabitable palace.

How did Consuelo manage, she wondered with a shudder, living day after day in such a dispiriting place? *She* couldn't endure it, she knew. Blenheim would suck all the life and creativity right out of her. Perhaps it was her American democratic spirit, but she knew she'd feel as if she were living in a vast imperial museum, full of relics of British conquest and domination, and she was its curator. Or a splendidly gilded jail, and she was both its jailor and its prisoner.

But the Park around the palace was lovely beyond words. This morning, the rising sun was a pale silver globe draped with ghostlike mists, and in the pearly light, Kate could see geese and ducks and swans sailing on the lake and hear them speaking to one another in low, comforting calls. However she might feel about the palace, she had fallen in love with the lake and woodlands and meadows, which seemed to change with each hour of the day, with the slightest change in the wind and weather. Early morning—before anyone but the staff was up and about, before the groundskeepers began their work—morning, for Kate, was the best time of all. Yesterday morning and the morning before, she had explored the East Park, the Cascades, and the Swiss Cottage, as well as the wilder, more sinister forests of High Park.

On this morning, Kate had risen just as the sun came up, dressed quietly, and set out in the company of her friend and coauthor, the intrepid, invisible, but very real Beryl Bardwell. Kate was carrying an artist's folding stool, a sketchpad and pencils, and a notebook. She and Beryl had visited Rosamund's Well on Tuesday afternoon—just a quick visit, to get the lay of the land and to give themselves something to think about. This morning, Kate wanted to sit in the grass below the spring, to sketch its setting and make notes, while Beryl wanted to dream about a time when there had been a pleasure garden and a cluster of buildings—the famous Rosamund's Bower—on the hillside above, as well as a royal hunting lodge, which over the centuries had been altered and enlarged until it became a palace as stately and substantial as Blenheim was now.

It was all gone, of course, dissolved into the mists of time and remembered only in legend and the occasional desultory conversation, like last night's table talk. Rosamund's Bower and the grand palace had fallen into ruin, the sites had been razed, and the building stones used to construct the foundations of the Grand Bridge. But the bower and the palace were still there, in Kate's and Beryl's imaginations— and so much clearer now, after Kate had read one of the books she'd bought in the bookstore, *The Early History of Woodstock Manor and its Environs.*

According to the book, the Norman kings of England had first hunted in the forests of Oxfordshire some nine hundred years ago. It was probably Henry I, at the beginning of the twelfth century, who enclosed a park near the village of Woodstock, for he had kept a menagerie there: a lion, leopards, lynx, and camels, and even a porcupine—all exotic creatures never before seen in England. Perhaps, Kate thought with a little smile, the stone wall around the grounds had been built to keep the porcupine from wandering off.

Henry's park, of course, was nothing at all like the open ornamental landscape that now existed. Then, there had been no lake, only the pretty little River Glyme winding through a marshy valley, its banks rising steeply on either side. The woodlands had provided venison for the royal table, sport for the royal household, and timber for royal buildings, while the river was dammed to create small fishponds, where pike, eel, and bream were impounded. No one could take fish or game or fell trees except by royal permission.

The second Henry came to the throne in 1154. At nineteen, he had married Eleanor of Aquitaine, a marriage between powerful political allies. Exceptionally beautiful, ambitious, and willful, Eleanor was the richest woman in the known world, the possessor of almost half the territory that is now France, and eleven years Henry's senior. Her age hardly mattered at the time of their marriage, and in the course of the next thirteen years, Eleanor bore her husband five sons and three daughters.

But Henry took a number of mistresses, the most famous of whom was Rosamund de Clifford. She was very young, perhaps only fifteen. Henry had already begun to expand his father's hunting lodge at Woodstock into a royal palace, and when he brought Rosamund there, he built her a house of her own: Rosamund's Bower, it was called, a *bower* being a rural retreat. Historians disagreed about the truth of this story, but that hardly mattered to Beryl Bardwell, who was quite happy when historical ambiguity gave Kate's imagination a freer rein.

What did matter was that the Rosamund legends had evolved over the centuries into a fascinating, if contradictory, literary tradition. In ballad and story, Rosamund's Bower became a palatial establishment of stone and timber, with 150 doors, surrounded by a maze "so cunningly contrived with turnings round about, that none but with a clue of thread could enter in or out." Some of the tales suggested that the king constructed the labyrinth to barricade the beautiful young girl against his jealous queen and against other rivals—one of whom, Roger of Salisbury, was said to have fallen so desperately in love with Rosamund that he tried to carry her off. Others hinted that Rosamund herself would have been glad enough to escape from the king, but she was now his captive, trapped in their sinful liaison (symbolized by the legendary labyrinth, of course).

In the legend, Henry's Herculean efforts to defend his mistress ultimately failed. Eleanor visited the palace at Woodstock. When Henry came to her one morning, she saw that his spur had snagged a golden thread. Following the thread through the maze, Eleanor discovered Rosamund. Shortly thereafter, Rosamund was found dead. She had been poisoned.

Had the aging, vengeful Eleanor murdered her beautiful young rival? Or had Rosamund been killed by a treacherous servant, or even by the desperate Roger of Salisbury? Or had she—stricken with shame, sick with scandal and disgrace, realizing that she was imprisoned for life—killed *herself*?

Beryl, of course, found these questions deliciously enthralling, for the legends offered a wealth of story material for their novel, some of it wonderfully lurid and exactly the sort of mystery she loved. Kate herself was always more circumspect and tried to keep within the bounds of the believable. If history said that Eleanor had been in Henry's prison at the time of Rosamund's death and hence could not possibly have killed her, that settled the matter.

But Beryl was bolder, and insisted on holding open all the possibilities as long as possible. *So what if the queen was shut up in jail?* she argued. *What makes you think she couldn't have hired a killer to do the dirty deed for her?*

To which Kate had no immediate answer. In such matters, Beryl was usually right, and Kate usually gave in. For now, at least, they would leave the questions open and see where the story took them.

By this time, Kate had arrived at the end of the bridge and was setting off along the narrow path that led down the hill to the left, in the direction of Rosamund's Well. The grass was damp and slippery, and she had to scramble to keep her footing. But the soft gray light was exactly what she wanted, and when she reached the Well, she unfolded her stool, opened her sketchpad, and set to work.

The spring, she saw, issued out of an ancient, moss-covered stone wall and fell into a square pool, about twenty feet by twenty, set within a paved area. When an observer had described the site some two hundred years before, there had been three pools, and a seat built into the wall, as well as the ruins of an old building and much stone paving. Now, Kate and Beryl had to use their imaginations in order to see what might have been there in Rosamund's time: a pleasant rustic bower, a paved courtyard, a pear orchard, a fragrant herb garden filled with birds and butterflies, and perhaps a series of bubbling waterfalls, where the waters of the spring danced down the rocky slope.

The mist swirled through the trees and over the lake, concealing Blenheim Palace on the opposite shore. Surrounded by the gray swirls, Kate could imagine herself carried back to Rosamund's time, on a morning when two lovers stood in a pleasant garden beside a spring, absorbed in their passion and seeing nothing of the turmoil around them. For a moment, she was swept by Rosamund's feelings—a tumble of delight, apprehension, and the reckless, headstrong abandonment that comes with passion. And Henry's—his desire, his need, his concern for Rosamund's well-being, his determination to keep what belonged to him. And Eleanor's, as well. The older woman, losing her husband to a younger; the queen, in danger of losing her kingdom and her freedom; the jealous wife, filled with a hateful bitterness.

Beryl was right. All the elements were here, and more.

Compelling characters and a tantalizing setting, within a rich background of legend, tradition, and history. She had only to let her imagination go free, and she would be able to create a wonderfully powerful story, perhaps the best she had ever written.

But as Kate sat, lost in a misty vision of the past, her attention was caught by something very real and entirely unimaginary: a scrap of burnished gold silk snagged on a low holly bush in front of her. She leaned forward and picked it off, turning it over in her fingers. The silk was exactly the shade of the dress that Gladys Deacon had worn to dinner the night before.

For Kate, the sight of the scrap of silk evoked the scene at the dining table: Marlborough's possessive hand on Gladys's wrist, Gladys's provocative smile, Lord Northcote's angrily jealous glance, Consuelo's sad mouth. And Gladys's idea for a folly, "a sort of Gothic ruin," she had said, "where people could go and pretend to be Rosamund and King Henry and fall madly in love." And then another image flickered across the first, like a blurry double exposure, the ancient story of adulterous love, annihilating jealousies, and bitter rivalries, reenacted in the present. Gladys playing Rosamund, Marlborough as Henry, Consuelo as Eleanor, and Botsy Northcote as Roger of Salisbury.

And in her mind, she heard Beryl, speaking in an ominous whisper. *Something awful has happened, Kate. There's been a tragedy here, a death. I know it. I can feel it!*

Kate shivered, for a moment overwhelmed with apprehension. But Beryl was often overly dramatic, and as she considered the situation, she could see no reason to imagine any sort of tragedy. Apart from the exchange of gesture and glance at the dinner table, and that silly business about the folly, the previous evening had been rather ordinary.

After dinner, they had adjourned to the Saloon. No one seemed to feel much like conversation, so Kate, Charles, Northcote, and Winston had played a hand of bridge. Pleading weariness and a return of her headache, Consuelo excused herself and went to bed. When she was gone, as if by a secret signal, Gladys and the Duke announced that they were going for a walk. A few moments later, Northcote flung down his cards, rose, and went to the window, where he stood for a while with his back to the room, smoking a cigarette and looking out at the moonlit garden. Then he, too, pled weariness and went off to bed.

"I'm not much for three-handed bridge," Winston had said. "Charles, perhaps you and I could enjoy a cigar while you tell me what you think of those chapters I sent you." So Charles and Winston had gone to the smoking room, and Kate had gone upstairs to her book. As evenings went, this one had been on the quiet side.

But what about Gladys and the Duke? Likely, Kate thought now, turning the golden scrap in her fingers, she had persuaded him to take her to the Well, after all. They could have rowed across the lake in one of the skiffs that were kept in the boathouse, then walked up to the spring, and Gladys had torn her dress on the bush. Kate's mouth tightened. The silk scrap might not be the golden thread that Eleanor had followed to Rosamund, but there was a connection here, and it made Kate uncomfortable.

She opened her pencil case and put the scrap inside. Gladys would want to have it, so that the dress could be repaired. But she would approach her privately, Kate decided.

The girl would certainly not want anyone to know where the scrap had been found, for fear of raising embarrassing questions.

Or would she? Gladys Deacon had struck Kate as the sort of young woman who preferred to be the center of everyone's attention, to be at the eye of every storm—and if there was no storm, she was perfectly capable of creating one. She probably wouldn't mind at all if she were publically confronted with the evidence of a moonlight tryst with the Duke, Rosamund to his Henry. She might even feel triumphant at the sadness in Consuelo's eyes and the scarcely concealed jealous rage on Northcote's face.

And with that in mind, Kate decided very firmly that Gladys Deacon should not have the opportunity to feel any sort of satisfaction. She would return the silk scrap privately, along with the suggestion that it was dangerous to play with people's hearts. Gladys would laugh and pay no attention, but Kate would at least have made the effort.

CHAPTER TEN

*No American heiress knew how to run the enormous household
her English husband expected her to manage—with no prepara-
tion or training or even assistance. She knew nothing of how
the food was purchased and meals made to appear on the table,
how the clean linen was accomplished, the dust done away
with, the tradesmen paid. Her ignorance often led to serious
problems with the servants, for they recognized her inexperi-
ence and exploited it to their best advantage.*

Dollar Duchesses
Susan Blake

Consuelo was in the habit of rising at seven, breakfasting
in her apartment, and then spending several hours at
the desk in the morning room where she conducted her
household duties: meeting daily with the butler, the housekeeper, and the cook; going over their household accounts;
checking inventories and seeing that the tradesmen were
paid; and dealing with staff problems. When there were
guests, she had the extra work of seeing to their comfort,
planning elaborate meals, arranging entertainment.

Of course, the four guests staying with them this week

posed no problem at all, compared to the thirty—King Edward and Queen Alexandra, together with an assortment of dukes and duchesses—who had been invited to Blenheim for a gala weekend at the beginning of August. This wasn't the first time the Royal couple had been guests of the Marlboroughs, and Consuelo knew what a daunting responsibility it was to feed and amuse not only Their Royal Majesties and the other luminaries, but to accomodate the various entourages of valets, maids, footmen, and grooms. Altogether, a hundred people would be sleeping in the house, and there would be a fine hubbub and hullabaloo below-stairs.

For Consuelo, visitors usually brought a welcome respite from the long, dispiriting days when she and Sunny were alone with nothing to say to one another, with nothing to share, certainly not love and scarcely even friendship. She would especially enjoy playing hostess to Edward and Alexandra, would enjoy dressing up and wearing her jewels, usually kept in the London bank—the nineteen-row pearl dog collar her husband had bought for her, the long rope of perfect pearls that had once belonged to Catherine the Great, as well as her diamond tiara. She hoped she would feel better by that time, not as tired and low-spirited as she was now. She had even left her guests early the night before, angry at her husband and irritated with Gladys, who was behaving like a spoiled child.

Consuelo had been barely nineteen when she came to Blenheim—much too young and inexperienced, she knew now, to have taken on the monstrous burden of administering such a huge enterprise. When she might have been enjoying the pleasures of a glamorous, carefree youth, the Duke had made it clear that her chief duty (next to producing a male heir, of course) was to manage the enormous house and its complex and often inharmonious staff. The situation was made even more uncomfortable because Marlborough's aunt, Lady Sarah Churchill, had acted as his hostess and chatelaine during his bachelorhood. The butler and housekeeper had been loyal to her, resisting Consuelo's efforts to undertake her new responsibilities and make necessary changes.

Even now, with six years of experience behind her, Consuelo felt that she didn't do a very good job. Marlborough felt so, too, and frequently took her to task for not paying the proper attention or for being too soft in her dealings with the staff. He told her she should try to be more like Lady Sarah, who was extraordinarily well organized and had a great firmness with everyone, especially those who were slow in executing her orders.

Looking over the accounts on her desk, Consuelo had to admit that they were rather in a muddle. The trouble was that she had to rely for everything upon Mrs. Raleigh, the housekeeper, and Stevens, the butler, who had both been in service at Blenheim for several decades. She was confident that she could trust them, although they were both getting on in years, Mrs. Raleigh especially, and she often found herself wishing that they would keep a tighter rein belowstairs, where some of the servants seemed unacceptably lax.

Of course, Consuelo thought with a sigh, it was becoming harder and harder to find good household help. Many young men had gone off to the Boer War, many young women were taking factory jobs in the cities, and service was not the attractive alternative to agricultural labor that it had once been. Stevens had just stepped in to ask permission to hire a new page to replace Richard, who had been promoted to third footman because the third footman had gone to America. And here was Mrs. Raleigh, wanting to hire yet another housemaid, a replacement for one who had apparently left without permission—more surprisingly, without asking for a character or for the pay that was due her.

Consuelo frowned. Page boys and housemaids and scullery maids came and went, but it was rather strange for one to just up sticks and leave. And now was a difficult time to hire a new maid. "This will be the second new housemaid in a fortnight," she said disapprovingly, "and with Royalty coming in less than three weeks. There will scarcely be time to train her."

"The new maid, Bess, has recommended a woman with whom she was in service at Wilson House, in London," Mrs. Raleigh said. "If she is as good as Bess, she will be a treasure."

"Bess *is* good," Consuelo agreed, "experienced and quite responsible." Bess had been with them for only a few weeks, but she had already proved her worth by volunteering to look after Gladys Deacon, whose own maid had been requisitioned by Gladys's mother. Gladys (who was hard to please) had spoken favorably of the woman. Consuelo frowned, going back to the previous subject. "The housemaid who has left, Mrs. Raleigh. When was she last seen?"

"I believe it was Friday night at bedtime, Your Grace," Mrs. Raleigh replied thinly. "Ruth, who slept with her, missed her in the morning when she woke up."

Friday night, and today was Thursday. "A search was made, I suppose," Consuelo said, thinking uneasily of the gardener who had drowned himself in the lake in a fit of despair the winter before.

"Oh, yes, Your Grace," Mrs. Raleigh replied quickly. "There wasn't a sign of her anywhere. She had been here just since May, so I supposed she got homesick and left. Nothing is missing," she added, pursing her narrow lips. "I made a careful check of all the rooms she worked in, just to be sure."

Consuelo felt a sudden impatience with the woman, although she understood Mrs. Raleigh's concern. Not long ago, a valuable china box had disappeared from a table in the Green Drawing Room. Marlborough had discovered it missing, and a housemaid was accused. After everyone was thoroughly upset, he had told Consuelo that he himself had taken the box to see if its absence would be noticed. Since then, Mrs. Raleigh had supervised the housemaids more closely, although her supervision did not appear to extend to the nighttime hours, or to the locking of doors. Presumably, the missing maid had got out through an unlocked door.

Consuelo tried to conceal her impatience. "What was the girl's name? Who on the staff knew her best?"

"Her name was Kitty, Your Grace." Mrs. Raleigh watched uneasily as Consuelo wrote it down. "I suppose Ruth would have known her best."

"Then I should like to speak to Ruth," Consuelo said, feeling that somebody ought to make an effort to get to the bottom of this, and if Mrs. Raleigh wouldn't do it, she would have to. What's more, she was curious. It wasn't like housemaids to disappear without their wages. "*Now,* if you please," she added firmly.

Ruth was summoned from her duties and stood nervously before her, a sturdy young girl, pleasant-faced, her thick brown hair bound up under her cap. She could scarcely be sixteen.

Consuelo softened her tone. "Tell me, Ruth, what you think might have become of——" She looked down at her notes. "Of Kitty."

"I'm sure I don't know, Your Grace," Ruth said, biting her lip. "She went to bed same as me, but when morning come, that would be Saturday morning, she was gone. Sneaked right out, she did. Quietlike, or I would've heard her. I told Mrs. Raleigh straightaway," she added, as though she were afraid she might be accused of concealment.

"Did she go off with someone, do you think?" Consuelo asked. "Did she have a young man?"

The girl frowned. "A . . . young man? I don't think so, Your Grace. She never said."

Consuelo tried another tack. "Well, then, where was she in service before she came here?"

"Welbeck Abbey, Your Grace," Mrs. Raleigh put in officiously. "She had a fine character from the Duchess of Portland's housekeeper. And before that, at Carleton House, in Manchester."

A fine character. Consuelo knew what that meant. It wouldn't surprise her if half the characters the new hires presented were forged, and although the housekeeper and butler were supposed to check, they didn't always. But perhaps Ruth knew where the girl came from.

"Where was her home, Ruth?" she asked in a gentle voice. "Where are her people?"

Ruth shook her head, and then, as if she felt she should explain, added, "Us maids don't talk much about ourselves, Your Grace. There's not hardly time in the day, what with the work and that, and at meals there's always somebody listenin'." Her voice became self-pitying. "And at night we're wore out. We're asleep soon's our heads hit the pillow."

Consuelo suspected that there was plenty of time during the day for the maids to share personal secrets and household gossip, but she could not deny that by bedtime, they would be exhausted. A servant's life was not an easy one. She would have done more to make it easier, if she could—would at least have heated the tower rooms where the girls slept, and laid on running water. But Marlborough disapproved of innovations in the house. Her Vanderbilt dowry was meant to restore Blenheim to its earlier glory, not to make it more habitable.

There was a little silence, and then Ruth added, almost as an afterthought, "But we did talk once, now that I think on't. We walked to the village together on our last half-day off. Kitty wanted to see Fair Rosamund's Well, and it was only a little out of the way, so we stopped for a look. She said she was meeting someone at the Black Prince, in Manor Road."

"Meeting someone?" Mrs. Raleigh stared at the maid disapprovingly, over the tops of her glasses. "A young man?"

Ruth shook her head. "Oh, no, not a *young* man. He was waiting in front of the Prince for her, and I'd say he's as old as my father. He had a red beard. She—"

"Well, then," Mrs. Raleigh interrupted, obviously relieved. "I expect he was a relation."

Consuelo wasn't so sure of that, but there was no use in speculating. "Very well, Ruth," she said. "Can you think of anything else?"

The girl glanced hesitantly at Mrs. Raleigh, then at Consuelo, then seemed to pluck up her courage. She licked her lips. "Well, yes, I can, Your Grace. You see, I've been wondering . . . ." Her voice trailed off.

"Yes?" With an inner sigh, Consuelo looked down at the seemingly endless list of chores in front of her. The weekend menu was next, a task she always dreaded, for the French chef was inclined to be a prima donna. Whenever he wanted to show his displeasure with her, he would serve ortolans—rare songbirds, considered a gourmet delight—to her guests for breakfast, because he knew that she considered these mortifyingly nouveau riche. One never knew what might set the man off. He hadn't been at all pleased, for instance, when she'd sent word that they wanted a picnic lunch today.

She looked up to find the girl still standing there. "What were you wondering, Ruth?"

The girl ducked her head. "Whether I could have Kitty's best dress. It would exactly fit my sister. She's—"

"Kitty's dress?" Consuelo asked, startled. "You mean, she went away and left her clothing behind, as well as her earnings?" She turned to Mrs. Raleigh. "Is this true?"

"I don't know, Your Grace," Mrs. Raleigh replied, flustered. "I didn't think to ask—"

"So her things are still in the tower?" Consuelo asked the maid.

"Yes, Your Grace," Ruth said, "in a trunk." She went on eagerly, "There's a skirt and blouse and winter cloak, if they're wanted for the other maids. But this dress is made of blue wool, you see, with blue and black braid, and my sister is getting married and—"

"I think we might wait a while before we give away Kitty's clothing," Consuelo said quietly. "Thank you, Ruth. That will be all."

After the girl had left the room, Consuelo sat for a moment, thinking. If the housemaid had left her clothing behind, especially her best dress, she had not gone off with some young man. But where could she be?

To Mrs. Raleigh, she said, "I think you should ask the other servants what they know about this missing girl. Since she has left both clothes and money, it is not unreasonable to think that she might have met with an accident."

Mrs. Raleigh looked uncomfortable. "Yes, Your Grace. I'll have it looked into right away. And about the clothing, I must say that I—"

"Thank you," Consuelo said firmly. "I also think that inquiries should be made at the Black Prince. The person Ruth mentioned, the man with the red beard, may still be there. Perhaps he can offer some clue as to Kitty's whereabouts. And if he is indeed a relative, he will need to know that she is gone."

Mrs. Raleigh stiffened. Even though she may have felt in the wrong about the girl, it was clear that she would go only so far to make amends. "If you will pardon me, Your Grace, inquiries at a village pub are the sort of thing the footmen should be asked to carry out. Shall I ring?"

Consuelo frowned. Perhaps it wasn't a good idea to send one of the footmen on this errand, for they would only gossip about it in the servants' hall. It might be better if she asked the butler, who could perhaps manage it himself, without causing a commotion or creating gossip among the servants.

"I'll speak to Mr. Stevens about it." She glanced at the ormolu clock on the desk, stifling a sigh. It was nearly nine-thirty. "It's time to get on with our work. Please tell Monsieur Carnot that I am ready to discuss the menus with him. And don't forget that lunch is to be a picnic. Be sure that it is sent over to the Well so it's waiting when we arrive. There's to be champagne, of course, so don't forget to arrange for the ice."

"Yes, Your Grace," Mrs. Raleigh said. She went to the door, then hesitated indecisively.

Consuelo looked up. "Was there something else?"

"Yes, Your Grace, I'm afraid there is. I don't like to mention it, but . . ."

"But what, Mrs. Raleigh?" Consuelo felt impatient. There was so much to do, and never enough time. "Please, we don't have all morning."

Mrs. Raleigh's lips thinned. "It's Miss Deacon, Your Grace."

Consuelo frowned. "What about Miss Deacon?" The week before, Mrs. Raleigh had reported that Gladys had accused one of the housemaids of having taken a silver comb. The comb had subsequently been found under the bed, but the hard feelings had lingered. She hoped this wasn't another report of the same sort.

The housekeeper spoke with obvious reluctance. "The maid went in to take her tea and open the drapes, and she— Well, she wasn't there."

Consuelo felt a chill of unease. "Well, then, she's gone out, I expect," she said. "Perhaps she's walking with Lady Sheridan, who loves early-morning tramps."

"Walking?" Mrs. Raleigh's tone was colored with a delicate disapproval. "Pardon, but I shouldn't think so, Your Grace. Bess says her bed hasn't been slept in. I realize that Miss Deacon has her own way of doing things. But if she intended to go off last night, she might at least have let someone know."

Consuelo swallowed, grasping for control. As a hostess, she was certainly very much aware of the customs of English houseparties, which involved a great many noctural frolics— surreptitious tip-toeings down the carpeted halls, delicate tappings on doors, and muffled sounds of pleasure from the curtained beds. But everyone, even Gladys, knew the rules. It was always the gentlemen who went tip-toeing down the hall, never the ladies. And all must be back in their assigned rooms before the housemaids came with tea and a pitcher of hot water. If Gladys had not slept in her room—

Consuelo put down her pen and stood. She could feel her knees wobbling, and when she spoke, she was surprised to hear her voice sounding normal. "I imagine that she's gotten back already," she said. "But perhaps we'd better go and have a look."

CHAPTER ELEVEN

She's only a bird in a gilded cage,
A beautiful sight to see.
You may think she's happy and free from care,
She's not what she seems to be.

"A Bird in a Gilded Cage," 1899
Words by Arthur J. Lamb, music by Harry von Tilzer

It had been shortly after eight-thirty in the morning when Kate returned to Blenheim. She went upstairs and changed quickly out of her walking costume and into the slim blue skirt and white silk blouse she planned to wear until dinner, with the addition of an embroidered tunic at teatime.

The usual rule for houseparties was four changes of clothing: a relatively simple morning costume; a more elaborate luncheon and afternoon dress; a loose, luxurious tea gown—a *teagie*, it was called; and a sumptuous dinner gown. Each costume, of course, had its own accessories and jewels. Ladies who cared about such things made sure they didn't wear the same outfit twice. For them, a four-day houseparty required sixteen different costumes and appropriate accessories, and since some of the skirts were voluminous, their luggage might include three or four large trunks.

Kate, however, viewed the business of multiple costumes as silly. She packed what she felt she needed—skirts and blouses for day, a tea gown, and one or two dinner gowns—and that was that. She did not require a maid to help her dress, and she wore her hair in a simple style that she could manage herself. If other guests were offended by her casual attitude toward dress and her natural look, well, so be it. Kate might have married into the peerage, but she valued her comfort and convenience much more than the opinions of ladies who chiefly dressed to impress.

A few minutes later, she was opening the door to the breakfast room—a lovely, light room wallpapered in green and ivory, with a wide window that overlooked the Italian garden. She had tucked the scrap of burnished gold cloth into her skirt pocket, hoping to see Gladys Deacon and give it to her privately. Winston and Charles were already there, discussing Chamberlain's Imperial Preference proposal over plates of eggs and kidneys.

In the last few weeks, Winston had come out hard on the side of free trade, creating a great deal of bad feeling among his fellow Tories, who stood with Chamberlain and his protectionist policies. "But they're going to have to hear me out," he was saying gruffly, as Kate came into the room.

"If you're not careful, Winston," Charles replied, "you'll find yourself crossing the floor and joining the Liberals."

"Would that be such a terrible mistake?" Winston asked. He pulled his brows together and pushed out his mouth in what Kate had come to think of as his "bulldog" look. "And don't smile, Charles. I'm in deadly earnest."

"I'm not smiling," Charles said soberly. "In fact, I should

think you could work far more effectively from the Liberal bench." He glanced up as the footman seated Kate at the table. "Good morning, my dear. Did you enjoy your walk to Rosamund's Well?"

"Yes, thank you," Kate said. She added strawberry jam to her buttered toast and accepted a cup of tea from the footman. "Thank you, Alfred," she said with a smile. Of all the Blenheim footmen, she liked this one the best—a tall, blond young man, with a sweetly pleasant look and an accomodating manner. "Has Miss Deacon come down yet, Charles?"

"Not to my knowledge," Charles replied. "You were here before I came down, Winston. Did you see her?"

"No, nor the Duke, either," Winston said, "which is a bit odd. He's always down for breakfast at half past eight." He grinned at Kate. "You're an early bird, Kate. Don't tell me you've been around the lake already this morning?"

"Just over the bridge and back," Kate said. "It's the best time of day to walk." She smiled back at Winston, whose energies she admired. "You're welcome to go tramping with me any morning you like."

"Thanks," Winston said earnestly, "but I'd rather not expend energy on walking that will be needed for writing. It's amazing how blasted hard it can be to write, especially when one is writing about one's father." He wrinkled his nose. "I hate to say it, but I do believe that he dared to offend every member of the party, at least twice."

They all laughed at that, and the men went back to their discussion. Kate ate quickly, listening with half an ear. Gladys still had not put in an appearance by the time she finished, so she stood and excused herself.

"I'm off to work," she said to Charles, putting her hand on his shoulder. "What are your plans for the morning?"

"I'm taking my camera into the Park. I plan to be back by picnic time, though."

"Enjoy yourself, then." She left the men, still talking politics, and went upstairs. It was nine-thirty, and Gladys was probably awake by now. Before she and Beryl settled down to a morning's writing, she would go to the girl's room and speak to her.

In the second-floor corridor, Kate paused in front of a heavy oak door, where a hand-lettered white card with Gladys's name on it had been inserted into the brass slot. She knocked, expecting a sleepily irate reply. Hearing nothing, she raised her hand to knock again. Just then, she turned to see Consuelo hurrying toward her down the hall, looking troubled. Behind her was Mrs. Raleigh, the housekeeper, a short, round, bustling woman with a bunch of jangling keys at her waist.

"Oh, good morning, Consuelo," Kate said, dropping her hand. "I was just looking for Gladys. She doesn't answer my knock, but perhaps she has gone out for an early walk."

Consuelo's lips were pinched and her voice was low and distracted. "The maid reported that she doesn't seem to have returned to her room last night."

"Didn't return to her room?" Kate asked, startled. Suddenly, the scrap of cloth felt like a flaming ember in her pocket.

"Yes," Consuelo said. "I thought perhaps I should see for myself. I'm very glad you're here, Kate. Please come in with me." She went to the door, squared her shoulders as if she were stepping into a lion's den, and turned the knob.

The large room was cheerful and bright, with an eastern view. The draperies had been opened to admit the morning sun, and a tray with a cup of tea and a single rosebud sat on the small table beside the window. Last night's fire had burned down and had not been relit. The coverlet and sheet had been neatly turned down but were undisturbed, and Glady's dainty lace-trimmed nightgown was folded on the pillow.

Kate looked at the Duchess. Her hands were clenched into tight fists, and there was a bewildered look on her face.

"What in the world could have—" Consuelo stopped. "I wonder if she came back here to change before she . . ." Her voice trailed off.

With the torn scrap in her pocket, Kate thought she knew the answer to that question, but she went to the wardrobe and opened the doors. The crowded rack was a rainbow of Gladys's stylish gowns in shades of blue, chartreuse, yellow, carnelian, ivory. But the burnished gold silk she had worn the night before was not there.

"She was wearing a diamond necklace," Kate said, half to herself, and went to the elaborate jewel box on the dressing table. It was full of bracelets, baubles, and bangles, some of them, Kate thought, quite valuable. But the necklace was not there. Wherever the girl had gone, she was still wearing her dinner dress and diamonds worth a small fortune.

Consuelo made a low sound of wrenching pain. In the doorway, Mrs. Raleigh was watching the scene with a puzzled frown, as if she failed to see why the Duchess should be so up-set about the vagaries of a guest, and particularly the flighty Miss Deacon. Kate felt it was time to take command.

In as authoritative a tone as she could summon, she said to Mrs. Raleigh, "Her Grace and I are going to sit down to a cup of hot tea in my room. Please see that it's brought as quickly as possible." And then she noticed the large bunch keys at the housekeeper's waist. "Oh, before you go, please let me have the key to this room. Perhaps it's a good idea to lock it."

With barely disguised displeasure, Mrs. Raleigh took out the key and handed it to her, then went off to see to the tea. Kate put her arm around Consuelo's shoulders and led her out of the room, pausing to lock the door behind them. As they turned, Kate saw that the door across the hall was open, a pair of white-capped, white-aproned housemaids peering out, saucer-eyed. Kate shook her head at them and they scurried back to their work, but she knew that within the hour, news of Gladys Deacon's unexplained absence—and the Duchess's reaction to it—would be on every servant's tongue. And if Kate knew servants, the tale would be full of exaggerations, intentional and otherwise. Why, they'd probably have Gladys murdered and her body in the lake, she thought, and shivered.

A few moments later, sipping a cup of hot tea in a chair in front of the fire in Kate's bedroom, the color had come back to Consuelo's cheeks, her hands had stopped trembling, and she looked rather better. But her voice was still bleak and thin when she spoke. "I'm sorry, Kate. I didn't mean to cause such a commotion, especially in front of the servants. They are such terrible gossips."

"You didn't cause a commotion," Kate said comfortingly. Holding her cup, she sat in the opposite chair. "It was the shock, that's all. I was every bit as surprised as you. Where on earth can the girl have gone?"

She had already decided not to say anything just yet about the scrap of gold silk. If Gladys reappeared with an explanation for her absence, she would speak to her privately about it. And if she didn't, well, the torn silk was a clue to where the girl had been. It was the sort of thing that

Charles, or the police, if it came to that, would want to know about. Kate found herself wishing that she'd had the presence of mind to scout around Rosamund's Well for any other signs that Gladys had been there—Gladys and someone else. She somehow doubted that Gladys would have gone there alone.

"I have no idea where she might be," Consuelo said miserably. "I must confess that she occasionally behaves . . . well, erratically. But she's never just disappeared like this." Her hand trembled, and she put down her cup on the small table beside her chair, as if she were afraid she might drop it. "May I . . . may I speak to you in confidence, Kate? I'm reluctant to burden you with my troubles, but there's no one else, and I feel as if I will go mad if I can't at least talk about it." She looked away. "I've begun to feel as if you're . . . well, a kindred spirit. After all, we are both Americans. And both married to Englishmen."

With a soft sound, a coal fell in the grate. They might both be Americans, Kate thought, but they were separated by an enormous chasm of class and upbringing. Consuelo was a Vanderbilt, heiress to one of the largest fortunes in the world, while she herself had been raised on the Lower East Side of New York.* But her Irish aunt and uncle had taught her to support herself by her own industry, while she suspected that Consuelo had been given few opportunities to make her own independent decisions or even to develop her own interests. And as to their both being married to Englishmen—well, Charles was nothing at all like the Duke of Marlborough,

---

* The story of Kate's life before she came to England is told in *Death at Bishop's Keep.*

thank heavens. Kate could comfort herself with the thought that he hadn't wanted her for her money (since she had none), while Consuelo was daily confonted with the fact that Marlborough had loved not her, but the Vanderbilt millions. All in all, there were a great many more differences between them than similarities.

But Kate said nothing of this. Instead, she replied softly, "Of course you may speak confidentially, Consuelo. Tell me anything you like. Your secrets will remain with me."

"I used to talk to Gladys about the way I felt," Consuelo said bleakly. "She's an American, too, and we've been friends for several years. But recently, I've come to realize that—" She stopped, took out a lace handkerchief, and blew her nose. "That she is more my husband's friend than mine." She looked at Kate. "I suppose you've noticed."

Not sure what she should say, Kate only nodded.

"They make no secret of it," Consuelo said miserably. "Everyone must know. I hear whispers whenever I'm in London."

Kate thought that gossip and rumor, real or perceived, must be very painful for the Duchess of Marlborough, who lived such a public life, herself and her marriage always on display. She felt a mix of emotions: pity for Consuelo's pain, anger at the causes of it, fear that nothing could be done to make the situation any better.

But she kept all this from her voice as she said, "How long have they known each other?"

"They met in London after our first child was born, while I was still confined." Consuelo gave a little laugh. "I was . . . well, naive, I suppose. For a time, I didn't notice what was going on, and when I did, I thought it would fade. After all, Gladys was barely sixteen then, and Marlborough is a man of few passions. He was so fully immersed in Blenheim's restoration that I honestly thought the flirtation would wear itself out." She bit her lip. "It's hard to know how Gladys feels, but his infatuation with her has only grown more intense."

"I don't suppose they are together that often," Kate said thoughtfully. "She lives with her mother on the Continent, doesn't she? And travels a good deal?"

"Marlborough invited her here several times last year, once for a full month. And earlier this spring, they were together in Paris." She made a little face. "I know, because her mother—such a wicked, foolish woman—told a mutual friend that she was afraid that my husband and her daughter would . . . would run away together." She said the words gingerly, as if to give them voice might make it happen.

"I'm quite sure the Duke would never do that," Kate said firmly. "He hates scandal. And he is so deeply attached to Blenheim." Then, fearing the omission had been hurtful, she added, "And to you and his sons, of course."

"To his sons, yes," Consuelo said, "since they represent the next generation of Churchills." Her voice became bitter. "He keeps reminding me that we are merely links in a long chain that stretches back into the past and ahead into the future. A *chain*," she said, with a sudden, angry emphasis. "A chain, yes, exactly, Kate! I feel as if I am chained to this awful place, and to this marriage. As if I live in a hideous cage, and I'll never break free. Can you understand that?"

"I think I can," Kate replied. "It must be a terrible thing, to feel imprisoned." She hesitated. "Have you spoken to Gladys about it? Or to the Duke?"

"Not to Gladys," Consuelo said dispiritedly. "I don't blame *her*, not really, you know. For all her sophistication, she's still an innocent child."

Kate stared at her, remembering the flirtatious, seductive Gladys she had seen at dinner the night before. An innocent child? It seemed to her that the Duchess was the innocent one, trustful and accepting, protected throughout her life from anyone who might want to harm her and without the experience that would help her see that her young friend Gladys was capable of betraying her.

"But I do blame Marlborough," Consuelo was going on sadly, "who is misbehaving badly. I've tried several times to talk to him about it, as recently as last week. But I'm not very good at confrontation, you see. He just gives me that . . . that hooded look of his, as if there's nothing behind his eyes, or if there is, he's hiding it from me. He refuses to talk. He says there's nothing wrong. Nothing to be said between us."

It was time, Kate thought, to say what she thought. "If you don't mind my speaking frankly, Consuelo, we see this situation from different points of view. I don't believe that Gladys is at all innocent. She's deliberately toying with Botsy Northcote, and casting eyes at Winston as well. And she's scarcely a child, although she loves to play the *jeune fille*." She paused. "I'm sorry to say this, Consuelo, but I think she's . . . well, dangerous. She's put your marriage in jeopardy and your happiness."

"Do you think so?" Consuelo's mouth twisted. "Oh, God, Kate," she said wretchedly. "My life is such an appalling chaos." Her voice rose. "What am I to do? I'm trapped. I'm chained. I want more than anything to be free, but that is a hopeless dream. The law makes divorce nearly impossible. And even if it didn't, Marlborough would never agree because of the scandal. And the money." She paused. "It's the money, more than anything."

"We can only take things a day at a time," Kate said, knowing that the words, offered no real comfort. "But at the moment, there is something we really *must* do. We must find Gladys."

"You're right, of course." Consuelo blew her nose again. "But where can we start?"

Kate thought for a moment. Charles had said that he was going out for the morning and would not be back until lunch, so she could not ask his help or advice. She would have to deal with this herself.

"What about the Duke?" she asked. "Shouldn't he be told that Gladys is gone?" She paused, seeing the look of wrenching pain on Consuelo's face, and she softened her tone. "Whatever else the girl is to him, you know, she is a guest in his house. You will have to tell him—and the sooner the better, I should think."

Consuelo seemed to brace herself against the thought. "You're right, of course. But I don't think I can face Marlborough alone, and I think he might find it easier if you're there." A smile ghosted across her mouth. "At the least he might feel that he has to make a civil answer. Will you come with me?"

"Of course," Kate said. She glanced at the clock on the mantle. The morning was more than half gone. "Where do you suppose we'll find him?"

"He spends several hours every morning in the office, with Mr. Meloy, his estate agent," Consuelo said. She stood. "It's in the East Court." Her lips tipped into a wry smile. "No more than a half-mile from here, actually. Oh, Kate, this awful place is so inhumanely huge. Whatever could they have been thinking about when they built it?"

Kate managed a laugh. "Perhaps Gladys has spent the

night wandering around the palace," she said in a joking tone. "I've been here since Monday, and I'm just now able to find my way to my bedroom without getting lost."

The estate office certainly was a distance, through the endless corridors of the private residence, down the stairs, and across the paved East Court to the far side. But when they reached it, the estate agent—a broad-shouldered man with graying mutton-chop whiskers, dressed in green tweeds and boots—was alone.

He rose when he saw them in the doorway. "Good morning, Your Grace." He inclined his head to Kate. "Madam."

"This is Lady Sheridan, Mr. Meloy," Consuelo said. "We . . . we need to speak to the Duke on a matter of some importance." She looked around the room. "I see that he isn't here. Can you tell me where I might find him? The stables, perhaps?"

Mr. Meloy tipped his head to one side with a slightly puzzled look. "I'm afraid I can't say, Your Grace. The Duke and I were to meet at nine to talk about the drains at one of the farms." He paused. "He was most insistent that we settle the matter today, but he hasn't come. I expect something happened unexpectedly, and he changed his plans."

"Oh, dear," Consuelo said faintly. Consternation washed across her face, and Kate saw the agent's sharply noticing glance.

She took the Duchess's arm firmly. "Thank you, Mr. Meloy," she said, forcing a smile. "Perhaps the Duke and Lord Sheridan have gone off together and forgotten the time."

"I'm sure that's it," Mr. Meloy said heartily, seeing them to the door. "When he comes," he added to Consuelo, "I'll tell him that Your Grace is particularly wanting to see him." He made his voice sound easy, but Kate knew that his searching glance had not missed the Duchess's discomfiture.

Outside the office, Consuelo turned to Kate, her dark eyes wide and luminous with distress, her face pale except for two bright spots of color high on her cheekbones. "What should we do?" she asked. "I can't imagine where he can be, except—"

"Perhaps the Duke's valet?" Kate interrupted, not wanting Consuelo to finish her sentence. The idea that the Duke had gone off with Gladys might be entirely obvious, but it was better not spoken, at least until they had more information. "At the least, he would know how his master was dressed when he left this morning. For riding, walking, perhaps a trip to town."

But when they finally found the Duke's valet, Mallory, a meek, mustached man with a pronounced lisp and beautifully manicured hands, he could be of no help. All he could say was that the Duke must have gone out quite early, for when he had gone to his rooms to wake him, he had already left.

"Most unusual, if Your Grace will forgive my saying so," he said with a downcast look. "I have shaved His Grace every morning since I came into his service. This is the first morning in our ten years together that he has risen and left without a word to me." A note of something like anguish crept into his voice. "I confess that I cannot imagine His Grace shaving himself. Nor can I imagine that he left unshaven, either. He—"

The Duchess put her hand on the little man's sleeve. "One other question, Mallory," she said thinly. "Did the Duke . . . did my husband sleep in his room last night?"

The valet's eyes dropped. "I believe so," he said, his voice suddenly guarded. Kate could not be sure whether he was lying or telling the truth, and she understood why. No servant, if he wanted to continue with his employment, would discuss his master's personal affairs with his master's wife.

Consuelo must have repented of the question, for she summoned a brief smile. "Thank you, Mallory," she said softly. "I know how much the Duke depends on you." To Kate, as they walked back down the long hallway, she added in a low voice, "I think the Duke and Gladys must have gone off together. There is no other explanation for both of them being gone."

"I think it's too early to come to that conclusion," Kate replied. She put her hand on the Duchess's arm. "Let's find Winston. He may have seen the Duke, or have some idea what should be done about Gladys."

Consuelo's face brightened. "Oh, yes, Winston," she cried. "He'll be able to think of something."

Her relief, Kate thought, was almost pathetic.

CHAPTER TWELVE

Several crime rings operated in London at the turn of the century, but one—known simply as the Syndicate—enjoyed enormous success. The mastermind, who was personally known to none of his associates, contracted the criminal work to gangs of thieves. According to Ben MacIntyre, in The Napoleon of Crime, *"the crooks who carried out these commissions knew only that the orders were passed down from above, that the pickings were good, the planning impeccable, and the targets . . . had been selected by a master organizer. What they never knew was the name of the man at the top, or even of those in the middle. . . ."*

The Social Transformation of England: 1837–1914
Albert Williams

Blenheim's six footmen, like the ten housemaids, had far more to do than they could reasonably be expected to accomplish—or at least, that was Alfred's considered opinion. Their days began early, so they could light the downstairs fires, lay the table in the breakfast room for the family and guests, and (wearing black jackets, vests, and white gloves) serve breakfast from the sideboard and hot plates. Then there were dishes to remove to the scullery, silver to polish, knives and lamps and candleholders to clean, guests' writing supplies to replenish, and fires to maintain. After that, there was the luncheon table to lay and the meal to serve. Lunch over, the afternoon began with visitors to announce (the footmen now dressed in their short maroon livery, with white knee breeches and powdered hair), messages to carry, and Her Grace's carriage to accompany should she wish to go out. Then tea to serve, the formal dining table to lay, dinner to serve and dishes to remove, coffee and liqueurs to serve in the drawing room, and the gentlemen's smoking room to attend. Throughout the day, it was the task of the footmen to sound the gongs that ordered the household's schedule, run errands for family and guests, and in general, meet the needs of the household. Alfred had heard of a footman at Harlington House, a large establishment in London, who had recorded his steps with a pedometer and measured eighteen miles in one day without leaving the house. He would not have been surprised to learn that he walked farther than that himself, for Blenheim was much larger than Harlington House.

Alfred, of course, would not have been satisfied with this situation if he had not known that his tour of duty (as he thought of it) would soon come to an end. He hated having to change his clothes several times a day, to wear the silly costumes that made him look like an organ grinder's monkey, and most of all, to powder his hair until he appeared to be wearing a white wig. Some people might think that he cut a handsome figure when he was tricked out in his powdered hair and gold-trimmed finery, but he felt completely ridiculous, and a fraud, to boot. The other footmen at least had the comfort of knowing that their dress and demeanor took them further toward their goal: becoming a butler in a great house.

But Alfred did not aim for butlerhood. He'd set his heart on buying into his cousin's pub near the Brighton Pier, and the position of barman gleamed a great deal more brightly in his imagination than any butler's place, even that of Mr. Stevens at Blenheim, who cut a grand figure indeed, even if he was an old man who couldn't see past the end of his nose.

Of course, Alfred's dreams now included Kitty as well as the pub in Brighton. And it was because of Kitty that he'd been so deeply and thoroughly miserable, especially since he'd come up empty-handed in his talk with Bulls-eye. He'd pinned his hopes on Bulls-eye's being able to tell him what had happened to her, but he had learned nothing, and now he was desperate.

Finally, just this morning, he'd managed to get a word with Ruth, Kitty's roommate. He'd been on his way to the morning room with a tray of freshly cleaned lamps, and he'd met Ruth on her way upstairs. He stopped her and asked, in a low tone, what she knew about Kitty being gone.

"Funny thing you should ask," she said, eyeing him. "Her Grace was just wantin' to know, too." She gazed at him frankly, taking him in from top to toe. "You're a friend of Kitty's, then?"

Alfred blushed and lowered his eyes. He was by nature a shy young man and inexperienced, not used to the appraising glances of pretty young women. "Yes, we're friends," he said, and then, feeling that he needed to stake his claim, raised his eyes and added, "we're promised."

"G'wan," Ruth said, in a tone of disbelief. "Kitty's not promised to nobody." The corners of her mouth turned up scornfully. "Anyways, she's a lot older'n you. Thirty, if she's a day. What'd she want with a boy like you, I'd like to know."

Thirty! Alfred was startled. He had not thought of the voluptuous Kitty in terms of age. "She's promised to me," he said stubbornly. "Since Welbeck Abbey, where we was in service together. We're gettin' married."

Ruth rolled her eyes at this foolishness. "Footmen don't get married," she scoffed, "leastwise not here at Blenheim."

"And who says we're stayin' at Blenheim?" Alfred retorted. He came back to the subject. "I need to know where she's gone," he said urgently. "You have to tell me."

"You and the Duchess," Ruth said, folding her arms across her white apron. "Both of you, hammerin' on me. But *I* don't know where she is, now, do I? All I know is, I woke up on Saturday morning and she was gone, and I got to do double work 'til Mrs. Raleigh hires somebody else."

Alfred's heart sank. "Just . . . gone?" he asked dismally. "She didn't leave you a note or tell you where she was going, or anything like that?"

"Not a note, not a word, not nothin'." Ruth gave him a softer look. "*You* don't know where she is, then? If you're promised, seems like she'd tell you she was goin' home or wherever."

"I'm sure she would if she'd had a chance," Alfred said stolidly. "She always tells me everything."

The truth was, of course, that Kitty told him very little. Their conversations had been mostly about the business, Welbeck Abbey being only his second job. At Welbeck, she'd told him generally about the scheme—what they should take, where it was, what they should do with it, and helped him through his case of nerves, since he was green at this sort of thing and scared half witless from start to finish, which Kitty had said was all right, since he looked so incapable that nobody would ever take him for a thief. And when the job was over and they had been together in London for those two incredible days, they hadn't talked at all, just tumbled in the sheets for hour after ecstatic hour, with nothing but moans of pleasure and little cries of delight. At the thought, Alfred's face burned, and he brought his attention back to Ruth.

"Did she take anything?" he asked. "Her clothes?"

"No, and that's the odd thing. That's what I told the Duchess, y'see. That she left her trunk and all her clothes, including her best blue wool dress."

"Her trunk?"

Ruth nodded. "I told Her Grace that, and about the man, too."

Alfred frowned. "What man?"

"I don't know, do I?" Ruth retorted crossly. "A man with a red beard, is all I know. Kitty and me walked into Woodstock and she met him, last half-holiday. I went on to my mother's house and left her with him at the Prince."

And then the Duchess and Mrs. Raleigh had come out of the morning room, and Alfred, still holding his tray of lamps, had pulled himself to attention and looked straight ahead, and when he relaxed, the hallway was empty and everybody was gone.

As he set out the morning room lamps, Alfred was deeply troubled. If Kitty had left her clothes, she must have meant to come back. His heart wrenched within him. Something must have happened to prevent her from returning, and he couldn't for the life of him imagine what it might be. Did it have something to do with the red-bearded man she'd met at the Black Prince? Was he a relative, a friend, a lover?

With a sharp stab of disloyalty, Alfred pushed that last thought away. He and Kitty might not be promised, but he knew in his heart that she loved him—if she didn't love him just yet, he was special to her. Maybe the man was connected to the Syndicate. He hadn't met any red-bearded men, but then, he hadn't been working for the Syndicate long, and he didn't know who was who, except for Kitty and Bulls-eye. Bulls-eye hadn't seen her, though, at least that's what he'd said, so Alfred was at a loss.

And it wasn't just his romantic hopes and dreams about Kitty that were threatened by her mysterious disappearance. Kitty was the one with the experience, the one who knew the general scheme, the signals, the arrangements for getting the things out of the house. And while he had a general idea what they were supposed to find out before the rest of the crew arrived, Kitty was the one who knew the details.

Alfred finished his task, went out of the room, and shut the door behind him, feeling bleak and abandoned. Without Kitty, he had no way of doing his job the way it was supposed to be done, and he knew enough about the Syndicate to know what happened to people who didn't do their jobs. But his chief thought was for Kitty—beautiful, sensual Kitty, whose lovemaking warmed him still—and his chief worry was that something dreadful might have happened to her.

The pub in Brighton, and the family of little Alfreds and Kittys, seemed suddenly very far away.

CHAPTER THIRTEEN

Restless—almost intolerably so, without capacity for sustained and unexciting labor—egotistical, bumptious, shallow-minded and reactionary, but with a certain personal magnetism. . . . (Winston Churchill's) pluck, courage, resourcefulness and great tradition may carry him far, unless he knocks himself to pieces like his father.

Our Partnership
Beatrice Webb

Winston had begun working on his father's *Life* the summer before, and was already nearing the end of what he planned as the first of a two-volume work. He knew, though, that he was going to have to spend quite a bit more time polishing the text than he would like. His task was to redeem Lord Randolph from the portrayals of his more malicious peers, as a conniving, capricious politician who had thrown up a promising career on a crazy whim. While others might suggest that Lord Randolph had been an angry, spendthrift, syphilitic husband and a cold and uncaring father, Winston saw him as a great statesman who was too busy about the affairs of the Empire to squander his energies on his family, and especially his undeserving eldest son. Lord Randolph was a Churchill, cast in the same mold as that noble duke, the first Marlborough, and it was Winston's job to guard that memory and the Churchill name, and to do all he could to enhance it.

This morning, Winston was scribbling away at a paragraph about his father's abrupt breach with his party. But he put down his pen when Consuelo came into the room, not stopping to knock. She was followed by Kate Sheridan. Both were breathless, and the Duchess wore an almost distracted look.

"Why, my dear Connie!" he exclaimed, rising and holding out his hands. "Whatever is wrong?"

"It's Gladys," Consuelo said wretchedly, "and the Duke. They're gone!"

"Gone?" Winston echoed stupidly. Her hands in his were very cold, and her fingers were trembling. "*Gone?* Both of them?" His thoughts immediately went to the gesture he had seen the night before, the public touch, the open declaration. What a wretched business! And where the devil was Marlborough? He hadn't gone off with that foolish girl, had he? By Jove, if he had—

But that was unthinkable. Marlborough might fancy himself in love, but he could never bring himself to drag the family name through the dirt, or risk a break with the Vanderbilts—and the Vanderbilt money.

Kate Sheridan put a steadying hand on Consuelo's shoulder. "What Consuelo means," she said in a calm, quiet voice, "is that Gladys did not sleep in her bed last night, nor change clothes."

"Did not sleep in her bed!" Winston exclaimed in agitation.

Kate nodded. "And since her absence struck us as a rather serious matter, we thought that the Duke ought to be informed—except that we've not been able to locate him." She paused. "We spoke to Mr. Meloy, who has not seen him. Mallory, his valet, did not see him this morning, either. It doesn't seem helpful to alarm the servants, so we thought that perhaps you might have a look for the Duke and—"

"Yes, of course," Winston interrupted. "I should be glad to, very glad." He kissed Consuelo's hands and let them go. "You can count on me," he said comfortingly, suppressing his own rising alarm. "I'll find Sunny, and then we can sit down together and discuss what should be done about Gladys." By heaven, he would *force* Sunny to come to terms on this business, and make a final break with Gladys. Marlborough had to be made to see the danger the woman posed. "She can't have wandered far," he added, putting on a reassuring smile, "not dressed as she was. In fact, she may have already returned to her room."

From the beginning of his acquaintance with Sunny's wife, Winston had gone out of his way to cultivate a strong friendship with her. That had not been difficult, for Consuelo was shy and lacking in confidence and had accepted him happily as an ally who helped her face her husband's family. He wanted her to see him in all matters as her advocate and champion, as well as her representative among the Churchills, who were quite a formidable lot, all in all, extremely judgmental and critical.

Of course, Winston realized that this advocacy position was not an entirely unselfish one. It was sometimes hard to know what was going on in the Duke's mind, but Consuelo was much more artless and transparent, and she confided in him things—private family matters—that her husband would have concealed. If Consuelo saw him as her confidant, Winston would always know what was going on at Blenheim, which, after all, was his home, too.

"Oh, thank you, Winston," Consuelo said, her voice lightened with relief, some of the strain in her face easing. "What do you . . . what are you going to do? And what do you think Kate and I should do?"

"Well, for a start," Winston said, with more careless confidence than he felt, "you and Lady Sheridan could take your little electric car and go for a drive around the Park. You might run into Sunny, he's probably just gone out for a morning ride. And you might even catch a glimpse of Gladys." Although as to why Miss Deacon would be wandering around the Park in her evening dress and slippers, Winston couldn't hazard a guess. But he had to say something, and apparently Consuelo was satisfied.

"Yes, of course," she said, sounding relieved. "The car. What a very good idea, Winston. Kate and I will go immediately." She paused, frowning. "But what will you do?"

"I? Why, I'm off to the stables," Winston replied easily. "Sunny may have mentioned to the groom which way he intended to ride." He bent over to kiss Consuelo's pale cheek. "Don't fret, my dear. I'm sure we'll find each of them, safe and sound."

And pray God, he thought fervently, *we don't find them together.* He had put the best face on things for Consuelo, but he was deeply troubled, and by the time he had reached the stables, Winston had worked himself into a fine frenzy. If it were just Gladys who had gone missing, it was probably just one of her madcap escapades. The girl was prone to pranks and high jinks and had little regard for proper conduct or for the feelings of others, although he had to admit that it was rather odd that she had disappeared in her dinner dress. The Duke's absence raised another urgent question, though, one that he hoped very much would be answered at the stables.

But Winston was to be disappointed, for no one at the stables had a clue as to Marlborough's whereabouts. Sunny had not taken one of the horses, and while there were any number of bicycles around the estate, Winston could not imagine his aristocratic cousin actually riding one. As to going off on foot, well, that seemed equally improbable. Unless he was hunting, the Duke did not enjoy tramping through the fields and woods.

Winston prided himself on his reputation as a man of action and a quick thinker who was never at a loss for ideas. But at this moment, Winston couldn't think of a single thing—except to turn out all the servants and question every one of them, which of course he could not do.

It was at that moment that a new possibility suggested itself to Winston in the person of Charles Sheridan, who was walking jauntily across the stable yard, dressed in a somewhat disreputable Norfolk jacket, with a camera bag over one shoulder and a tripod over the other. He was whistling.

Winston suddenly discovered that he had been holding his breath and let it out. He strode toward Charles, speaking eagerly.

"I say, Sheridan, might we have a private word?"

CHAPTER FOURTEEN

It is of the highest importance in the art of detection to be able to recognize, out of a number of facts, which are incidental and which vital. Otherwise your energy and attention must be dissipated instead of being concentrated.

"The Reigate Puzzle"
Sir Arthur Conan Doyle

Charles, a photographer of some note, had spent the morning with his camera on the eastern side of the Park, where he had photographed the picturesque Swiss Cottage, a timbered house with roundel windows and a curious spired turret, set within a grove of trees that made for some rather pretty pictures.

But on the whole, the photographic expedition had been a pretext to get away from the palace and reflect upon a number of puzzling facts, some of which might be entirely unimportant, or vital to some sequence of events that he did not yet understand. While Charles pointed his camera here and there, he was reviewing what he knew about the theft of the Warrington Hoard—an inside job, so to speak, accomplished with the aid of a recently hired char woman and a certain mysterious lady who offered the stolen items for sale to Mr. Dreighson. He was also thinking of what he knew of the theft at Welbeck Abbey, where the Duchess of Portland's famous emeralds had disappeared, along with a great deal of valuable jewelry belonging to her guests.

News of the theft had been hushed up to protect the Duchess from embarrassment, but Charles had learned of it from Leander Norwood, the chief of the Yard's burglary division. Norwood had been called in to conduct the investigation, which had been so far fruitless. He'd told Charles that the theft looked to him to be the work of employees, even though servants did not usually steal significant and unique items of property because of the difficulty involved in selling them. The Portland emeralds, for instance, which had once belonged to Marie Antoinette, would be almost impossible to fence. It was Norwood's opinion that the job had been managed by a ring of sophisticated thieves with connections on the Continent, where the jewels might be more easily got rid of, sold to collectors who would not question their pedigree. And that one or more servants had been involved, as well as, quite possibly, one of the female guests, who might have had access to the bedrooms. Norwood wouldn't offer details, since the investigation was continuing, but he had also hinted that there may have been a similar theft or two in the past year, during large weekend house-parties at other country estates.

With these things in the back of his mind, Charles was thinking of what John Buttersworth had told him about the mysterious woman who had showed him the seal stones— stones that reminded Buttersworth of the Marlborough Gems. Buttersworth's first thought seemed to be that the Duchess of Marlborough was offering them for a clandestine sale, something that was not too unusual in these days of declining personal fortunes. A great many titled ladies, duchesses among them, were forced to sell what they could to keep ahead of their dressmakers' and jewelers' bills—and their gambling debts. While Consuelo did not strike Charles as the kind of woman who would squander a fortune, it wasn't entirely out of the question. Even as wealthy a lady as the Duchess of Marlborough, née Vanderbilt, would not necessarily be immune from financial exigencies, especially a temporary one that had thrown her into a sudden panic.

Charles, however, was beginning to suspect that there might be a very different game afoot, and that the woman who appeared at Dreighson's, offering to sell the Hoard, might also be associated with the robbery at Welbeck Abbey. And there was more. Thieves had struck at Welbeck during one of the Portlands' houseparty weekends, when the ladies had brought their favorite jewels. Blenheim was an even more tantalizing target, and the natural time to strike was the weekend set for the visit of King Edward and Queen Alexandra, three weeks hence, Winston had told him last night. The King loved seeing gentlemen dressed in splendid uniforms and ladies wearing silk and their finest ornaments, so there would be several fortunes in jewels lying about the bedrooms, when they weren't fastened at their owners' throats, ears, and wrists.

And at Blenheim as at most other country houses, there would be no attention paid to security, except for the one or two special agents who were assigned to safeguard the Royal persons. Such events, with the influx of the guests' personal servants and additional help hired from the local village, always involved a state of general household confusion and chaos, below-stairs and above. A Royal houseparty at

Blenheim would be perfect pickings, to use an American phrase, for a ring of thieves.

Given these facts and speculations, Charles was becoming increasingly concerned, to the point where he was almost ready to lay his suspicions before the Duke, who would certainly not want to be disgraced by a theft at Blenheim Palace. However, where the Duke was concerned, there was one additional bit of information that troubled Charles, although he had no way of knowing whether it was incidental or vital. Buttersworth had said that the woman who showed him the gemstones had a nose like that of Sappho, a female poet of classical Greece, a description which, Charles thought, fit Miss Deacon remarkably well.

Was it possible that it had been Miss Deacon who presented the stones at the Ashmolean?

Was she somehow involved with the thieves?

A ridiculous idea, on the face of it, or so the Duke would certainly think. But the preceding year, the *Times* had carried the story of a certain Lady Tallarde, who had been found guilty of a similar association in France and sentenced to a lengthy prison term. And Chief Norwood had mentioned that a woman guest had fallen under suspicion at Welbeck. Charles could not discount the possibility.

But this was only speculation, and Charles had no way of determining the truth. Because of this, he felt that it would not be quite prudent to discuss the matter with the Duke, at least, not yet. He needed more inside information, and he had thought of a way to get it. But he would first have to consult with Winston. If the Duke's cousin could be convinced that the matter was urgent, he was in a position to help implement the scheme . . .

These were the thoughts that were passing through

Charles Sheridan's mind as he went across the stableyard on his way back to the palace, his camera bag over one shoulder and his tripod over the other, whistling tunelessly as he walked. In fact, he was so preoccupied that he scarcely knew where he was, and didn't hear Winston calling until he nearly bumped into him.

"Ah, Winston," he said, blinking in surprise. "I was just thinking about you. I'd like to discuss an important matter with you. I think you might be able to—"

"I need a word with you first, Charles," Winston said urgently.

Within a few minutes, Charles had heard the news that Miss Deacon had disappeared the night before, dressed in evening clothes and wearing her diamond necklace. And that Marlborough seemed to be missing as well.

Charles felt a sharp stirring of concern. "You've checked the Duke's room? And Miss Deacon's? Is there any luggage missing, or any indication that they went off together? What about horses? Motor cars?"

"I haven't checked the rooms," Winston said, "although Kate and Consuelo have done so. There are no horses missing, and the only motor car on the property is Consuelo's little electric runabout. Consuelo and Kate have driven it out to look around the estate, hoping that they'll catch sight of one or the other of our—" He cleared his throat and said dryly, "Our missing persons."

Charles heard the crunch of wheels on gravel, and looked up. "And there they are," he said, with a strong sense of relief, seeing a small electric motorcar, with Consuelo driving. Kate was sitting beside her, and on the engine box behind them sat the Duke of Marlborough, holding a fishing rod and wearing a distinctly disagreeable look.

Ten minutes later, they were all back at the palace. Winston and the Duke went off together, Charles agreeing to meet them shortly in the Duke's private study. Consuelo said she had a wretched headache and went to lie down, and Kate had followed her upstairs, but not before telling Charles privately how she and Consuelo had chanced on the Duke walking along a narrow lane near High Lodge, on the west side of the Park. Marlborough had told them he had been fishing at the southern end of the lake since very early in the morning, although he did not seem to have caught any fish and volunteered no explanation for missing his appointment with the estate agent. He had seemed astonished to learn of Gladys's disappearance and kept shaking his head and muttering darkly that it must not be true, that he could not believe that Gladys would leave without a word of explanation to *him*.

"Which hurt Consuelo deeply," Kate added with a sober expression. "Really, Charles, this affair, or whatever it is, is becoming very difficult for her. And here is something that makes it even worse." She put her hand into the pocket of her skirt and brought out a scrap of gold silk. "I found this at Rosamund's Well before breakfast this morning, caught on a bush. I believe it's from Gladys's dress, the one she was wearing last night. When I saw it, I immediately assumed that she and the Duke had rowed over there together, a sort of romantic tryst. You remember that she talked about the Well at dinner."

"I remember," Charles said, taking the scrap and looking at it closely. "She cast herself in the role of Rosamund, with Marlborough as Henry, and the Duchess, implicitly, as the jealous Eleanor."

"And Botsy Northcote as Roger of Salisbury," Kate said.

"A ready-made cast for a tragic theatrical." She paused. "There's something odd about that torn piece, Charles, now that I come to think about it. I found it on a small bush, but the bush wasn't sturdy enough to have snagged and torn that heavy silk."

"Rosamund's Well," Charles mused, pocketing the scrap. "Thank you, Kate. I'll have a look around the place." He leaned forward and took her arm. "Listen, my dear, it's very important that Miss Deacon's bedroom be immediately locked. Can you find the housekeeper and make sure that's done? I don't want the maids going in there until it's been thoroughly searched."

With a little smile, Kate put a key into his hand. "It's done already," she said. "I locked the door when Consuelo and I left this morning. No one's been in there, at least since we left."

"Ah, my Kate," Charles said with pleasure, and kissed her cheek. "What a treasure of a wife you are." He paused, thinking. "But perhaps it would be better if you'd search the room. I have a number of urgent things to see to, and you may find something that should be acted upon right away. Would you mind?"

"Of course not," Kate said with satisfaction, taking the key back. "It will make me feel that I am being of some use."

"And one more question," Charles said. "Have you seen Lord Northcote this morning?"

"Botsy?" Kate's hazel eyes widened. "Oh, my goodness, Charles. No, I haven't seen him!"

As it turned out, no one else had seen Northcote, either. An inquiry of the housemaids—deliberately casual, so as not to raise suspicion—told Charles that Botsy's bed had not been slept in, and that all of his clothing, together with the Gladstone bag he'd brought it in, was gone from his room.

Charles then made a quick visit to the butler's pantry, a large, well-lit room off the main corridor below stairs, where he found Mr. Stevens reviewing the wine and spirits inventories and preparing an order for the King's visit.

The butler, a man in his sixties, was stooped and almost frail, but he still held himself with a dignified reserve. He listened gravely to Charles's question and explanation and agreed to look into the matter. "Rest assured, m'lord," he said with equanimity, "that if there's anything to be learned, it will be reported to you at once."

Charles thanked the butler, and then, telling himself that he had done as much as one reasonably could in such a short while, he took himself off to the Duke's study.

CHAPTER FIFTEEN

*Some circumstantial evidence is very strong, such as when you
find a trout in the milk.*

Journal, November 11–14, 1850
Henry David Thoreau

"Northcote's gone *too?*" the Duke croaked in a voice that
was harsh with alarm and disbelief. He dropped back
into a leather chair so large that it made him look like a boy.
"Bag and baggage?"

"So the housemaids tell me," Charles replied evenly. "I
haven't yet checked his room."

With a moan, the Duke buried his face in his hands.

"Old Northcote," Winston muttered. "Didn't think he
was up to it."

"Up to what?" Charles asked, thinking of the torn scrap
of fabric Kate had given him. Had Botsy Northcote taken
Miss Deacon to Rosamund's Well, assaulted her and torn
her dress and, perhaps, inflicted some physical harm on her?

But Winston seemed to have something rather different
in mind. "Of convincing Gladys to go off with him," he said

in a low voice. "Of course, he's a good-looking chap and all that, but after all, he was a guest here. And it's not exactly—"

"What makes you think he convinced her to go off with him?" The Duke's voice was muffled by his hands.

Winston looked surprised. "Why, what other explanation can there possibly be? Northcote considered that she engaged herself to him when she accepted his family diamonds at Welbeck. Of course, it seems a bit strange that Miss Deacon went off in her evening dress and without taking leave. But we both know . . ." He paused, cleared his throat, and said, rather pompously, "We both know, my dear Sunny, that she has on occasion behaved in rather an eccentric fashion."

The Duke, his face still buried, made a low sound.

"At Welbeck?" Charles asked.

Winston nodded. "That's where the engagement took place, I understand. Family heirloom, that necklace. Rumor has it that Botsy's mother is furious with him." Squaring his shoulders, he turned to his cousin. "We've got to face facts, Sunny. Can't let ourselves be misled. Fact is, she's gone off with—"

"I don't want to hear it!" Marlborough shouted, jumping out of his chair and pacing up and down in front of the fire. "I don't believe it! She'd never agree to go off with that blathering fool. I want her found, do you hear? I don't give a damn about Northcote, but I want Miss Deacon found and returned, safely." He whirled upon Charles, the muscles in his jaw working furiously. "You're supposed to be something of a detective, aren't you, Sheridan? Well, *find* her, damn it! And make it quick! There's not a minute to lose. She's in danger. She must be, or she would have contacted me."

Charles felt a flare of irritation at the imperious tone, but did not allow it to show in his voice. "I think," he said steadily, "that we might come closer to finding both of them if we understood what went on last night. What time, for instance, did you leave Miss Deacon? And where?"

"What time?" The Duke's eyes narrowed. "Why is that important?"

"We need to establish who saw her last," Charles said, "and when. The Duchess and Lady Sheridan retired early. Northcote left the Saloon not long after you and Miss Deacon went into the garden, saying that he was going up to bed. Winston and I went off to the smoking room, where we stayed until past eleven, and then went upstairs. I left Winston at his door, and neither of us saw Miss Deacon after she went out with you." He paused. "Did you take leave of her in the garden? In the Saloon? Or upstairs, perhaps?"

There was a silence. "In the . . . the garden," Marlborough said in a despairing tone. He turned toward the fire, his hands behind his back. And then, when the silence had lengthened still further, he added stiffly, "We had a . . . a bit of a row, if you must know."

Winston opened his mouth to say something, but Charles shook his head. To Marlborough he said, "What kind of a row?"

Marlborough's narrow shoulders became taut. He did not turn around, but Charles could guess the look on his face by the strain in his voice.

"Gladys—Miss Deacon can become upset very easily. Her feelings . . . matter to her, you see. They matter enormously. Her heart is so tender, and when she cares, she cares with such a passion that it is . . . astonishing. Somewhat frightening, in fact. One does not quite know how one ought to take it."

He turned suddenly, holding out his hands and saying angrily, "The deuce of it is that she can't seem to understand how things are *done!* How a man in my position must behave. What's proper and what's not." The anger held a desolation. The Duke was like a boy who has seen something he cherished taken from him through no fault of his own, and now believes that he has lost it forever.

His voice dropped. "Miss Deacon—Gladys is very like her mother, you know. Nothing is ever enough for her. She always wants more, and then more, and more. And when she can't have it, she . . . well, she can become rather childishly violent. It won't do, of course. That sort of thing really doesn't, but there it is. That's what we rowed about." He stopped, and dropped his head, and then sank back down in his chair, hiding his eyes with his hand.

Winston said nothing, but his glance at Charles spoke volumes of embarrassment and chagrin.

Charles thought he understood what had happened. Gladys had pressed the Duke for some sort of verbal pledge as openly declarative as his light, impulsive touch on her wrist at table. Perhaps she had insisted that they go away together. Or even that Marlborough separate from his wife, unthinkable as that was. When he refused, pleading public scandal, she might have become distraught. A woman scorned can be dangerous, Charles knew, and Gladys Deacon—willful, impulsive, untrustworthy—seemed to him to be a potentially dangerous woman. Believing herself rebuffed, Gladys might have even threatened the Duke with some sort of public exposure, which would undoubtedly terrify him. What would he do then? To what lengths would he go to keep her from creating a public scandal?

But Charles said nothing of this. "What time did you leave her in the garden?"

"Ten, half-past," Marlborough said dully. "Perhaps as late as eleven. I don't know."

Charles doubted that. The Duke struck him as a man who always knew what time it was. "Did anyone see you after that hour? Your valet, perhaps?"

Angrily, Marlborough started up. "What the devil gives you the right to pry—"

"Sunny," Winston said, laying a cautioning hand on his cousin's arm. "If Miss Deacon can't be found, the police may have to be involved."

"The police! No, no!" the Duke said wildly. "We can't have the police! Anything but that!"

"Well, then, let Sheridan have his head," Winston urged. "He's a good man. We can trust him. Northcote can go to the devil if he likes, but we absolutely *must* find Miss Deacon."

"All right, damn it." The Duke's voice was thin and flat. "The answer to your question is no, Sheridan. I did not require my valet's services when I retired. No one saw me after I . . . after I left her."

Winston coughed slightly. "Well, then, perhaps someone saw you this morning, when you went off to the lake to go fishing."

The Duke tensed, then seemed to force himself to relax. "No. I . . . I couldn't sleep, so I got up and dressed and went out very early. It was still rather dark."

There was a polite tap at the door. Stevens, the butler, appeared and motioned to Charles with a white-gloved hand. "If I might have a word with you, m'lord," he said quietly.

Charles excused himself and went out into the corridor,

closing the door behind him. "Yes, Stevens?" he asked. "You've learned something?"

Mr. Stevens, despite his age and frailty, held himself like a man of some personal authority, as well he might, Charles thought. The task of being butler at Blenheim must be a formidable one, not least because of the size of the place.

"Forgive the liberty of the interruption, m'lord, but I believe I may have uncovered the information your lordship requested. Alfred, one of our footmen, has some information he would like to impart." Stevens motioned to a tall, well-built footman who was standing several paces behind him. "Alfred, this is Lord Sheridan, the gentleman who is making inquiries on behalf of His Grace. You may tell his lordship what you witnessed."

Alfred stepped forward. Like Mr. Stevens, he was wearing morning dress, white gloves, and his own hair, which Charles infinitely preferred to the idiotic business of powdering.

"I saw Lord Northcote, m'lord," Alfred said in a voice that had something of the north country richness in it. "I had late duty last night, y'see, sir, and I was just lockin' the east door when he came flyin' down the stairs." Alfred's eyes were bright, and Charles thought that he was relishing the report.

"Did he have anything with him?" Charles asked. "And what was his demeanor?"

"He had his Gladstone in his hand, sir. And his demeanor, if I may be permitted, was abrupt. Hasty, y'might say. He came down the stairs like the devil himself was after him. He didn't speak a word, just shoved me to one side and dashed out the door."

"If I may be permitted an observation, m'lord," Stevens put in ponderously. "This sort of thing is most irregular. We are not accustomed to such behavior on the part of our guests at Blenheim. It appears that Lord Northcote said nothing of his departure to anyone—that he did not even take proper leave of Her Grace."

"Irregular, indeed." Charles looked at Alfred. "Was there a horse waiting for him, Alfred? Or a motor car?"

"No, sir," Alfred said, shaking his head. "He was afoot. I thought p'rhaps—"

"His lordship does not wish to know what you thought, Alfred," Mr. Stevens said in a tone of rebuke, "only what you saw. You may go."

"On the contrary," Charles said. "What *did* you think, Alfred?"

Alfred spoke tentatively, as if he were not accustomed to being asked his opinions. "Well, I thought p'rhaps his little talk with the young lady in the garden had changed his plans, m'lord, and that he'd decided to walk into Woodstock and stay at one of the pubs. P'rhaps catch the early train out in the morning."

Charles was opening his mouth to ask about Northcote's talk with the young lady in the garden, but Mr. Stevens interrupted.

"Just to inform you, m'lord, that the train goes at six," he said. "Gentlemen guests with next-day business in London occasionally prefer to stay in the village, so that they don't rouse the household with an early departure." He pulled himself up with an expression of deep offense. "They do not, however, rush out of the house in the middle of the night."

"I see," Charles said. "You mentioned Lord Northcote's talk with the young lady, Alfred. That would be Miss Deacon, I take it. When did that take place?"

"Oh, that was earlier, m'lord," Alfred said. "About half-past ten. Yes, it was Miss Deacon. She was alone in the garden, and he went out, and they talked. Well, he talked, mostly. I could hardly keep from seeing them, could I?" he added diffidently. "They was right under the Saloon windows, and I was putting out the lights."

"I'm sure you couldn't avoid noticing them," Charles said, with a small smile. "Do you have any idea what they were talking about?"

Alfred shook his head. "No, m'lord. But it did seem that Lord Northcote was . . . well, put out, is how I'd describe him. Heated, if you don't mind my taking the liberty, m'lord."

It was always a marvel, Charles thought, how well-informed the servants were about matters that family and guests thought were entirely private. "And the young lady? How would you describe her?"

"Oh, cool, sir," Alfred said promptly. "Entirely cool. Hardly had a word to say. Which made his lordship even more . . ." He searched for a word and found it. "Inflamed sir."

"Did you see either of them leave the garden?"

The footman shook his head. "I had other duties to attend to. I drew the curtains and left the room."

"And what time did you see Lord Northcote leaving the house?"

"Just going twelve-thirty, sir." Alfred slid a glance at Mr. Stevens. "I was a bit delayed in my rounds. I'm meant to lock the east door at midnight." He hesitated, then went on eagerly, "I understand, sir, that you're trying to find a missing—"

"That's enough, Alfred," Stevens broke in. "You may go now."

"No," Charles said. "I want to hear this. Go on, Alfred.

You were asking about the young lady who's gone missing?"

"Well, yes." Alfred knit his hands together nervously. "Y'see, I know her, m'lord." He paused and dropped his eyes. "And I've been worried about her."

Charles stared at him in surprise. It was hardly the response he would have expected from a footman. "You've been *worried* about her?"

"Well, yes," Alfred replied. "You see, I—"

Stevens rustled nervously. "M'lord, if I may be so bold, I hardly think that this matter should be of concern to—"

"You say that you know the young lady who's disappeared," Charles said firmly, taking no notice of the butler.

"Yes, m'lord." Alfred, too, seemed to have forgotten Mr. Stevens. His eyes were fixed on Charles, and there was something like hopefulness in them. "I know her from before Blenheim. From Welbeck."

"I . . . see," Charles said, feeling as if ideas that might have seemed merely incidental had suddenly become vital, ideas that concerned Gladys Deacon. "Then you were at Welbeck, too, I take it."

"Yes, m'lord," Alfred said earnestly. "It was my second place as footman, y'see, and the young lady and me, we—" He stopped and drew in a deep breath as if he were not quite sure what to say next.

"Quite right, Alfred," Stevens said with a dark look. "His lordship is not interested in the experience of a footman at Welbeck, or a young person who—"

"But I *am* interested," Charles said. "And I am most particularly interested in the young lady." He was surprised to hear that Miss Deacon had become familiar with a footman, but perhaps it was not so extraordinary, after all. She had more than a hint of her mother's famed recklessness about her, and young ladies were often known to be attracted to the handsome young men who served them. He was also somewhat bemused that Alfred would be so ingenuous as to tell him this, but he was not one to look a gift horse in the mouth.

"Go on, Alfred," he said encouragingly. "Tell me more. You were saying that you met her when you were both at Welbeck. That was recently, I assume."

"Yes, m'lord. It was my last post before comin' here, m'lord." Alfred was speaking eagerly now, leaning forward. "After we left th' Abbey, we went down to London and spent a few days together, and then—"

"Alfred!" Stevens exclaimed with a horrified look. "Remember your place, young man! You are speaking of a *lady!*"

"A lady?" Alfred looked suddenly confused. "But I—But I wouldn't say that she—"

Charles put his hand on Alfred's sleeve. "No matter, Alfred, just go on with your story. You and Miss Deacon spent a few days together in London. And then you came here. Did she come with you, or later?"

Alfred's eyes went wide. "Miss . . . Miss Deacon?"

"Yes," Charles said impatiently. "Miss Gladys Deacon, the young lady you saw last night in the garden, talking with Lord Northcote. You were saying that—"

"Oh, but it's not Miss Deacon, m'lord!" Alfred exclaimed, with something like relief in his voice. "No, not Miss Deacon, at all, sir. It's Kitty I'm speaking of."

"Kitty?" Charles blinked. "And who is she?" He turned to the butler. "Stevens, what the devil is going on here?"

"If your lordship will permit me, it seems that Alfred has inadvertently misled us." Mr. Stevens gave the footman a sharply reproving look. "It appears that he has been speaking not of Miss Deacon, as your lordship and I might have naturally assumed, but rather of one of our housemaids, a certain Kitty."

This was beginning to sound like a melodrama. "And this . . . this Kitty—she's gone, too?" Charles asked.

"So it would seem, sir, although I was not informed of her absence when it occurred. Mrs. Raleigh, our housekeeper, has just informed me that the girl left without giving notice. And Her Grace, who is understandably anxious, has requested that I make inquiries about her at the Black Prince, in Woodstock, where she recently went to meet a . . . a certain person." He shot another dark glance at the footman. "It appears that Alfred is somewhat concerned about her, as well."

"Somewhat concerned!" Alfred exclaimed hotly. He clenched his fists. "I've been off my head with worry, is what I've been!" He turned back to Charles with a look of entreaty. "I know you're not the police, m'lord, not that I'd be wantin' the police, since I cert'nly hope it won't come to that. But Mr. Stevens says you're making inquiries, m'lord, and I was hopin' you'd be able to find out what happened to Kitty." He choked back something that sounded like a sob. "I just know that something's gone awful wrong, sir."

"So it was a housemaid who was with you at Welbeck," Charles said, beginning to see things in a new and different light. "Kitty, you say?"

"Yes, m'lord," Alfred replied hopefully. "That's her name. Kitty Drake."

Kitty Drake. Charles pressed on. "But perhaps you were also acquainted with Miss Deacon during your service at Welbeck, Alfred. I understand she was a guest there."

"Miss Deacon, m'lord?" Alfred's eyes narrowed slightly.

"Well, not to say *acquainted,* of course, m'lord. But you're right, she was a guest there. She and Lord Northcote both."

"Ah," Charles said. "And did the two of them seem to be . . . on friendly terms?"

"Oh, yes, m'lord. Quite friendly, especially her. Not at all like here. Once I even——" He stopped suddenly, his eyes going to the butler as if he expected a rebuke, then back to Charles.

"Please go on, Alfred," Charles said. "I am not asking you to repeat gossip or carry tales about the guests. But Miss Deacon disappeared last night, and anything you know about her, even something that seems entirely incidental, may help us to find her."

"Miss Deacon's gone missing, *too?*" Alfred asked, taken aback. "Well, I don't really . . . that is, all I know is what I *saw,* m'lord. At Welbeck, I mean." The footman looked flustered.

"And that was——" Charles prompted.

"Well, they was kissing," Alfred said hesitantly. "In the Welbeck conservatory. And he was telling her that he loved her. And then he gave her something in a box. I couldn't see what it was, actually, but she said she thought it was beautiful and she kissed him again, and said she'd have him."

Charles felt his eyebrows go up. "It was your impression that she agreed to be engaged to Lord Northcote?"

Alfred nodded. "And then she came here, and a few days later, Lord Northcote came, and it didn't seem like——" He stopped. "I mean, it seems like Miss Deacon and His Grace——" He was flushing from jaw to temple. "Miss Deacon . . . well, she was very cool to Lord Northcote, and warm to His Grace, if your lordship will forgive me."

"Yes," Charles said. "Yes, indeed. I see." This whole affair was beginning to seem extraordinarily complicated. He took a deep breath and turned to the butler. "You said that Kitty Drake went off without notice. When was that?"

The butler drew himself up. "The housemaids are not my responsibility, as I am sure your lordship is aware. But I believe that it was the beginning of this week. I—"

"It was Friday, sir," Alfred interjected, "which would be nearly a week ago. And she left without saying a word to me, which she would not have done, I'm sure, sir, and without asking for her wages. And she left her trunk, too, Ruth says."

"Ruth?" Charles asked.

"Another of the housemaids," Stevens said.

"Her roommate," Alfred put in. "And she met somebody at the Black Prince, a man with a red beard, m'lord, and I'm thinking that—"

"Alfred," Stevens said firmly. "Lord Sheridan has a great deal to do just now. If he wishes to know further details of this housemaid's precipitous departure, he will ask to be informed. Now, go back to your duties."

"Thank you, Alfred," Charles said. "You've been very helpful."

Yes, helpful. The evidence against Northcote might be circumstantial, but it was very strong, Charles thought regretfully. Very strong indeed.

CHAPTER SIXTEEN

History will be kind to me, for I intend to write it.

Sir Winston Churchill

Winston turned away from the window as Charles Sheridan came back into the Duke's study.

"Marlborough was feeling indisposed," he said apologetically. "He said to tell you that if you have additional questions, he'll be glad to speak with you later." Marlborough had not been quite so accomodating—he had, in fact, said that Sheridan could go to the devil and stay there, by damn—but Winston wanted to put his cousin in the best light. This was family business, after all. The honor of the Marlboroughs was at risk, and a mistake could come at a very high price.

Sheridan sat down in the leather chair the Duke had vacated. It appeared to fit him far more comfortably. "It's just as well," he said, reaching into his pocket and taking out his pipe and a pouch of tobacco. "I need to talk something over with you, Winston. Confidentially, if you don't mind." He looked down at the pipe. "May I smoke?"

"Of course," Winston said, with a wave of his hand. He sat

down in the other chair and took a cigar out of his pocket. Lighting it, he stretched out his legs, feeling that it was very lucky that Charles Sheridan was here, and able to help with this matter of Gladys Deacon. They had to do all they could do to keep her disappearance private, out of the hands of the police and away from the newspapers. He glanced up at a portrait of the first Duke, hanging over the mantel. He had to do all *he* could, and the responsibility this imposed on him was suddenly almost overwhelming.

"How may I help you, Charles? I'll be glad to do anything I can. Anything," he repeated with a special emphasis.

"I asked the butler to inquire among the footmen about the events of last night," Sheridan replied. "One, a chap named Alfred, reports that Northcote had a conversation with Miss Deacon in the garden last night, about half-past ten. Northcote appeared to Alfred to be 'inflamed.' Miss Deacon seemed 'cool.'" Sheridan applied a match to the tobacco and pulled on the pipe. "The same footman reported that he saw Northcote leaving Blenheim, bag in hand, about twelve-thirty this morning. It was a rather abrupt departure."

"Ah-ha!" Winston exclaimed. He jumped up excitedly and began to pace. "Well, that throws a new light on the matter, doesn't it?" He spoke around the cigar jutting out of his mouth. "Northcote is behind Gladys's disappearance. He either persuaded her to go with him, or he carried her off. Damn the man! It took some nerve to do something like this at Blenheim, right under Marlborough's nose."

On the other hand, Winston reflected, he should not be too angry, for Botsy might have done them a great service, quite unintentionally, of course. Confronted with what had happened, Sunny would have to see the true Gladys Deacon: a duplicitous woman who was capable of engaging herself to one man while at the same time entangling the affections of another.

"Northcote must certainly be considered," Sheridan conceded, "although I'm not sure we should jump to any conclusions just yet." He drew on his pipe. "What can you tell me of the man?"

Winston took a turn in front of the fireplace and summarized what he knew. "His family have property in the Midlands—mines, I believe. First Battalion, Scots Guards, invalided out during the Boer War. Never married, reputation as a ladies' man, known to be hot-tempered, especially when he's had too much to drink." He paused, dredging in his memory for anything else, and came up with it, something quite satisfying, too. "Said to have landed himself in a spot of trouble two or three years ago with Lady Luttersworth's youngest daughter." He grunted. "Exactly the sort to carry off Miss Deacon, with or without her consent."

Sheridan looked up quickly. "What kind of trouble?"

"No idea, but I'm sure I can find out. Cornwallis-West knows the man quite well, I believe. They were in the same regiment. Would you like me to do a spot of checking?"

Winston topped the ash from his cigar into the fireplace. He had not yet come to terms with his mother's marriage to George Cornwallis-West, who was only sixteen days older than himself. But when she announced her decision to marry, just five years after Lord Randolph's death, the Churchills' approval had ratified the business, so what was Winston to say? That he distrusted George? That he was jealous of his mother's love for this ridiculously young husband? But Jennie Churchill (as she would always be to him) and George Cornwallis-West had been married for three years now, and Winston was learning to make the best of something he could do nothing about.

"I think it would be helpful to have more specific details about Northcote's background," Sheridan said. "If I might impose upon you, Winston, I'd be grateful if you would go to the railway station and inquire as to whether he may have left Woodstock by the early morning train. It goes at six, according to Stevens." He puffed on his pipe. "You will, of course, want to find out whether he was alone or accompanied, and learn anything you can about his destination. And if you know his London club, perhaps you could check and see whether he has gone there."

"Certainly," Winston said. "Is there anything else?"

"Northcote is said to have left here at twelve-thirty, on foot. He was not likely to have gone far. Perhaps you might inquire at The Bear—it's the nearest accomodation—or the Marlborough Arms. If he asked for a bed at that late hour, it's bound to be remembered."

"Alone and on foot," Winston mused. "If Gladys didn't go with the fellow, where the devil is she? What did he *do* with her?" He shook his head. Yes, on the one hand, Northcote might have done them all a favor. On the other, this was the sort of thing that led to newspaper stories and scandalous rumors and trouble for the family. "Damn and blast, this is a bad business."

"Yes," Sheridan replied gravely, "and it may even be worse than we think." There was an expression on his face that Winston could not quite read, a mixture of apprehension, concern, and something else—interest, was it, or intrigue? At some level, the man looked as if he found all of this, well, stimulating. "There's something else I must ask of you, in complete confidence," he went on. "I think the Duke should not be bothered about it at the moment, so I am turning to you. I hope you can help."

"Of course I'll help," Winston replied urgently. "Anything, Charles. Anything at all."

Sheridan puffed on his pipe and rings of smoke rose over his head. After a moment, he said, "What can you tell me about the Marlborough Gems?"

"The Gems?" Winston was taken aback by the question, which seemed to him to take the conversation in an unnecessary direction. However, since he was asked, he did his best to comply.

"They were a famous collection of carved gemstones assembled by the fourth Duke. There were quite a few of them, some eight hundred or so, I've been told, some—from ancient Greece and Ptolemaic Egypt—truly priceless. The Duke was obsessed by them. He had Reynolds paint him with one of his favorites. And he kept the lot in this very room, in red Morocco cases lined with velvet."

"Indeed," Sheridan murmured, looking around as if the gems might still be there.

"He even commissioned engravings of the hundred finest stones and had them privately printed in two large leatherbound folios," Winston went on, warming to his subject. He sighed regretfully. "But the engravings are all that's left, I'm afraid. The gems themselves were sold by my grandfather."

At the words, Winston felt his heart twist. It wounded him deeply to think that any true Churchill could be such a philistine as to plunder Blenheim's precious treasures, but that was what had happened. A high-living spendthrift who was perennially short of money, the seventh Duke had first sold the priceless gemstones for a paltry thirty-five thousand guineas, then persuaded Parliament to put through the Blenheim Settled Estates Act, stripping the family heirlooms of their entailment so that they could be sold as well. Paintings, art objects, silver, jewelry—everything of value had gone on the auction block in a matter of just a few days. And worst of all, he'd sold the Sunderland Library, that splendid collection of twenty-four thousand beautifully bound volumes, classics, bibles from early presses, rare county histories, illuminated medieval chronicles. Winston had been only eight when the precious books were sold, too young to have actually read any of them. But he had loved to creep into the Long Library and imagine all of the wonders stored between the embossed leather covers on its shelves and dream of the day when he would turn the pages himself and learn all the wisdom that could be gained from them. He had been struck as if by a physical blow when he saw the shelves standing empty. The Duke had died not long after, and Winston could not help feeling that his grandfather had been struck down by a vengeful deity in retribution for the pillaging of the library's treasures.

Sheridan's question broke in upon his consciousness. "Were *all* the gemstones sold? Might a few have escaped?"

"As a matter of fact, some did," Winston replied. "The story goes that the seventh Duke's secretary deliberately left a half-dozen or so out of the inventory that was conveyed to Christie's before the auction. The stones—seal stones, all of them—were found, loose, some years later, in a cabinet in the Saloon. I used to play with them myself, when I was here on holiday as a child." He smiled a little. "I imagined them as having a special magic."

And who knows, he thought fondly, perhaps they did. His magic lantern, his steam engine, his lead soldiers, and the last few Marlborough gemstones—together, they constituted the enchantments of his too-brief childhood. And Blenheim, of course. He had always loved to come here. And if things had been different, if Sunny had died before he fathered a son, he himself—Winston Leonard Spencer-Churchill, grandson of the seventh Duke—would have become Duke of Marlborough. He often thought of that and wondered despairingly whether anything he might accomplish in his life would equal that never-to-be-achieved glory. How would history remember him, if not for that? What could he do to merit—

Sheridan coughed as if to get his attention. "Do you know where the gems are now?"

Winston frowned. Why was Sheridan so interested in the Marlborough Gems? "Why, yes, as a matter of fact, I do. They are kept in a box in the Red Drawing-Room. Why?"

"I'm not at liberty to tell you," Sheridan replied quietly. "All I can say is that I was instrumental in resolving an art theft in the district, and that I have coincidentally learned something about a theft at an estate in a northern county. I have reason to suspect—no facts, mind you, just suspicions, some of which may be entirely unfounded—that there may be a similar plot afoot here at Blenheim. If it goes true to pattern, it may occur during the weekend of the Royal visit."

Winston felt his jaw drop. "The Royal visit!" he sputtered. "But that . . . can't be permitted, Charles! It's totally and completely out of the question that thieves should strike Blenheim! Think of the newspaper headlines! Imagine the scandal!" He struck his forehead with the heel of his hand. "Something *must* be done to prevent it."

"That's what I wanted to discuss with you," Sheridan said. "But first let me ask you whether among the servants there are any who are especially devoted to you, any whom you feel you can trust implicitly."

The servants? Winston puffed out his cheeks. "Well, the butler and the housekeeper have been here since my father's time, although neither of them have any special relationship to me. Both are getting on in years, and they don't keep a very tight rein on the lower servants. And sad to say, there have been a great many changes among the staff in the last few years. Poor Consuelo frequently laments the difficulty of finding good people who will not take advantage." He paused, not liking the idea suddenly borne in upon him that the house might be full of untrustworthy servants. Who could tell what conspiracies they were hatching? Winston might be feel himself a Liberal at heart, but he was not enough of a Liberal to fancy that people of the lower classes were inherently good.

"In that case," Sheridan said, "I have a proposal to make to you. We need someone below-stairs whom we can trust, someone who will be our ears and eyes among the staff. What do you think of this, Winston?" And he began to outline a plan.

Winston listened intently, commenting here and there. The scheme was full of merit, it seemed to him. A bit of a conspiracy, but how else were they to get to the bottom of things? He was sure that Marlborough wouldn't agree to it, of course, and if he knew anything about the plan would deny his permission. But Winston would do his best to ensure that the business would not reach his cousin's ears until it was all over, and they were successful in averting the danger. Then he could be told, and Winston had no doubt that the Duke would be appropriately grateful.

When Sheridan was finished, Winston said without

hesitation, "I shall go and speak to Stevens at once, Charles, without giving him any clue to the significance of this business. I believe I can guarantee that he won't give us any trouble."

"Very good," Sheridan said, rising from his chair and going to the fireplace to knock the tobacco out of his pipe. "And when you go into Woodstock to inquire at The Bear and the railway station, there is one other thing that you might do. It seems that one of the housemaids cannot be located, although her personal effects are still in her room. Her name is Kitty. Her roommate mentioned that she spoke with a red-bearded man at the Black Prince. Could you ask there and see what you can find out about the fellow?"

"A housemaid, too?" Winston asked, shaking his head. "Miss Deacon, Botsy Northcote, a plot among the servants—good God, Charles, what's *next?*"

"I don't think we should try to look too far ahead," Sheridan said dryly. "We might not like what we see."

"There's wisdom in that." Winston put out his cigar in an onyx ashtray. "Well, I'm off below-stairs, and then to Woodstock. What are you going to do?"

"I have one or two things to look into," Sheridan said vaguely. "Please let the Duchess know that I shall miss lunch, but that I expect to be back by teatime. And tell Stevens that our young man will be arriving this afternoon. At least," he added cryptically, "so I sincerely hope."

CHAPTER SEVENTEEN

[Gladys Deacon] is an enchanting but naughty, untruthful child. It is terrible the way one gets to feel with her after a very short time, the impossibility of believing a word she says, but the equal difficulty of disbelieving everything . . . but all the same she is an Enchantress!

Mary Berenson, Diary, 28 March 1905

Kate left Consuelo, went to the morning room, and rang for Mrs. Raleigh. When the housekeeper arrived, she told her that the Duchess had cancelled the picnic lunch and that they would be eating, instead, in the family dining room. Then she went back upstairs and down the hall toward Gladys Deacon's room.

Kate had left Consuelo lying on her bed with a cool compress over her eyes. She could not help feeling a deep pity for the Duchess, whose wealth and title had brought her nothing but unhappiness. If Consuelo had been a woman of ordinary means instead of a Vanderbilt, she wouldn't have been compelled to marry a man she didn't love—a man who ridiculed her in front of their guests—and live in a house that felt to her like a prison. And even worse, live with the fear that her husband was courting public scandal and disgrace in an affair with a very foolish young woman. A woman who had unaccountably disappeared, dressed in her evening finery and—perhaps this was also important—wearing a valuable piece of jewelry. Where *was* she? What had happened to her?

Kate stopped in front of Gladys's door and rapped twice, just in case she had turned up while they were looking for the Duke. Hearing nothing within, she inserted the key in the lock, turned it, and went in, locking the door behind her so that she would not have to worry about being disturbed.

Or being accused of snooping, Beryl Bardwell whispered cattily in her ear. *Of looking for material for your novel about Fair Rosamund.*

Kate lifted her chin. She was not snooping. Gladys had disappeared and she was assisting her husband in his inquiries into what was obviously a very serious matter. And whatever resemblance Gladys Deacon might bear to the young mistress of Henry II lay mostly in Gladys's imagination, although Kate had to admit there were certain intriguing parallels among the relationships. Henry, Rosamund, Eleanor, Roger of Salisbury. Marlborough, Gladys, Consuelo, Northcote. Enough parallels, no doubt, to satisfy Gladys that she was acting her part in the unfolding drama that was her life.

Kate stood with her back to the door for a few moments, looking around the room, wondering where she should begin and what she should look for. Something that might explain what had happened to Gladys? Some clue to her whereabouts?

But Kate was not optimistic that she would find anything bearing directly on this situation. The best she could do, she thought, was to develop a more complete picture of Gladys, which in turn might offer Charles some sort of guidance.

This was not Gladys's personal room, however; it was only a Blenheim guest room. Although Gladys might stay here frequently, the room would bear few traces of her personality.

But Kate had been commissioned to search, and search she would. She went to the wardrobe and opened it, noticing that the gowns were elaborate and expensive, several rather flamboyantly exotic. The clothing was that of a wealthy young woman who spent a great deal of money on personal finery, some of it in questionable taste, or at least so it would be perceived by the more conservative ladies of Society. The garments bore Gladys's favorite scent, musky and provocative. Closing the wardrobe, Kate made a mental note to ask Bess, the Blenheim maid who had the task of looking after Gladys, whether any garments were missing. (Gladys's own maid would not be with her until the following week; she was in Naples, with Gladys's mother.) She wasn't sure Bess would know very much about the clothing, but it was worth an inquiry.

A chest of drawers stood against one wall, and Kate went to it next. On the marble top was displayed a jewelled Cartier clock, a blue porcelain bowl, a jade ash tray, and a Fabergé cigarette box filled with cigarettes bearing the gold Marlborough crest. Several seemed to be missing, and Kate remembered that she had seen Gladys smoking after dinner. There were also two silver-framed photographs of handsome young men, one in cricket whites, the other in a yachting jacket and jaunty cap, both photos inscribed to their darling Gladys in terms of such effusive endearment that Kate had to smile, thinking that Gladys seemed to win men's hearts wherever she went.

There was another, larger photograph in a gold frame— a mustachioed man with eyeglasses, signed "To little Gladys, from her loving Papa." Edward Deacon, Kate thought, the jealous husband who had shot his wife's French lover. The story had been in all the newspapers while she was still living in New York. Gladys's mother was reputed to be a foolish woman with an endless string of European lovers, playing one of them against another in a dangerous game. Like mother, like daughter? Kate wondered, her glance lighting on a tiny snapshot of Botsy Northcote, stuck crookedly in a corner of one of the frames—not an indication of a very great affection.

However, there was another photograph, this one unframed and hidden. Kate found it, face-down, beneath a stack of lace underwear in the top drawer. It was a studio portrait of the Duke, inscribed "Ever only your own Marlborough." Kate stared at it for a moment, at the hooded eyes, void of any expression, the arrogant mouth framed by a delicate mustache, the smooth boyish cheeks, the hair swept back from the brows. There was no hint of passion in that perfectly composed face, no hint of emotion, of desire, even of ordinary human tenderness. If she were choosing a lover or a husband, Kate thought, she would not choose this chilly, remote little man, who had only his title and the family estate to recommend him. Of course, Consuelo's ambitious mother had chosen him for her—or so Kate had heard—but Gladys had chosen him freely. What did the choice say about *her*? With a shiver, Kate turned the photograph over and replaced it.

The other drawers seemed to contain nothing but untidy heaps of clothing: lingerie, nightgowns, filmy stockings, lace shawls, silk scarves, all of it very expensive. In the bottom drawer, however, she found something much more interesting. It looked to be a diary, bound in supple blue leather and fastened with a tab inserted into a small golden lock. Kate turned it over in her hands, intensely curious.

Go on, Kate, Beryl whispered urgently. *What in the world are you waiting for? It's a tiny lock, of no consequence at all. You can pick it with a bent pin. Just think of the secrets inside!*

Kate held the diary for a moment, considering. If she opened and read it, she would be privy to Gladys's secrets, all of them profoundly intimate, most of them embarrassing, and some of them childish and silly. How would she choose which ones to confide to Charles, and which to keep to herself? If Gladys had not safely returned by the time she had reported to Charles, she decided, she would tell him where to find it, and he could determine for himself whether it should be opened and read.

This plan did not satisfy Beryl, of course. *Oh, pooh!* she said disgustedly. *Your heroines would not hesitate to read something like this, would they? So why not you?*

But Kate stood firm against Beryl's urging, and put the diary back in the drawer. As she did so, her fingers touched a pouch made of supple leather. She took it out and opened it, spilling small five tissue-wrapped bundles onto the marble-topped chest. She pulled the tissue off and saw five polished stones. The most intriguing was a blue-green piece she recognized as an Egyptian scarab, with marks carved into it. The other four—red, green, blue, and smoke-colored—also had engraved marks cut into various polished faces. Perhaps Gladys had collected them as a child and they had some sentimental value. She rewrapped them and replaced the pouch beside the diary.

Finding nothing more of interest in the chest of drawers, Kate turned her attention to the glass-topped dressing table, which was crowded with baskets of ribbons and silks and natural hairpieces, exactly the color of Gladys's hair, and bottles and jars of lotions and cosmetics. Kate picked up a small pot of French rouge, recollecting the heightened color of Gladys's lips and cheeks the night before. It was easy to conclude that she was a woman deeply concerned with her physical appearance, a conclusion borne out by something Consuelo had mentioned to Kate this morning: that Gladys had paraffin wax injected into her nose to enhance its Hellenic profile.

Kate put down the pot of rouge with a wry face. She was of the opinion that one took what one was given, although there was no special harm in making the best of it with rouge or powder or other cosmetics. However, paraffin injection—which had become popular over the past decade or so, especially among those who frequented Continental beauty salons—was not only foolish, it was dangerous, and Kate had seen photographs of the misshapen faces which proved it so.

The dressing table and jewel box, filled with elaborate, ornate jewelry, had nothing special to offer, and Kate turned her attention to a shelf of books beside the bed. It contained a somewhat surprising collection of titles, reminding Kate of something else that Consuelo had said: that Gladys was not only beautiful but genuinely brilliant, having learnt seven languages and studied art, literature, mathematics, and music. There were several books of poetry with Gladys's name in them; a much-thumbed-through book of photographs of classical statuary with the text in Greek; books of German philosophy, with passages underlined; several rather risqué French novels with playful notes in the margins, in French; and Edith Wharton's just-published and much-discussed first novel, *Valley of Decision*. It was an eclectic collection, to say the least, Kate thought, and it forced her to modify her assessment of Gladys Deacon. The young woman might not be wise, but she was certainly intelligent.

And then, lying half-hidden under a book of French poetry on Gladys's bedside table, Kate found something of much greater interest. It was a note written in a square masculine hand on the thick, creamy Blenheim stationery which was kept in every room, and dated Tuesday, 12 May, just two days before. Kate hesitated only a moment. This note was not locked with a key, like the diary, and it was clearly of current interest. And besides, Beryl was prodding her, even more urgently than before. *Oh, for pity's sake, Kate. Read!*

Kate picked up the note and read it.

My dearest darling,

I am beside myself with anxiety and apprehension at the cruel indifference you are showing toward your own, your devoted Botsy. You say that my passion distresses you, but surely you must realize and excuse the depths to which I am stirred by my love for you and my desire to make you my wife. (Do I need to remind you that you pledged yourself to accept me when we were together at Welbeck? or that my passion did not distress you then?) You simply must hear me out, Gladys, and agree to set a date for our wedding. And if you refuse, why then I shall simply carry you off straightaway and the devil take he who tries to stop me—Marlborough or anyone else!

With the most ardent passion

N

Well, there was no doubting the relevance of this letter, Kate thought, reading it for the second time. Northcote hadn't yet been seen this morning. What if he had spirited Gladys away, as he threatened in this letter? She suspected that such a violent and precipitous action was not the way to win the young lady's heart, but perhaps she was wrong. Perhaps an extravagant gesture was exactly the thing that would sweep Gladys off her feet and get her to honor her promise. And Botsy Northcote, Kate had no doubt, was exactly the kind of man who would do it.

She glanced at the Cartier clock on the chest of drawers. The bell for lunch would ring in an hour. She would find Charles straightaway and give him the letter. She locked the room, pocketed the key, and went to inquire after Charles.

Learning that he had left for Oxford and feeling at loose ends, she went downstairs and out into the rose garden, walking slowly along the gravel path, reflecting on the events of the night before. The last time she had seen Gladys, the girl was going into the garden with Marlborough, and yet a scrap of her dress had been found on a bush at Rosamund's Well, on the other side of the lake.

On the other side of the lake? Beryl mused. *And just how do you suppose she got there?*

Kate paused in the act of burying her nose in a large pink cabbage rose with a delightfully spicy scent. Beryl had raised a very good question. Come to think of it, just how had Gladys crossed the lake?

"She walked over the bridge?" Kate hazarded aloud.

Gladys Deacon walked? Beryl laughed shortly. *Don't be ridiculous, Kate. Can you see that young woman taking a half-mile tramp after dark, along a gravel path and down a steep hill? In her evening dress?*

"I suppose you're right," Kate murmured. The road across the bridge was graveled, and the path that led from the bridge to the Well was steep and overgrown. It wasn't something one would do unless one were wearing proper boots.

"Of course I'm right," Beryl replied. *And what sort of foot gear was Gladys wearing last night? Evening slippers, that's what! Gold evening slippers, to match her dress. No woman in her right mind would walk about the countryside in those shoes.*

Kate didn't remember noticing Gladys's feet, but it was Beryl who was always took notes on details of dress and manner, and Kate didn't doubt the truth of her observation. She bent to sniff another rose. Well, then, if Gladys didn't walk around the lake, how *did* she get to Rosamund's Well? As Kate straightened, her glance happened to light upon the boat house, a rustic building far down at the foot of the garden, behind some shrubbery, next to the lake.

Congratulations, old girl! Beryl exclaimed triumphantly. *That's it! Our Gladys rowed across the lake!*

"Rowed?" Kate replied, with a mildly sarcastic chuckle. "Oh, come, now, Beryl. Gladys Deacon wouldn't have the slightest idea of what to do with an oar. She could never row a boat all the way across that lake."

Beryl chuckled maliciously. *Who says she rowed it? Maybe Botsy rowed it for her. After all, he promised to carry her off—and what's more romantic than a rowboat on a moonlit night? Come on, Kate, let's have a look.*

"A look at what?" Kate asked. "The lunch gong will be sounding in just a few minutes. We don't have time to go anywhere."

It won't matter if we're a little late. Anyway, what's more important? Sitting down to lunch on time, or finding out what happened to Gladys?

With that, the intrepid Beryl flew off down the path. And Kate had no choice but to follow.

CHAPTER EIGHTEEN

All men dream, but not equally. Those who dream by night in the dusty recesses of their minds wake in the day to find that it was vanity: but the dreamers of the day are dangerous men, for they may act their dream with open eyes, to make it possible.

The Seven Pillars of Wisdom
T. E. (Ned) Lawrence

Ned Lawrence had been bitterly disappointed when he learned from John Buttersworth that he had missed Lord Sheridan's visit to the museum. He had been hoping to see him, and hoping that his lordship would take another criminal case in the Oxford area and, this time, ask him to assist. He admired Lord Sheridan for the cool and careful way he used his wits, but there was more, some of which Ned would not have been able to recognize and acknowledge, at least at this point in his life. He respected men who showed strength of character and physical bravery, and yet were deeply sensitive to the feelings of others; who were sure of themselves but not brazen about it; who were intellectuals but not snobs; who were attractive to women but resisted their power. He would be glad to play Watson to his lordship's Holmes any day, and he'd told him so, straight to his face. Ned's mother may have taught him to be deferential to his elders and betters, but his father had taught him to ask for what he wanted from men who had the means to give it, and Ned thought that his best course was to follow both their teachings. Of course, he already knew how to get what he wanted for himself, whenever that was necessary.

Today was one of the days when he was getting what he wanted. He had asked Buttersworth for a day's holiday from his work at the Ashmolean and—clad in tweed knickers, a sweater, and a tweed cap—had ridden his bicycle to All Saints, a small stone church with a square Norman tower in the country near the hamlet of Derwood. He'd brought his brass-rubbing kit and planned to spend the day making rubbings from some brasses he had noticed in the church when he'd gone scouting there some weeks before.

Ned's passion for antiquarianism had become an obsession, all but taking over his life. He worked at the museum during the summers and on Saturdays throughout the school year. As he prowled through the city, he loved to stop at new building sites and search for medieval artifacts: coins and tiles and bits of pottery and metal. He would often trade his pocket money to the laborers for things they'd found, and some of them had learned to save promising items for him. He kept everything on the shelves in the room he shared with his older brother—there were five boys in the Lawrence family—and his growing collection fueled his enthusiasm for the Middle Ages.

Imagining himself already an archaeologist and adventurer, Ned dreamed of traveling through Egypt and Africa, crossing perilous wildernesses, fighting savage tribesmen, and giving his life in the defense of a doomed city, as General Gordon had done. He devoured the action-filled adventure stories of G. A. Henty, whose fictional boy heroes met real men—Robert the Bruce, Sir Francis Drake, the Duke of Marlborough, Napoleon—in a variety of historical situations. He dreamed of performing great deeds in the company of someone like Charles Sheridan, who had distinguished himself as a military officer in the Sudan, very nearly getting himself killed in a brave attempt to rescue General Gordon and free Khartoum from the awful onslaught of the Mahdi's Dervishes.

Yes, Sheridan would be a perfect companion, although Ned knew that he had a great deal of work to do before he was ready. He was planning to read Modern History when he got to Oxford, so he'd understand the politics and history of the places they would go. He'd have to win a scholarship for that, though, for although his father was a gentleman with an independent income, the income was small and five boys were rather a lot to send to school.

Brass rubbings were one of Ned's recent obsessions, and over the past few months, he had bicycled to almost every church within a half-day's ride of Oxford to record the brasses he found there. Brass-rubbers were supposed to get written permission from the appropriate authority, but Ned had never bothered. Somebody who cared as much about the brasses as he did ought to be entitled to do whatever he liked with them, as long as he didn't damage them, of course. And anyway, being where he shouldn't be, doing something he shouldn't do, only lent a greater sense of danger and intrigue to the adventure.

The heavy wooden door of All Saints stood ajar when he arrived, shortly before one. The church was deserted, as he'd hoped it would be, so he hid his bicycle behind some shrubbery and went inside, closing the door behind him. He looked around, reveling in the dusky quiet, redolent of old hymnals and lemon-polished oak. Ned sometimes dreamed of becoming a monk—when he wasn't dreaming of being an adventurer. He loved the idea of the introspective, ascetic life, with regular fasts and rigorous physical exercise and long days when he was entirely alone, when he spoke to no one at all.

But he wasn't thinking of that at the moment. The brasses he had come to rub—three small, square ones, two feet wide by two feet high—were attached to the stone wall near the altar. On their faces, they were all Tudor, one engraved with a coat of arms, two with Latin texts, and dated 1598. Well and good, and he was glad to have them for his collection. But Ned had the idea that they might have been looted from a local monastery and bought as reusable metal by the engravers. To test his theory, he took a screwdriver out of his kit, unfastened the four screws securing one of the brasses to the wall, and took it down. Holding his breath, he turned it over.

To his inexpressible joy, he was right! On the reverse, there was what looked to be the head and shoulders of a priest in Mass vestments. He stared at it, feeling his heart pound. It was extraordinary, really, this idea that an object from the sixteenth century—old enough, certainly—might conceal an object from the fourteenth century, both hidden away in a church that itself had been built sometime in the twelfth century.

Reflecting reverently on these mysteries, Ned took out a brush, tape, a roll of paper, and his heelball, a cake of black wax that fit neatly into the palm of his hand. Getting down on his knees, he dusted the grit from the brass, taped the paper to it, and began to rub, working carefully, watching with amazement as the artistry of the long-ago engraver—dead some five centuries, unseen for three—appeared as if by magic under his hands.

Ned was so intent on his work that he did not hear a motor car approach the church and stop along the verge. Congratulating himself on being skilled enough to do the whole job in less than fifteen minutes—and a good job it was, too, one of his best—he removed the paper, rolled it, and prepared to refasten the brass to the wall.

But the brass was easier to take down than to put back up. He was struggling with the unwieldy object when he heard the creak of the door opening. Startled, he lost his grip and the brass fell to the stone floor with an echoing metallic clang. He turned to see Lord Sheridan strolling toward him down the aisle, his hands in his pockets and a severe look on his face.

Ned's heart plummeted into his boots. Of all the people to find him here, it would have to be Lord Sheridan, whom he admired and respected so highly. In an instant, his fantasies of doing heroic deeds with this man vanished like a puff of cloud. His dreams for the future were gone, his work at the Ashmolean a thing of the past. He would be publically disgraced, perhaps even sent to jail or—

"Doing a little investigation on the sly, are you, Ned?" Lord Sheridan asked.

Ned let out his breath and bent to pick up the brass. "You startled me. Sir," he added.

"Be glad I'm not the sexton or the vicar," Lord Sheridan said with a half-smile. "Or the local constable. He might have you up before the magistrate for something like this, especially if you haven't asked permission." He paused. "Let me see what you have there."

He took the brass from Ned and examined both sides. Then he handed it back and picked up the rubbing. "Quite nice," he said after a moment. "Quite nice indeed." He rolled it up again and put it with Ned's kit. "You'll be sure to sign and date it, won't you? And include the name and location of the church."

Ned squirmed, suddenly aware that the rubbing was evidence of his trespass. "It's for my private collection, sir," he muttered. "No one else will see it."

"Doesn't matter. You may think this is private, but you have no idea where it might end up—in a public museum, for instance. And if you don't properly identify your work, you'll have people prying brasses off church walls all over the kingdom, trying to locate this one." Lord Sheridan leaned one shoulder against the wall. "I came to take you up on your offer, Ned. If it's still good, that is."

Ned stared at him. "My . . . offer?"

"Yes. It turns out that I need an assistant." The corners of his mouth rose. "A Doctor Watson, so to speak. As I recall, you mentioned something of the sort to me, a short time ago."

Ned felt the joy and excitement rise in his throat, but disciplined his expression and forced himself to sound casual. "Well, if old Buttersworth can spare me, I s'pose I might be able to lend you a hand. What's doing?"

There was a glint in Lord Sheridan's eyes. "I wonder whether you've ever considered going into service."

Ned felt the disappointment twist in his gut and knew that it showed on his face. He had thought, he had *hoped,* that Lord Sheridan was asking something more than mere service of him, for if that's what he wanted, Ned would be forced to say no. It was true that he did not come from a wealthy family, and that boys from his class did not usually aspire to great heights of social ambition. But while his mother had been a nanny, his father was the grandson of a baronet and sprang from a family of Irish gentry that included (or so it was said) Sir Walter Raleigh. Ned was determined to make what he could of the noble blood that flowed through his veins, and service was demeaning. But it was Lord Sheridan who was making the proposal, so he replied with more tact than he might have done otherwise.

"I was hoping that your lordship might have something different in mind. Something with a little more . . . scope."

"A little more scope, eh?" Lord Sheridan smiled. "Actually, I do, Ned. What I have in mind is a spot of espionage, a bit of secret agent work. The servant's role—you would work as a page in a large country house—would be, in effect, your disguise."

"I say, that's jolly good!" Ned exclaimed happily. He clicked his heels together and swept off his cap in an exaggerated bow. "Indeed, I am entirely at your service, m'lord. Ask and I shall perform your every command, m'lord! What would you have me do, m'lord?" And he made another bow.

Lord Sheridan chuckled. "That's a bit strong, I'd say, but you have the right idea, and with coaching, I daresay you'll do just fine. Most of your work as a page won't involve the upstairs people, though. What I need you to do is definitely below-stairs work." He paused. "However, I shall have to ask your father's approval for this, since it will involve your being away from home for perhaps as long as a fortnight."

"A fortnight!" Ned said breathlessly, feeling that he must be dreaming. Either that, or he had just stepped into the pages of one of Mr. Henty's grand adventure stories.

"I trust that Mr. Buttersworth will release you from your work at the museum for that period of time," Lord Sheridan said. "Of course, you will receives wages as a page and a stipend as an informant. It should make up for the loss of the museum's wages."

An informant, Ned thought, elated, not quite believing it. *I'm going to be a spy. A real spy!*

"I can assure both you and your father that your work will not involve any danger," Lord Sheridan continued. "And I will always be close at hand, as will one or two other people to whom you can go in the event of . . . difficulty. You will not be on your own."

"Danger," Ned scoffed carelessly. "I have no concerns for my personal safety."

Lord Sheridan eyed him. "I don't believe you do," he said thoughtfully. "A young man who is daring enough to pry a brass off a church wall has more than enough audacity to carry out my small task." He pursed his lips. "However, I hope you will not have to learn your first lessons about real danger when you have been put in command of other men. It wouldn't hurt you to face a hazard or two now, if only to see what it feels like. You might then have more respect for those who are mindful of the dangers you so eagerly disregard."

Ned had the vague sense that this was a rebuke, but since he didn't know how to reply, he ignored it. "Where am I to work?" he demanded eagerly. "A country house, you said?"

"We'll be at Blenheim Palace."

"Blenheim Palace!"

Now Ned was sure that he was dreaming. He had gone through the palace on Tourist Day, of course, and more than once. He had reveled in its architectural glories, its martial magnificence, which symbolized all the achievements of the Empire. He had stood at the foot of the Column of Victory and imagined himself as the first Duke of Marlborough, riding out to battle, flags and pennants flying. He had stood at Rosamund's Well, across the lake from the palace, picturing himself as Henry, with all of England and the Aquitaine at his feet. And now he was to be a spy. A *spy* in Blenheim Palace!

Lord Sheridan nodded. "The King and Queen will be arriving for a visit the first weekend of August. I should think our work will be over as soon as they have left, and you'll be free to return home." He paused, eyeing Ned. "Will that be satisfactory, do you think?"

Satisfactory! It was splendid, it was magnificent, it was . . . Ned had run out of superlatives and could scarcely speak for crowing. He would be at Blenheim Palace during a visit by the King and Queen of England!

"Of . . . course," he managed. "It will be most . . . satisfactory."

Lord Sheridan became serious. "I should caution you, though, that everything you learn from this moment on must be kept entirely confidential, Ned, now and in future. You may want to boast about your exploits with your friends, but you must not share this with anyone." He paused. "Do you understand? Can I trust you?"

Solemnly, Ned raised his hand. "I'll never say a word to anyone. I swear it."

A smile flicked across Lord Sheridan's mouth and he nodded. "Right, then. I'd like to get on with the business, so if you wouldn't mind replacing that brass I'd appreciate it. Let's fasten your bicycle onto the back of my motor car, and go to Oxford. Are we likely to catch your father at home?"

"Yes, *sir*," Ned said smartly.

What were a few brasses compared to the opportunity to serve as a spy at Blenheim Palace?

CHAPTER NINETEEN

We hold several threads in our hands, and the odds are that one or other of them guides us to the truth. We may waste time in following the wrong one, but sooner or later we must come upon the right.

The Hound of the Baskervilles
Sir Arthur Conan Doyle

The boat house, which Kate had noticed on one of her previous rambles, stood at the edge of the lake, partly concealed by a screen of shrubbery. It was a utilitarian wooden building, rather ramshackle, constructed on pilings sunk into the lake bed. There was a crudely painted sign on the door—NO ADMITTANCE—and a padlock, but the hasp was unshackled and the door hung open. Ignoring the sign, Kate cautiously pushed the door wide and went through.

Inside the boat house, the air smelled of weeds and rotting wood, and the silvery light danced across the surface of the water. Off to the left, in the shadows, Kate saw a pile of fishing gear, a heap of netting, and some fishing poles. To her right, there was a stack of wooden crates and baskets. A dock extended some six or eight feet into the water in front of her. A green-painted rowboat was tied to the dock on one side, with a pair of oars in the bottom. A yellow-painted rowboat was tied on the other.

Kate hesitated for a moment, as her eyes became accustomed to the shadowy gloom and the dazzling reflections. Then she stepped forward onto the dock, to a point where she could see down into the rowboat.

Look! Beryl exclaimed, with an excited nudge. *What's that in the bottom of the boat? It looks like—*

Kate got down on her knees, bent over the boat, and picked up a golden evening slipper, somewhat damp from lying in a puddle.

It is! Beryl cried. *It's Gladys's shoe!*

Kate straightened up, still on her knees. It was indeed Gladys's shoe—at least, it was the same color as the dress she had worn the night before. So Gladys really *had* gone across the lake in the rowboat.

There was a moment's silence. *But did she go by herself?* Beryl asked, in a significant tone.

Kate frowned. Then, with no hesitation at all, she gathered her skirts, clambered down into the rocking boat, and began a thorough search, from prow to stern. She had just picked up several bits of litter when a dark shape loomed over her and a rough male voice demanded, "Here, now, Miss! Wot d'ye think yer doin'?"

Kate's head snapped up. The man was small and wizened, with a gray beard and a thick shock of gray hair, as shaggy as a terrier. He was dressed in worn corduroy trousers, a jacket made of sacking, a brown leather hat, and workmen's leather boots.

"I . . . I was just looking for something," Kate stammered, straightening hastily and thrusting her left hand into her pocket. The boat rocked wildly, and the man leaned over and grabbed her right arm.

"Hey, now, Miss!" he cried. "Steady! Watch wot yer doin' there, or ye'll find yerself in the water!"

Kate recovered her balance. "Thank you," she said. Accepting his extended hand, she climbed out of the boat, adding, somewhat breathlessly, "What did you say your name was?"

"Di'n't," the old man growled. "Badger's wot they call me."

"Well, thank you, Badger," Kate said briskly, dusting her hands. "Are you responsible for these boats?"

The man looked even fiercer. "'Deed I am," he said. "I'm 'sponsible fer the fish'ry on this lake, and I minds the boats. These be *workin'* boats," he added with a dark emphasis. "If ye're wantin' one o' the Duke's boats t' go out for a row, ye need t' go down the shore 't the Duke's boathouse."

"I see," Kate said. "So guests aren't encouraged to take these boats?"

Badger pushed his hands into his pockets. "These be workin' boats," he growled again. "T'other boats're better 'n' cleaner. They're fer the Duke's guests. Wish they'd tell 'em that, up 't the house," he added in a disgruntled tone, "so people 'ud stop botherin' me. Damn nuisance, is wot it is."

"Bothering you?" Kate asked. "Have other guests inquired about these boats?"

Instead of answering, Badger squinted at her. "What's that ye've got in yer hand?"

"Something I found in the boat," Kate said, holding it up. "A woman's slipper. It appears that one of the other guests, Miss Gladys Deacon, was in this rowboat last night, and may have gone across to Rosamund's Well. Most likely, she was with someone—a man. Might you have seen them?"

A crafty look crossed Badger's face, but it was gone as soon as it came. "Nobody but me uses these boats," he said, in a gruff, ill-humored tone, evading Kate's question. "Anyway, it's dang'rous here. Rotten boards, deep water, nobody 'round to hear ye if ye call fer help." He paused and added, ominously, "Nivver kin tell wot might happen in a place like this. Losin' a shoe 'ud be a small thing, compared."

Hearing the warning—or was it a threat?—in his tone, Kate nodded. "Thank you," she said, thinking that Badger knew more than he was willing to tell her. It might be a good idea if Charles talked to the man. "And how do I reach the Duke's boats?"

Badger jerked his thumb. "That way. Take the path."

Feeling Badger's dark glance following her until she was out of sight, Kate did as she was bid, taking a path that meandered for fifty yards along the shore of the lake. The Duke's boathouse, it turned out, was large and ornate, rather like a picnic pavilion. However, as Kate discovered, it was securely locked, which answered one question that had come to her mind: why Gladys—and her rowing partner, if she was not alone—had taken one of the working boats instead of the boats available for guests.

In the distance, Kate heard the resounding gong that signaled luncheon. She'd have to hurry, or she'd be late. But as she went up the hill toward the palace, she couldn't resist taking her finds from her skirt pocket and looking at them again.

Gladys Deacon's golden slipper, slightly damp.

A cigarette bearing the Marlborough crest, half-smoked, also damp and trodden upon, found in the bottom of the boat.

And what looked like a letter written in ink in an un-skilled hand on a ragged piece of paper, crumpled and much blotted, found with the cigarette.

Dearest Kitty,

I need to talk to you, soon as ever posibel. You know I luv you dearest and long too hold you close.

Yours 'til death
Alfred

A touching little love note, Beryl sniffed, *but I doubt it has anything to do with Gladys.*

Kate agreed. It had probably been written by one of the male servants to a female servant, and suggested that Badger's rowboats were more commonly used than he liked to acknowledge. It might even have been one of the servants who arranged for the lock to be unfastened.

But the slipper certainly belonged to Gladys, and the cig-arette, too, most likely, although Kate would have expected that if it were Gladys's cigarette, it would have borne traces of her lip coloring. It did not. Kate wondered whether it was possible to take a fingerprint from a half-smoked cigarette, and handled it carefully. She was anxious to see Charles and give everything over to him, including Northcote's letter.

And if Beryl was feeling smug about the course of their investigations this morning, who could blame her? They had, after all, answered their initial question. But the an-swer raised still other questions, and Kate frowned as she pondered them.

Gladys seemed to have gone across the lake in the row-boat. Did she go voluntarily, or against her will, as the shoe seemed to suggest? And who had rowed the boat back across the lake and returned it to the boat house? The passionate Northcote, who threatened to spirit Gladys away? The secretive Duke of Marlborough, whose taciturnity might conceal an even greater passion? Some as-yet-unidentified third man, perhaps a spurned lover? And where in the world could Gladys have gone, minus one shoe? Kate shivered, liking neither the questions nor the possible answers, all of which seemed to her to be ominous.

And as she went into the palace through a rear door, a line from one of Conan Doyle's recent novels came into her mind. "We hold several threads in our hands," Sherlock Holmes had said to Watson, "and the odds are that one or other of them guides us to the truth."

She held several threads of a mystery in her hand, like the golden thread that had led Eleanor straight to the heart of Rosamund's labyrinth.

But what exactly was the mystery?

And did *any* of the threads lead to the truth?

CHAPTER TWENTY

Circumstantial evidence is a very tricky thing. It may seem to point very straight to one thing, but if you shift your own point of view a little, you may find it pointing in an equally uncompromising manner to something entirely different.

The Boscombe Valley Mystery
Sir Arthur Conan Doyle

Winston Churchill thought of himself as a man of some importance, and under other circumstances might have resisted the suggestion that he make inquiries at an hotel or a railway station, as if he were a policeman or a private inquiry agent.

However, he knew that it was of the utmost urgency that he and Charles discover Gladys's whereabouts and get her safely back to Blenheim Palace. Since he refused to believe that Sunny might have had anything to do with her disappearance, that left only that blasted Northcote. Or some unknown person, of course—a possibility that, where Gladys was concerned, ought perhaps not be discounted. Miss Deacon had a great many suitors, both past and present, and one never knew how a disappointed fellow might take it into his head to behave.

But first there was that other business to attend to—Charles Sheridan's scheme designed to obstruct a possible robbery attempt during Edward's and Alexandra's visit. It was very hard for him to imagine a ring of thieves daring to infiltrate Blenheim Palace and target its illustrious guests. But even Winston had to admit the awful possibility of such a thing, and he was all for any plan that would keep the family from the public humiliation of a jewel theft during a Royal weekend! And when it was all over and the danger had passed, he would be glad to receive the Duke's gratitude for having rescued the Marlborough name from disgrace.

So, spurred by a sense of familial responsibility, Winston had located the butler and informed him that Lord Sheridan wanted to find a place for a worthy young man of his acquaintance and that he, Winston, had agreed to look into the possibility of obtaining a page's position for the boy at Blenheim. Lord Sheridan hoped to send the young man along later in the afternoon, and both he and Winston would very much appreciate it if Stevens might accomodate him.

Bowing, Stevens had conceded that it would indeed be possible to find a place for Lord Sheridan's young acquaintance, since he had only that morning obtained Her Grace's permission to hire a new page. Winston assured Stevens that he and Lord Sheridan could vouch for the young man's suitability, and suggested that Alfred be assigned to supervise the boy.

"Alfred, sir?" Stevens asked with a frown. "But he has not been here long himself and—"

"Yes, Alfred," Winston said peremptorily. He did not intend to explain. "As well, I should like you to allow the young man some latitude in the execution of his duties, in case either Lord Sheridan or I have special tasks for him."

Stevens's audible sigh was resigned. He was obviously accustomed to dealing with peremptory persons. "Certainly, sir," he said.

"Very good, Stevens," Winston said. "I regret that both Lord Sheridan and I shall have to miss luncheon. Would you convey our apologies to the Duchess, please?" Then he went out to the stables, where he got a cart and pony and drove off to Woodstock with the intention of seeing if he could discover any bit of information relating to Northcote and Gladys Deacon.

His first stop was The Bear, an old coaching inn that boasted of serving Woodstock since the thirteenth century. It was located on Park Street, a short distance beyond the Triumphal Arch and across from the Woodstock Town Hall. Winston had stayed at The Bear on occasion, when he had arrived too late to be let into the palace, where the gates were usually locked by midnight. He knew of his own experience that the pub would still have been open when Northcote arrived, and that the man who presided over the bar was also available to provide latecomers with a key and a reasonably clean bed.

"Lord Northcote?" the hotelier asked, with pretended doubtfulness. He scratched a scabby ear with a pencil and said again, even more doubtfully, "Northcote, was that wot ye said?"

"A friend of mine," said Winston, and pushed a half-crown across the desk. "He would have procured a room quite late— or rather, quite early this morning, sometime after twelve-thirty."

"Ah, well, a friend," said the hotelier heartily, pocketing

the half-crown. "Well, that do make all the difference, do'ant it, sir?" He ran a grubby finger down the hotel register, paused, and asked, "Henry Northcote?"

"That's him," Winston said excitedly. "So he was here?"

"Here, sir, and gone," the hotelier said with a cheerful grin. "Checked out, the gentl'man did, quite early. Five-thirty in the mornin', it was. B'lieve he was off t' the early train." He chuckled under his breath. "Ill-tempered fellow, if ye'll fergive me fer sayin' so."

"Ah, well, there it is, then," Winston said. "I've missed him." He made as if to leave, then turned back. "Oh, I nearly forgot," he said. "Would you happen to have registered a lady, late last evening or early this morning? A Miss Gladys Deacon?"

The hotelier's eyebrows rose significantly. "Another friend, sir?"

Winston sighed and produced a second half-crown.

The hotelier made a great show of studying the register. "No Miss Deacon, I'm sorry t' say, sir," he reported in a regretful tone.

"No single ladies at all?" pressed Winston, thinking that Gladys might well have used another name.

"No single ladies," the hotelier confirmed. He gave Winston a knowing look. "And in case ye're wonderin', sir, Lord Northcote was all alone. Both when he registered and when he left. Weren't no lady with him, is wot I mean t' say. O'course," he added, with the air of a man who wants to consider every possibility, "he might've met 'er on the way to the station. Can't be sure 'bout that, ye unnerstand."

"Yes," Winston said. "I understand." If Gladys had gone voluntarily with Northcote, she might well have chosen to stay at a different hostelry. But there wasn't time to check them all. He would get on to the railway depot.

The station was a red brick building next to the tracks that stopped at the north edge of town. Woodstock was located on the branch line that joined Great Western Railway's main line at Kidlington. In a bit of local whimsey, the locomotive that served Woodstock had been named "Fair Rosamund" when it was put into service in 1890. And just now, Fair Rosamund, trailed by three attached carriages, was waiting at the station, steam hissing from its boilers and smoke pouring from its smokestack. A trio of schoolboys stood nearby, hands in their pockets, watching—truant from the nearby National School, Winston guessed.

The stationmaster lifted his hand and dropped it, and Fair Rosamund began to pull out of the station, blowing her whistle shrilly, much to the delight of the schoolboys, who cheered and threw their caps into the air. The stationmaster turned, saw Winston, and said, "If you've a ticket, sir, and look smart, you can just catch 'er. She's going slow enough for you to hop onto that last carriage."

"Thank you, no," Winston said. "I've come for some information. Were you on duty this morning?"

"Since Bob Pomeroy took the first run out at six," the stationmaster said, hooking his thumbs into his blue serge vest. "And I'll be here 'til he brings 'er back at six this evening. Same thing every day, six t'six."

"I wonder," Winston said, "if you happen to know whether Lord Henry Northcote was on that train."

" 'Fraid I couldn't say, sir," the station master replied with a cheerful air. He bent over and began to load a stack of boxes onto a hand trolley. "He's not one I know. Now, if you was to ask me if His Grace the Duke took the train, or the mayor of Woodstock, or Mr. Budd, the baker, I'd tell you right off, 'cause I know 'em well. But lords and other such, they come and go here all the time, on their way to Blenheim and back to Lonnun, and I couldn't tell one from another, if y' take my point, sir. Lords all look the same to me." He straightened, lifted his blue cap, and wiped his forehead with his coat sleeve.

"A tall gentleman," Winston persisted. "Military bearing, dark mustache."

The stationmaster replaced his cap. "A tall military gentleman? Well, now, come to think on't, believe I did see such a one go out on the first train." He grinned slightly. "In rather a foul mood, he was."

"Thank you," Winston said. It was as good an identification as he was likely to get. "And perhaps you noticed a lady," he added hopefully. "A very pretty young lady. She might have been in the company of the tall gentleman. Or she might have been traveling alone, either on the early train, or a later."

"A lady, sir?" The stationmaster pulled his brows together. "And how would she be dressed, sir?"

Winston was nonplussed. Quite obviously, if Gladys Deacon had taken the train, she would not have been wearing the gold evening dress in which she had vanished. "I can't say, I'm afraid," he replied ruefully. "But she has red-gold hair." He put on a knowing smile. "And rather a fine figure."

Pulling his mustache, the stationmaster considered for a moment. "Sorry to say, sir, but I don't b'lieve such a lady rode out on Fair Rosamund today." He gave Winston a wink. "B'lieve I'd remember a lady like that, sir. Fine figure and all, I mean."

"I see," Winston said, swallowing his regret. He had almost convinced himself that Northcote had persuaded Gladys to go off with him—a preferable outcome, of course. Sunny would then have realized that the relationship promised nothing but trouble and would have given it up. Unfortunately, this did not appear to be the case. Still, the circumstances of Northcote's abrupt departure suggested that the man had something to do with Gladys's disappearance. Winston frowned. One did not like to dwell on the possibility of violence, of course, but Botsy was known for his difficult temper. What if—

With a shudder, Winston turned back to the stationmaster. "I should like to send a telegram," he said, hoping that George Cornwallis-West was at the London house and would be willing to tell him what he knew about Lord Henry Northcote's background.

Some twenty minutes later, the telegram to George having been composed and dispatched, Winston tied up the pony beside the Black Prince at the other end of Woodstock, a seedy-looking pub on the main road from Oxford to points north. It was not the sort of pub that catered to gentlemen, and he had never been inside. But Sheridan had asked him to find out what he could about the housemaid who had gone missing, and—

Winston frowned. That wretched housemaid. Damn it all, what *was* the girl's name? He furrowed his brow, trying to remember, but all he could recall was that she had been seen at some point chatting up a man with a red beard. Well, it wasn't likely he'd turn up anything important at the pub, but he wanted to report to Sheridan that he had done all he was asked, so he would inquire and see what could be found out.

As Winston went inside, the fragrance of hot eel pie reminded him that, in his haste to carry out his investigative duties, he had missed his luncheon. He stepped up to the bar and bought a pie, a chunk of bread, and a mug of ale, which he carried to an empty table.

It was bright daylight out-of-doors, but the pub was windowless and lit only by gas lights that hung from the low ceiling. A dozen or so men were in the dusky room, several lounging at the bar, the rest seated around tables. The air was flavored by beer and unwashed clothes. Winston put his hat on the chair beside him, settled down to his lunch, and finished it in good order, finding the eel pie all he might have wished. As he was wiping his mouth on the back of his hand (a napkin not being part of the service), he happened to notice a pair of fellows in a far corner. One of them had copper-colored hair and a reddish beard.

Recalling his errand, Winston pushed back his chair, put on his hat, and sauntered over to the table. The men looked up at him, not cordially. The one with the red beard was nattily dressed in a black jacket, blue waistcoat, and red-striped cravat, with a blue silk handkerchief in one pocket—a commercial traveler, no doubt. The other, of a more common appearance, was stout and thick-chested, with broad shoulders, beefy hands, and thick black hair. He was dressed in a dark corduroy jacket, rather out of repair, and fustian trousers. A red kerchief was tied around his neck.

"Good afternoon, gentlemen," Winston said, adopting the amiable manner with which he usually addressed his Oldham constituents when he went electioneering. He pushed his hat to the back of his head and put out his hand. "My name is Winston Churchill. I'm—"

"Wot's yer bus'ness, Churchill?" growled the dark-haired man, ignoring the outstretched hand.

"Forgive my companion, sir," the red-bearded man said with a genial deference. He jumped up and pumped Winston's hand vigorously. "Pleased to meet you, Mr. Churchill, and I do mean pleased, sir. I've heard you speak about your experiences in South Africa. Thrillin' escape that was, sir! Bloody good show all 'round! Flummoxed them stinkin' Boers right proper, you did, sir!"

Winston felt himself warmed by the man's admiration. "Thank you," he said modestly, retrieving his hand. "Very kind of you to say so." He paused and added, apologetically, "I've taken the liberty to introduce myself because I'm looking for someone, and wondered if you might be that person, sir. One of the young women at Blenheim—the household of my cousin, the Duke of Marlborough—seems to have gone off without letting anyone know. It's thought that she might have spoken to a red-bearded man here at the Prince. That wouldn't by any chance have been yourself, sir?"

The red-bearded man laughed easily. "A young lady from Blenheim? Not jolly likely, I'd say, Mr. Churchill. I just arrived here not two hours ago, on business." He looked inquiringly at his companion. "You wouldn't happen to know anything about a young woman, would you, Bulls-eye?"

Bulls-eye drained his mug of ale in one large gulp. " 'Fraid not," he muttered. "Not 'xactly in my line."

"I fear we can't be of much help to you, sir," the red-bearded man said.

"Well, then, I'll wish you good day," Winston said, and tipped his hat. "Forgive me for intruding, gentlemen. I'll be on my way."

"Oh, no intrusion at all, sir!" cried the red-bearded man with enthusiasm. "It's a great pleasure to have shaken the hand of a man who escaped from them bloody Boers and lived to tell the tale. I wish you luck in the House, sir. We need men like you there, sir, 'deed we do!"

It wasn't until Winston was nearly back to Blenheim that he recalled with some chagrin that he had not asked the man's name.

CHAPTER TWENTY-ONE

It's just as easy to steal a hundred thousand dollars as a tenth of that sum . . . the risk is just as great. We'll, therefore, go out for the big money always.

Adam Worth, known to Scotland Yard
as "the Napoleon of the criminal world"

"Bloody hell," growled Bulls-eye.

"Too bloody right," said Dawkins, sinking into his chair. "Rotten damned luck, his showing up here. But it would've been worse, if I hadn't kept my head."

"You don't think 'e knows, d'ye?" Bulls-eye heard the nervous tinniness of his voice and hoped that Dawkins hadn't noticed. He shouldn't like Dawkins to know that he was afraid.

"Knows? Knows what?" Dawkins was careless. "The way he asked about her, he didn't strike me as a man who knows much about anything."

Bulls-eye lowered his glance. "Well, ye didn't 'ave to jump up and jaw away like you wuz some jolly old barracks mate," he said defensively. "You could've sent him out the door, flat."

"And have him suspect we'd something to hide?" Dawkins retorted. "Soon as he said he was a Churchill, I knew we could be in for it. But now when he thinks of me, it'll be as one of his admirers." He grew thoughtful. "He did tell us something useful—that she's been missed upstairs, and they're looking for her."

"Don't see 'ow that's of any use," Bulls-eye said darkly. He stroked his chin and added, after a moment, "Don't suppose she told 'em anything, do you?"

"How could she? She didn't know anything. Well, not much."

"She said she knew the name of—"

"That's enough," Dawkins said, his voice flat and hard, all geniality vanished. "We won't talk about that." He narrowed his eyes. "You did say it's taken care of, right?"

"Oh, right," Bulls-eye said nervously. "I told you. All taken care of." He felt a tic at the corner of his left eye. He did not like to think how it had been taken care of. That sort of thing wasn't in his line, either. "But there's the other one, y'know. Alfred's 'is name."

Dawkins's glance sharpened. "You don't think she told him, do you?"

Bulls-eye didn't like to think so, for he did not want to hear the instruction that he knew would follow on the admission. But he had to reply. "I think it's likely," he said glumly. "'E's a cool one, 'e is. Acts simple, but 'e's dang'rous as 'er."

Dawkins gave him an evil grin. "We'll deal with him later."

Bulls-eye sighed. The whole affair had got entirely out of hand. Violence was not his way, nor Mr. N's way, either, come to that. He leaned forward on his elbows and lowered his voice. "Listen, Dawkins, I'm thinkin' that mebee we should make our play an' get out. Wouldn't take more'n a day or two to get the others 'ere, and—"

"We're sticking to the plan, and no argument." Dawkins's glance was severe and chastening. "Anyway, there's no point in making a play now. That place may look like a treasure-house from the outside, but inside it's empty, nothing but a hollow shell, a show, a sham. The Marlboroughs had plenty of valuables once, but they're all gone now." He made a wry face. "Hadn't been for that Vanderbilt woman, the Duke wouldn't have a shilling in his pocket."

"But what about the paintings?" Bulls-eye ventured. "Place is full of 'em. Crikey, they got to be worth something, a'n't they? We could—"

"Paintings?" The red-bearded man laughed contemptuously. "Bloody huge things, and mostly family stuff that no one else wants."

"All right, but what about the silver? Got to be plenty of that. Gold plate, too."

Dawkins was emphatic. "I told you, Bulls-eye. Mister N surveyed the place when he went through on Tourist Day and decided there's nothing in the lot worth the trouble. You know what he always says—there's no more risk in stealing big than there is in stealing small, so we go for the big money. And there's nothing big in the house until their Royal Flapdoodles get there, and all the fancy ladies with their fancy jewelry. *That's* when we make our play and not a minute before. That's how Mister N planned it, and that's the way we'll play it, and that's that."

At the mention of Mister N, Bulls-eye abandoned his objections. The *N,* he knew, stood for Napoleon—the Napoleon of crime. Of course, Bulls-eye didn't know his real name and identity, and didn't want to. No one knew it, in fact, so it was something of a mystery as to how the girl had found out. Some lucky chance, Bulls-eye guessed, or unlucky, rather.

Mister N, whoever he was, masterminded the entire Syndicate. He chose the targets, organized the members, and crafted the impeccable plans that made everything work. He sat at the top of his command network like a general ordering his troops to attack here and there, but a *covert* general, working in the shadows through various intermediaries, watchfully but anonymously overseeing all the details of half-a-dozen simultaneous operations—forgeries, frauds and swindles, thefts of registered mail from strongboxes carried by train, and (the Syndicate's specialty) thefts of art objects and jewelry. The subordinate felons who carried out the chief felon's orders knew only what they were supposed to do, and when, and how. What they never knew was the name of the man at the top, or even the name of the man just above them. Dawkins, for example, was probably not the real name of the red-bearded man sitting across the table from Bulls-eye at this very moment.

"So that's the way of it," Dawkins was saying emphatically. "We stick to the plan. Anyway, the girl's replacement is already in and settled. Has been for over a week."

Bulls-eye bristled angrily. "Whose idea was that?" He was supposed to be in charge of the Blenheim job, and here was Dawkins, pushing his way in. "And why didn't I know anything about it?"

"Now, don't get all frazzled," Dawkins said in a more conciliatory tone. "It was Mr. N's idea. When he heard about your little problem, he sent instructions. The replacement is the one he's been grooming special, y'see, not your usu'l East End lurker, and accustomed to working in the best places. She's been there over a week already. And as far as you not knowing," he added blandly, "Mr. N thought it 'ud be best. The fewer who know, the better."

Bulls-eye was not happy to hear what had been done behind his back, but did not feel that he was in a position to object. "I 'ope this one's not goin' to be any trouble," he said in a grudging tone. "Not like the other one."

"No trouble at all, I guarantee it," Dawkins said soothingly. "She's got a great deal more experience, and a cool head." He leaned forward and lowered his voice as if imparting a secret. "And she's a screwsman, to boot."

"A screwsman!" Bulls-eye said, genuinely surprised. "A *female* screwsman?" A screwsman was a specialist in locks and keys—screws—and had the ability to make the wax impressions from which duplicate keys could be created. It was a useful skill, and Bulls-eye knew that a female screwsman would be a valuable asset in a country-house game.

"Yes, and a prime one at that," Dawkins said smugly. "She can be depended upon to keep her trap shut and do what she's told—and use her brain, too. She'll see that we get the schedule of the weekend's activities, the layout of the guest and family bedrooms, *and* the keys."

"The keys'll make all the diff'rence," Bulls-eye said thoughtfully, beginning to see the merit in the plan. And it wouldn't hurt to keep Alfred in the dark as well. The boy was young and inexperienced, and Bulls-eye suspected that he'd lost his head over the girl. Once that kind of thing got started, it caused problems for everybody.

"The keys'll help," Dawkins agreed. "But as I said, we'll stick to the plan. There'll be the usual commotion belowstairs when the guests arrive with all their servants and baggage. 'Specially the Royal Flapdoodles. They'll have two dozen servants and a trainload of trunks, and nobody'll know who's who or what's what. That's when the rest of the crew'll go in disguised as extra help. And when they come back out, they'll be loaded with all the fine jewels those fine ladies have brought to show off to the King."

Bulls-eye nodded. The plan sounded good. It always sounded good, and it always worked. He had been temporarily rattled, that was all. The girl had rattled him, and he was rattled thinking about her. He pushed the thought away, comforting himself with the idea of a female screws-man, especially groomed by Mr. N himself for jobs in the best places.

Dawkins smiled agreeably. "There, now, Bulls-eye. Feeling better?"

"I b'lieve I am," Bulls-eye said.

"Well, good," Dawkins said. His smile was gone. "Now, maybe we'd better talk about the other one. Alfred, is that his name?"

Bulls-eye sighed, feeling rattled again. It was time for another mug of ale.

CHAPTER TWENTY-TWO

An American heiress who married an English Duke was more likely to be a character in a tragedy, rather than a fairy tale. "You're going to be put in a cage," warns Ralph Touchett when Isabel Archer considers a European marriage in Henry James's The Portrait of a Lady, *a warning that came true for too many. For instance, Consuelo Vanderbilt Marlborough's fabulous dowry came entirely under the control of her husband, and she had no funds of her own. But for Consuelo, even worse was her husband's coldness toward her and the dismay she felt about Blenheim, the "monstrous house," as she called it, which seemed to be her prison.*

"American Heiresses, English Duchesses"
Susan Blake

Kate had been only a little late for the luncheon, and as it turned out, there were just the two of them, Consuelo and herself. Charles had driven to Oxford, Winston had taken the pony cart to Woodstock, and the Duke had gone off with Mr. Meloy to have a look at a distant hay field. Botsy Northcote and Gladys Deacon were still absent.

Kate was tempted to share the results of her morning investigations with Consuelo, but she reluctantly decided against it. For one thing, she thought perhaps she ought to keep what she had discovered private until she had a chance to discuss it with Charles. For another, she wasn't entirely sure that Marlborough was clear of suspicion, and until that was so, she ought not to involve his wife in what she (or Beryl, rather) was coming to think of as an investigation. And of course there were the servants, hovering over the luncheon table, taking in their every word. Kate did not feel comfortable mentioning Gladys's name or bringing up anything of a personal nature.

After lunch, under the delicate shade of their lace parasols, Consuelo and Kate walked to the aviary, beyond the Italian Garden. There, hundreds of exotic birds collected from various parts of the British Empire, their bright feathers glowing like irridescent jewels, were confined within a two-story cage of wire netting. It stood adjacent to a heated building where the birds—most were from the tropics and would freeze in the Oxfordshire winters—spent the colder months. Today was very warm, however, and they were all in the outdoor cage.

"They're beautiful," Kate said, watching a parrot with gleaming yellow and red and blue wings dashing itself against the wire netting. "But sad, don't you think? They don't belong in England, somehow—like the leopards and camels and lion that King Henry kept here, when Blenheim was a Royal park."

"I'm sure," Consuelo said gravely, "that they would much rather be back in their own native jungles. But now that they're here, they must be confined. If they were released, you know, they'd be dead by the first frost." Her laugh was poignant. "There's a parallel here, I suppose. A moral to the story."

"I'm not quite sure that I know what you mean," Kate said quietly.

"I think you do," Consuelo said, as they strolled down the gravel path. "In some ways, we are alike, you and I. Both of us are American women, married to British peers—birds of a feather, one might say. In other ways, though, we are very different. You seem to have made a happy marriage, and I envy you for that. But you must know, Kate, that I have not."

Perhaps it was the stress of the events of the last day or so, or perhaps the Duchess had begun to feel that Kate was not only a fellow American but a compassionate and reliable confidant. Whatever the reason, she linked her arm in Kate's and spilled the story of her life.

It was, Kate thought later, one of the saddest tales she had ever heard. At a time when most women had to depend upon men because they had no money of their own and no means of earning enough to support themselves, Consuelo Vanderbilt had been a woman of independent fortune, who (most would assume) could have done whatever in the world she chose to do. But she was very young when her marital destiny was planned and executed, and of a pliant and yielding nature. It was that which had made her a victim—first of her mother, who had insisted upon her marriage to Marlborough even though Consuelo loved another man; and then of Marlborough, who having successfully married her fortune, paid no attention whatever to her.

They reached a bench in the shade of a large copper beech and sat down. "I'm grateful for the children," Consuelo said pensively. "They give purpose to my life." She had, Kate knew, two boys, Bert and Tigsy. "But between the governess, the head nurse, and the groom with whom they ride their ponies," she added, "there is little time left for mother." Her voice was forlorn. "And soon they will be off to school, and I shall lose them altogether, forever. Then what shall I do?"

Kate listened sympathetically. She herself had no children, having suffered a miscarriage several years before. For a time, she had been distraught, but she had lately been more reconciled to the situation, realizing that her inability to have children gave her a greater freedom. And she was sure that she would not have been able to tolerate the English system of childrearing, where the parents lived their own separate lives while their children were cared for by others. Patrick, the young boy she and Charles had taken into their home and their hearts, was now seventeen and she was happy to see him embarked upon his own path. But if she had borne him, she would not have been content to put him in the nursery and see him only when he was clean and combed and on his best behavior.

"Having the children go off is not the end of the world," Kate said at last. "You did relief work during the war, and enjoyed it. Once the boys are gone, you can do more of that."

"Yes, that's right." Consuelo brightened. "When Sunny was in South Africa with Lord Roberts, I was able to go to London to work with Jennie and the others to raise money for the hospital ship." She paused. "Well, you know, Kate. You were involved, too."

"That was a wonderful project," Kate said reminiscently. *The Times* had called them the American Amazons—more than a dozen energetic American women led by Winston's mother, Jennie, with the goal of raising two hundred thousand dollars to outfit the *Maine*. And they had done it, too.

Consuelo nodded. "That's where my interests lie, you know—in social work and philanthropy. But Marlborough allows me to pursue neither, except in the most desultory

way." She made a face. "Taking beef tea and jellies to the vil-
lagers, for instance, and blankets, and hats and gloves to the
children. That's all the Marlborough women have ever done,
apparently, and all I am meant to do."

"But it's something," Kate said. "It's important." And it
was, she knew, as much as other women in Consuelo's position did.

Consuelo sighed. "Yes, of course. Every little bit eases the
burden of poverty. But it's not enough, not nearly enough. I
am capable of doing more, if only he would *let* me. Sometimes
I feel so . . . so hopeless." She glanced up at the aviary, where
a pair of elegant white-crested cockatoos sat on a branch, and
tears filled her eyes. "Like those birds, Kate. Fed and cared for,
pampered, even—no danger of going without food or water,
no danger of predators, or any sort of threat. But they'll live
their entire lives cooped up in that cage. They'll never know
the joy of flying free, of flying as high as they like, or as far."

Kate could not answer. There was no reason for Marlborough to change, and nothing in Consuelo's situation that
suggested any alteration. She could think of nothing, short
of separation or divorce, that would free Consuelo from her
prison. So she could only press the Duchess's hand and mur-
mur a few consoling words, consoling, but meaningless.

Consuelo's face darkened and she turned her head away.
"And now, of course, there is Gladys," she said, with even
greater melancholy, "and Marlborough making a fool of
himself over her. I think I could bear the coldness, and even
the rebukes. It is much harder to bear the thought of his . . .
unfaithfulness."

Kate released her hand. For a moment, they sat in silence,
Kate thinking of what she had found at Rosamund's Well,
and in Gladys's bedroom, and in the rowboat. But the more

she thought, the more muddled things seemed to become. "Do you think," she asked at last, "that something . . . serious may have happened to Gladys?"

"I hope not," Consuelo said. There was another silence. Then she added, almost reluctantly, "The girl has many moods and fancies, Kate. She's a strange, whimsical creature, and sometimes quite . . . unpredictable." She gave a little shrug. "Perhaps that's why I have enjoyed her so much. She's playful, she's enchanting, like a child, like one of those birds. She raises my spirits. She brightens Blenheim's gloom."

She obviously raises the Duke's spirits, too, Kate thought wryly. Aloud, she repeated Consuelo's phrases. "Strange and whimsical. Like a child."

"Yes, very like a child," Consuelo said reflectively. "I've sometimes thought that Gladys lacks any sense of consequences, and that's why she takes the risks she does. Like that horrible business with her nose, for instance. That paraffin injection." She shuddered. "It might do very well for now, but I hate to think what will happen in another few years."

No sense of consequences. "Is it possible, do you think," Kate asked slowly, "that she might be . . . well, playing some sort of game with us?"

"A game?" Consuelo frowned. "What do you mean?"

"I don't know," Kate confessed. "I'm just thinking out loud, I suppose. I was wondering whether Gladys might take pleasure in something . . . well, something childish, like hide-and-seek, perhaps."

Consuelo stared at her incredulously. "But why would she do such a thing, Kate? She surely knows that we would be frantic."

Kate said nothing. She could imagine any one of a half-dozen reasons, although she doubted that any of them would occur to Consuelo, who struck her as inexperienced and rather naive. Gladys might do it to make the Duke realize how much he loved her, or to teach him some sort of lesson. Or to make Northcote even more insanely jealous. Or even to mock her friend Consuelo.

The silence stretched out, filled with the raucous sounds of birds, an occasional sweet melody rising plaintively above the tuneless racket. At last Consuelo said, in a doubtful tone, "I suppose it's possible, Kate. Once, when she and I were visiting Versailles together, she went off to Paris with her sister, without telling me."

"I'm sure you must have been wild with worry," Kate said.

"Oh, yes, of course." Consuelo frowned. "But that was . . . well, it was a lark, in a way, and I'm sure her sister egged her on. They seized the opportunity of a moment. She couldn't have done that here, of course. Where would she go? And how? It was night when she disappeared, and she was wearing evening dress. I just don't see—"

"I'm probably wrong," Kate said, not wanting to trouble Consuelo further. "Let's not talk any more about it."

But that did not mean that Kate and Beryl would not think about it. Or that Consuelo would not think about it, either.

CHAPTER TWENTY-THREE

Most people, if you describe a train of events to them, will tell you what the result would be. They can put those events together in their minds, and argue from them that something will come to pass. There are few people, however, who, if you told them a result, would be able to evolve from their own inner consciousness what the steps were which led up to that result. This power is what I mean when I talk of reasoning backward, or analytically.

A Study in Scarlet
Sir Arthur Conan Doyle

Mr. Lawrence had been surprised by Charles's request to borrow his son Ned for a fortnight or so. But having heard Ned's urgent plea and Charles's promise to keep an eye on the boy, he rather thought, on the whole, that the proposal presented no difficulty.

From Mr. Lawrence's dithery response, Charles got the idea that the man himself was too good-natured to refuse any reasonable appeal, but that it was just as well that Ned's mother was absent, for she would have been likely to have raised a strenuous objection which both Ned and his father would have had no choice but to honor. Charles surmised that, in the Lawrence household, the mother firmly ruled the roost, a fact which the father did not contest but the son deeply resented.

On the way back to Blenheim in the motorcar, Charles explained in some detail what was wanted of Ned and who among the servants the boy should observe most closely— Alfred, especially, the footman who had been at Welbeck around the time of the robbery there. He also mentioned Kitty, whose disappearance might or might not have some relevance, and gave Ned instructions for communicating with himself, or at a pinch, with Winston or Kate.

"I shall probably ask to see you this evening," he said. "If questions are asked, you might say that I am an acquaintance of your father." He smiled at the boy, who was trying, without success, to look confident and self-assured. "Lady Sheridan, Churchill, and I—all three of us will be looking out for you. You shan't have any problems."

Privately, Charles was not quite so confident. There were several potential problems, especially since the stakes were so high and the people with whom they were dealing were experienced and unprincipled. But of course, he reminded himself, all this business about a ring of thieves operating in Blenheim lay entirely in the realm of theoretical speculation. Sometimes, when one was reasoning backward (as Conan Doyle had put it in one of his Sherlock Holmes stories), one saw illicit activities where there were none, or invented criminal conspiracies where none existed—especially when one was beginning with a conjectured result. Charles had to admit that this might be one of those times, and that the whole thing was a fabrication of his too-vivid imagination, the sort of fantasy that Kate and Beryl Bardwell loved to create. Ned might search and search and come up empty-handed, simply because there was nothing to find.

"Whatever happens, I'm not afraid," Ned said staunchly. He pushed the blond hair out of his eyes. "I only want to do a good job, that's all. If there's something secret going on below-stairs, I'll ferret it out."

"That's the spirit," Charles said approvingly. In many ways, Ned reminded him of Patrick, the boy whom he and Kate had taken to live with them. Like Ned, Patrick had many gifts, chief among which was his talent for working with horses. He was now riding as a jockey at George Lambton's stables at Newmarket.* Ned was more of an intel-lectual than Patrick, Charles thought, but the two boys had the same energetic spirit, the same eager willingness to please.

They had come to the Hensington Gate, where the lane to Blenheim intersected the Oxford-Woodstock Road. Charles pulled onto the grassy verge and stopped.

"I'll leave you here," he said. "Walk down the lane, and when you come to the East Gate, tell the porter that Mr. Stevens is expecting you. When you're taken to Stevens, tell him that you are the young man recommended by Mr. Churchill. He will put you to work straightaway."

"I will, sir," Ned said, jumping out. "And don't worry about me," he added with a brash grin. "Compared to prying brasses off church walls, this should be easy."

That brought a smile to Charles's lips, and he was still smiling as he put the Panhard in gear and drove off down the lane, leaving Ned to come along behind him. But the smile had faded by the time he drove across the Grand

---

* Patrick's story is told in *Death at Rottingdean* and *Death at Epsom Downs*.

Bridge toward the Column of Victory, parked the motor car, and stood, surveying the scene.

It was getting on to five in the afternoon, and threatening clouds were piling up in the western sky. There was no breeze, and the lake was quiet, its placid surface disturbed only by several flocks of ducks and geese, a half-dozen elegant white swans, and an old man in a yellow boat, rowing in the direction of the Fishery Cottage at the north end of the lake. Charles knew he was going to be late to tea, but it could not be helped, for he could not put off having a look at Rosamund's Well any longer.

As an afterthought, he opened a compartment in the side of his motorcar and took out his camera bag and a small wooden box—a field collection kit he used when he was pursuing his natural history researches. It contained small glass vials, muslin bags, and celluloid envelopes, all for collecting specimens, as well as a hand lens, tweezers, needles, and a penknife. Carrying his gear, he walked down the slanting hill and along the lake shore, following the narrow footpath to the well.

As he walked, he was thinking of Gladys Deacon and the telltale scrap of gold silk Kate had found that morning, snagged on a bush. While Miss Deacon had last been seen in the Blenheim garden with Botsy Northcote, the torn piece of silk seemed to suggest that she had also been here, on the far side of the lake.

But when? After her conversation in the garden with Northcote? With Northcote or with someone else?

And how had she got here? On foot—which seemed to Charles unlikely, given the young lady's dinner costume—or by boat? He glanced over his shoulder at the yellow rowboat, disappearing under the arches of the bridge. There must be several such boats on the lake. He should have to have a look in the boathouse.

Charles had no difficulty finding Rosamund's Well, which bubbled out of a stone wall and into a shallow pool constructed of square-cut stones and surrounded by a flagstone pavement. The spring had in medieval times been called Everswell, in recognition of the fact that it had not stopped flowing through all the centuries of recorded history, not even in the worst of droughts. No wonder, he thought, that it had become the source of so many powerful legends—the stories about Fair Rosamund and Henry and Eleanor, for example.

He glanced up the hill above the spring, wondering where Rosamund's Bower might have stood, some six hundred years ago. On the brow of the hill, overlooking the River Glyme? Was that where Henry II had built the legendary labyrinth to protect his mistress? But the labyrinth had not kept Rosamund safe, if that's what it was designed to do, for if legend could be believed, she had been murdered.

But that was in the distant past, and Charles's errand had a much more immediate urgency. He had no difficulty finding the bush on which Kate had discovered the scrap early that morning, for several gold threads still clung to it. Upon close examination, however, he agreed with Kate: The little bush was not stout enough to have snagged and torn the heavy silk. So how had the scrap come to be there?

Not finding an immediate answer, Charles put down his camera and prowled around the pool, moving slowly, eyes on the ground, looking for anything out of the ordinary. It didn't take long to find it, on the front side of the pool, the side nearest the lake. A brownish, pinkish stain that looked very much like blood, on the flagstone pavement beside the pool.

Charles took his hand lens out of his pocket and knelt down, studying the stain intently. Overall, it was ten inches or so in diameter and surrounded by a number of spatters, as if the blood had forcibly sprayed from an open wound. All of it had dried, either by the action of the air or by soaking into the porous stone, or both.

He had no way of judging, of course, how fresh the blood was; it might have been there for some hours or some days. And there was no way of deciding, short of an analytical test, whether the blood was human or animal. The test, which distinguished among the proteins of different blood residues, had been only recently developed by Paul Uhlenhuth, a German professor. It could be used on any bloodstain, regardless of the size of the stain, its age, or the material on which it was deposited. Charles had none of Professor Uhlenhuth's serum, of course, but it could be obtained, and with that in mind, he took a penknife out of his kit, scraped a sample of dried blood into a glass vial, and corked it tightly. For the present, he would proceed on the assumption that it was human blood— an assumption which threw, he thought glumly, a new and disturbing light on the question of Miss Deacon's disappearance.

Having found the blood, he broadened his search, and almost immediately discovered a bloody heel print, remarkably clear and well-defined, on a nearby flagstone. He studied it for a moment, then set up his camera and made several photographs of it, and of the blood spatters. At the edge of the paving, he noticed the track of disturbed dirt and leaves left by something heavy, dragged in the direction of the lake. He photographed what he could see, then followed the track until it ended at the edge of the lake. There were several deep V-shaped indentations along the shore which might have been made by beached boats, and a welter of indistinguishable footprints in the soft earth, but nothing else.

Charles turned and looked in the direction of Rosamund's Well, some thirty feet away. Reasoning backward from the evidence, it looked to him as if someone had been standing beside Rosamund's Well when he, or she, was attacked. The assailant had left the print of a shoe, and the dead or unconscious victim—Miss Deacon?—had been dragged to the lake, perhaps to a waiting boat.

And then what?

Was the victim alive or dead?

If dead, had the corpse been taken to a less-frequented area and buried? Or weighted with stones and dropped into the deepest part of the lake?

In spite of the warmth of the afternoon, Charles shivered.

CHAPTER TWENTY-FOUR

There is a thread here which we have not yet grasped and which might lead us through the tangle.

The Adventure of the Devil's Foot
Sir Arthur Conan Doyle

When Kate went back to the house after her conversation with Consuelo at the aviary, she remembered that she had intended to talk to Bess, the housemaid who was looking after Miss Deacon. Kate found her tidying the housemaids' closet on the second floor, which was stocked with cleaning supplies, brooms and brushes, fresh linens, and everything necessary to make up the bedrooms.

"Pardon me, Bess," she said, "may I trouble you for a moment?"

Startled, Bess turned from her work. She was a woman in her late twenties with dark hair tucked up beneath her white cap, a firm mouth, and quick, intelligent eyes under thick, strong brows. She was wearing a neat black afternoon dress and a ruffled apron.

"Of course, m'lady," she said. She closed the closet door. "How may I help you?"

It was a pleasant response, Kate thought, different from the careless replies of most of the servants. "I wonder," she said, "if you would accompany me to Miss Deacon's room for just a moment. I shan't keep you long."

"Yes, m'lady." As they walked down the hall, Bess's face grew troubled. "Miss Deacon seems not to have returned to her room last night," she said in a low voice.

"So I understand," Kate said. "You were the maid who reported her absence to Mrs. Raleigh?" They had reached Gladys's bedroom door. Kate took the key out of her pocket and unlocked it.

"That's right, m'lady," Bess said, following her inside. She gestured. "I turned down her bed last night, and laid out her nightgown, same as I always do. You see? It's just the way I left it. Hasn't been touched."

"Yes, I see," Kate said. She went to the wardrobe door and opened it. "I would appreciate it if you would look through Miss Deacon's clothing and tell me whether anything is missing."

"Missing, m'lady?" Bess asked. She cocked her head, her eyes bright with curiosity.

"Yes," Kate said. She knew the maid wanted to know why she was making the inquiry, but she had no intention of telling her. "Either here in the wardrobe or in her chest of drawers. And please have a look at her footwear, as well."

If Bess thought this an unusual request, she didn't say so. Without a word, she began to look through the clothing, while Kate went to the dressing table and, in a desultory way, glanced through the perfumes and cosmetic items.

Parisian Pleasures, Beryl remarked in a snide tone, as Kate picked up a scent bottle. *Sounds like something Gladys would enjoy, doesn't it?*

Kate put down the scent bottle and took up a ceramic dish with a gilded picture of a country house surmounted by the arms of the Duke of Portland. Gladys had used it as an ashtray. "Welbeck Abbey," she mused.

Welbeck Abbey, Beryl said. *The scene of Gladys's crime.*

"The scene of the crime? At Welbeck?" Kate reflected aloud, setting the dish down. She hardly thought that pinching an ashtray amounted to a crime. But that wasn't what Beryl had in mind.

Not the ashtray, silly. Welbeck is where she accepted Northcote's hand and Northcote's diamonds, remember? Beryl chuckled maliciously. *If that's not a crime. I don't know what is.*

Bess finished with the wardrobe and went to the chest, where she was now pulling out the third drawer. She stopped, cocked her head, and turned.

"A crime at Welbeck?" A breath later, as an afterthought, she added, "M'lady."

Kate laughed a little. "A jewel theft, of sorts."

That's exactly what it was. Beryl replied flatly. *Gladys accepted those diamonds under false pretenses. As good as thieving, in my book.*

"A jewel theft?" A sudden, wary look crossed Bess's face.

Kate was about to correct herself and say that she was only playing with words, but something stopped her. Instead she said, "Have you been to Welbeck, Bess?"

"Welbeck?" A short, hard laugh. "Oh, no, m'lady. Not me. I just wondered what you was saying, that's all." She pushed in the drawer, folded her arms, and went on, in a matter-of-fact tone, "It appears that a pair of trousers and jacket are missing, m'lady. Brown, they were. Dark brown flannel. It was . . . well, it was rather like a man's lounge suit. I believe there was a tie, as well."

"Trousers!" Kate couldn't help exclaiming.

Trousers! Beryl echoed, intrigued. Kate herself owned several pairs of corduroy trousers, which she found useful for outdoor work at Bishop's Keep and for tramping across the fields and woods. And she knew that American women were wearing trousers for bicycling. But it was a little more difficult to picture Gladys Deacon in trousers.

Unless, Beryl whispered excitedly, *she wanted to disguise herself.*

A disguise! Kate thought. Of course. They were all imagining that Gladys had gone off, or been spirited off, in the dress she had worn the night before. But what if she had—

"I think a white shirtwaist is gone, too," Bess was saying, "although I can't be sure. And a pair of brown suede walking boots." She cleared her throat. "I noticed the trousers particularly," she added in an apologetic tone. "Quite . . . well, quite manly looking, if your ladyship wouldn't mind my saying so."

Of course she would notice them, Beryl remarked slyly. *I'll wager nothing gets past this 'un. Look at those eyes. Bess is a sly puss, if you ask me.*

Kate agreed. Nothing escaped the attention of a good maid, particularly something as extraordinary as a man's brown flannel lounge suit in a woman's wardrobe. And Bess struck her as a remarkably discerning person, the kind of housemaid who would be promoted to housekeeper, if she stayed in service. That made her question about the jewel theft that much more puzzling. A good servant would have allowed such idle words to pass unremarked.

Aloud, Kate said, "What about Miss Deacon's luggage, Bess? Do you remember seeing a small bag?"

"P'rhaps," Bess said thoughtfully, "when I did the unpacking. But the luggage has all gone downstairs, m'lady, where it's seen to by the odd man." She tilted her head, frowning slightly. "If your ladyship will forgive me asking, are you thinking that Miss Deacon might have . . . well, gone off?"

"I'm not at all sure," Kate replied. "Do you have an opinion?"

"No, m'lady."

No, m'lady, Beryl mimicked. *But if she did have an opinion, she wouldn't venture it, especially to you, Kate.*

Again, Kate agreed. An experienced maid kept her own counsel, although she might have a confidante among the other servants. She led the way to the door and closed and locked it behind them. "If you think of anything else, Bess, please come and tell me. And thank you for your help. I shan't keep you any longer."

Bess dropped a quick curtsey. "Yes, m'lady," she said, and went off, keys jingling, in the direction of the maids' closet. At the corner of the corridor, she turned and cast an appraising glance over her shoulder.

I wonder, Beryl said thoughtfully, *about those keys.*

But Kate didn't have time to think about that just now. She turned and went in the other direction, toward the service stairs. Below-stairs was normally out-of-bounds to guests, but Kate managed her own servants at Bishop's Keep and knew her way around their work area very well. She did not hesitate to open the green baize door and go down the stairs.

Once below-stairs in the maze of the servants' area, it took her a little while to locate the odd man, who was cleaning wax drippings from brass candle holders in the lamp-and-candle room. Back in America, such a person would have been called an odd-job man, but the words "odd man" seemed to fit this fellow rather well. He was a very small man, one shoulder higher than the other, with wire spectacles and only a fringe of gray hair around his bald head. He seemed a little surprised to see Kate, perhaps because ladies usually sent their maids to fetch their luggage. But upon her inquiry, he led her to the luggage room, where the empty trunks and valises belonging to the family and their guests were kept.

"Yer ladyship is wantin' her trunk, I s'pose," he said, scratching his head. "Let's see, now. B'lieve it's this'n." He pointed to Kate's leather trunk, with Charles's smaller trunk perched on top. "Or did ye want me t' fetch both yers and his lordship's?"

"Actually, it's Miss Deacon's luggage I'm asking about," Kate said, adding, "She said I might borrow one of her small bags for a day or two."

"That's the lot there," the odd man said, nodding to a towering stack of trunks that completely filled one corner of the room. "All but the small valise. She come and got that 'un day 'fore yestiddy."

"She did?" Kate asked, trying to keep the excitement from her voice.

"Yessum, her very own self," the odd man said, adding, with a private grin, "Give me a shillin', too." He looked around the room. "If yer ladyship is wantin' a valise, ye might take that carpet bag. B'lieve it b'longed to the Duchess of Manchester, and was left behind when she was last here." He rubbed his hands together with a hopeful look. "I'd be glad to bring it up to yer room, if ye like."

"Thank you," Kate said, wishing that she had brought a shilling to give him. "Now that I know it's here, I'll send for it when I'm ready."

Trousers, a jacket, walking boots, and a bag, Beryl said as Kate went along the back passage the way she had come, past the lamp-and-candle room and the large panel of electric bells that were connected to the upstairs bedrooms. *Sounds to me as if our Gladys was preparing to go off somewhere, dressed as a man.*

Beryl's idea might seem far-fetched, but Kate had to acknowledge that it was a possibility. However, Gladys had an abundance of long, red-gold hair. If she planned to masquerade as a man, she'd need to pin it up on top of her head and conceal it under a hat or a cap.

A cap? Beryl asked with a knowing grin. *Like one of those, d'you mean?*

Kate stopped. On her left was the service stairs. On her right was a door that led up a short flight of concrete steps to the outside. And next to the door was a row of wooden pegs on the wall, from which hung a motley assemblage of mackintoshes, umbrellas, and several sorts of headgear—tweed caps, leather caps, a felt beret, several straw hats, and even a battered yachting cap. If Gladys Deacon had wanted something under which to hide her long hair, all she had to do was help herself.

While Kate and Beryl were chatting with the housemaid and the odd man, Consuelo had gone to her room to read. Books had always been her consolation, her escape from her dictatorial mother and now her escape from the prison of her marriage. As a girl, she had loved fairy tales, imagining herself as the enchanted princess set free by the prince's kiss, then sentimental fiction—the sort of thing that fed romantic dreams, dreams of being loved, desired, and cared for.

But Consuelo had also been a bright, quick student, and by the age of eight, she could speak and write fluently in French and German, as well as English. Her favorite governess, Miss Harper, had encouraged her in a secret ambition: to attend Oxford University and take the modern languages Tripos. But the opportunity for formal education had been denied to her: girls of her class were not educated, for education was thought to make them unfit for marriage. But that didn't mean that she couldn't educate herself, and she continued to read as widely as she could. She loved poetry, and this afternoon, she sat with Shelley's *Prometheus Unbound* on her lap.

The volume remained unopened, however, for Consuelo's attention was elsewhere. She was looking out the window, beyond the Italian Garden toward the aviary where she and Kate Sheridan had gone for a talk that afternoon. She was thinking about Gladys Deacon.

Where *was* Gladys? What could have happened to her? Had she eloped with Northcote? Had she gone off with someone else? Or had she simply run away, as she had when she left Versailles and went off to Paris with her sister? Consuelo hadn't wanted to tell Kate the whole story behind that dreadful escapade, but it had been more than a childish prank, much more. The two of them had had a terrible row, for she had felt responsible for Gladys and refused to allow her to spend an evening with a German military cadet who was infatuated with her. That night Gladys had disappeared and was gone for four days. Four whole days, while Consuelo fretted and worried and finally alerted the police, only to have Gladys reappear, as blithe and carefree and unapologetic as if she had been gone only a few hours.

Consuelo sat back in her chair and closed her eyes, thinking over the events of the last fortnight: She and Gladys had taken the pony cart to Woodstock, had been driven to Oxford in the phaeton, and had taken several drives over the estate and the Blenheim farms in the electric car. In all that time, had Gladys said or done anything that gave a clue as to where she might go, or what she might do, if she suddenly vanished?

And then, as Consuelo thought longer and harder, an idea began to form. Yes, perhaps there was a clue, after all. She put down her book and stood. She would—

The echoing reverberations of the gong shivered through the air, and Consuelo sighed. She could do nothing now, for it was time to dress for tea, and after tea, time to read to her children in the nursery. And when that was finished, it would be time to dress for dinner.

And with a clear, painful awareness, Consuelo suddenly knew how desperately she envied Gladys Deacon's freedom, how wonderful it would be to vanish from Blenheim, how marvelous to take wing and, like a hawk or a falcon, simply fly away.

CHAPTER TWENTY-FIVE

Here begins the Great Game.

Kim
Rudyard Kipling

Ned had lied when he told Lord Sheridan that he was not afraid. His knees were beginning to quake even before he approached the terrifying East Gate, carrying the small bag he had packed at home, and he had to swallow a fearful stutter as he told the liveried porter his business. His fright mounted still higher as he was escorted down a narrow staircase and through a seemingly endless maze of dimly lit passages, at last arriving in the main servants' area, where he was deposited at the door to the butler's pantry and instructed to wait there for Mr. Stevens. He was almost tongue-tied with fear by the time that gentleman appeared some ten minutes later and listened to his stammering introduction and his explanation that he had been referred by Lord Sheridan and Mr. Churchill.

The butler, impeccably attired in black coat and trousers and white gloves, frowned over his gold-rimmed glasses. "Well, I dare say you'll do," he said, "if you can get over that stammer." In an appraising tone, he added, "You're certainly a good-looking lad, which will no doubt please the Duchess. If you are quick on your feet and reasonably nimble in your wits, you should get on here, particularly as you come so highly recommended. It does not hurt to have gentlemen like Lord Sheridan and Mr. Churchill in one's corner, as I am sure you are aware. You are a fortunate young man."

"I am fortunate indeed, sir," Ned said, assuming a deeply deferential tone. It was true, though. He was lucky to have someone like Lord Sheridan behind him, a strong man who would stand for no nonsense from anyone—unlike his own father, who could never be counted on to defend Ned or his brothers when their mother fell into a rage. "I will do my best to be quick, sir," he added obsequiously, "and to live up to the expectations of those who have recommended me."

Mr. Stevens nodded as if he were pleased with Ned's reply. "Well, then. We shall have to see you properly attired. Pages at Blenheim wear white shirts, short red jackets, and black trousers and tie."

"Of course, sir," Ned said. One had to dress as one was expected to dress. He would think of it as his disguise.

Mr. Stevens looked up as a liveried footman wearing a maroon jacket and satin knee breeches approached, carrying a silver tray stacked with white damask napkins, folded in a mitre shape.

"Ah, Alfred," he said. "I was just going to send for you. This is young Lawrence. He is to be our new page, in Richard's place. Give me that tray and take charge of him, would you? See that he's outfitted properly, then show him around. He's to have duty with you until he learns what's expected of him, so he might as well sleep with you, now that Richard has moved into Conrad's room."

So this was Alfred, Ned thought, a resplendent-looking fellow, to be sure, with his powdered hair and white-stockinged calves and the large gold buckles on his shiny black shoes. He had an amiable face and rather a confiding manner.

Alfred eyed him casually at first, it seemed, and then with a sudden interest, as if he had recognized him. "Cert'nly, Mr. Stevens," he said, putting his hand on Ned's shoulder. "He looks a fine, sturdy boy. With a bit of training, I'm sure he'll do well." He dropped his hand and smiled at Ned. "Come along, then, lad. We'll get you something to wear."

Trying not to appear surprised at anything that had happened in the last few moments, Ned hurried along behind, almost running to keep up with the footman's long strides. What good fortune he had tumbled into! This could only be the Alfred whom Lord Sheridan had instructed him particularly to observe—one of those involved in the robbery his lordship thought might be planned. Well, meeting him had been easy enough, Ned thought in some relief, and the fellow had the kind of look—open and almost transparent—that suggested an easy approach. Now, all he had to do was pump him for information about the plan, if there was one. This whole business might turn out to be very easy, after all.

Ned was right. They had no sooner reached the wardrobe closet where the out-of-service liveries and such were stored, when Alfred closed the door, shutting them both inside. He took a candle from a shelf, struck a match, and leaned forward.

"You're the lad Bulls-eye sent to carry messages?" he demanded, in a harsh, hurried whisper.

Ned had not the foggiest idea what the question meant or who Bulls-eye might be, but Lord Sheridan had told him to go along as well as he could with whatever game seemed on offer. He nodded, not quite sure he could trust his voice.

Alfred let out his breath with such gusto that the candle flame flickered. "That's good," he said, almost seeming to sag with relief, "that's damned good. Because I tell you, lad, I was beginning to feel that I'd been stuck in this place and forgotten. For all the word I've had, the play might have been dropped."

Alfred's great relief made him seem somehow vulnerable, and Ned took heart. "Oh, no," he said, affecting a careless assurance. "The play hasn't been dropped, and you haven't been forgotten, Alfred, not in the least." He paused, feeling he ought to say something more comforting. "Bulls-eye says to say that he's been busy, but he'll make it up to you."

"Well, then," Alfred said, "you undoubtedly have some word for me. What's Bulls-eye's plan, eh? What's the game? Who's t' be the cracksman?" He became more urgent. "And what's the word on our Kitty, boy? Has she been found?"

Our Kitty. The housemaid Lord Sheridan said had gone missing. "I'm afraid I don't know anything about Kitty," Ned confessed truthfully, and added, "and as for the game, Bulls-eye said to tell you he's still working on it."

"Still working on it!" Alfred exclaimed in a tone of hollow dismay. "But the King and his party are due in a fortnight. Who's to do the work? How's the job to be done? That's what I want to know!"

"Take care, there," Ned said in a frowning whisper, "unless you want someone to hear you." Inwardly, however, he was rejoicing. Lord Sheridan had been right! There was a scheme afoot and the Royals were the target—and *he* was in a position to thwart it!

"Sorry," Alfred said nervously. "I'm rattled, that's all. I tell you, lad, I'm glad you're here, if only for the company. I don't half like being left all alone in this monstrous place, where I run my legs off, days on end, with 'yes ma'am, thankee sir, right away sir' over and over again, and never a kind smile from anyone. And I'm worried about Kitty, worried half to death."

"Worried?" Ned asked encouragingly.

Alfred gulped. "She and me . . . well, I've been thinking that the two of us could go off together to Brighton, where my brother wants me to buy a share in his pub. I fancy owning a pub, I do. But not without Kitty. I couldn't do it without her." His face crumpled and his voice ran up the scale, cracking at the top. "I tell you, lad, I just can't make out what's happened to her. She wouldn't go off without telling me where she was going, I know it! And 'specially not when we've a job to do."

Seeing Alfred's distress, Ned began to feel a growing compassion. It must be hard for him, feeling left alone here, without Kitty, who had most likely cut and run, having found a better game elsewhere. But he also felt an increasing confidence. Lord Sheridan had reckoned that it might take him some little time to establish a connection with Alfred, but he had accomplished that within an hour of his arrival. From Alfred's question, he had to assume that Bulls-eye was his point of contact with the thieves, or perhaps the mastermind himself. And if Alfred thought that Bulls-eye had sent him, Bulls-eye must not be far away.

"Well, I'm sorry about Kitty," Ned said. "And I'll be sure to let Bulls-eye know that you're awf'lly bothered about her. Anyway, he said to tell you that if you had any special messages, to pass them along by way of me." Improvising rapidly, he added, "He said I'm to meet him late tonight, in the reg'lar place."

"That's all right then," Alfred said, apparently satisfied. "You can tell him that I'm waiting for instructions. And hoping to hear news of Kitty," he added urgently. "If he knows anything, anything at all, you need to tell me."

"I will," Ned said. Now came the tricky part, where he had to pick his step. He contrived a half-apologetic look. "Odd thing, though. Bulls-eye forgot to tell me where the reg'lar place is, and I was in a hurry and didn't think to ask. But I'm sure you must know."

"What?" Alfred gaped. "You didn't meet him at the Black Prince, in Woodstock?"

Ned almost gave himself away with a chuckle. Too easy. This spying game was all too easy. Or perhaps Alfred just wasn't very smart. "Not there," he said. "We met in the churchyard, y'see."

"The churchyard?" Alfred asked doubtfully. "A strange place to meet, i'n't it, amongst the tombstones?"

"Not at all," Ned said with a little smile, now more confident than ever. "My father is the rector, y'see."

"Ah," Alfred said wisely, nodding. He affixed the candle to the shelf. "Well, then, we'd best get you your jacket and trousers and white gloves, so you can look the part of a page. And then I'll show you where you're to eat and sleep and what you're to do. I doubt you'll find any of it very difficult."

"Thank you," Ned said, feeling that the most difficult part of the game was probably over. "You're awf'lly helpful, Alfred."

But such confidence was foolish. Ned could not know it, but the most difficult part was yet to come.

CHAPTER TWENTY-SIX

✦━━⊙━━✦

He who asks questions cannot avoid the answers.

Old English Proverb

As Charles had feared, he was very late to tea. In fact, as he came down the hall toward the Saloon, the Duke was just leaving.

"Ah, Sheridan!" Marlborough seemed tired and nervy, and an almost pathetic eagerness was written across his aristocratic face. "What news have you? Has Miss Deacon been found?"

Charles shook his head. "I'm sorry to say, Your Grace, that she has not. It is rather more complicated than——"

"She has *not!*" the Duke exploded angrily. "Why, man, what have you been doing all day? I thought you were supposed to be an equal to Holmes!"

"I doubt, Your Grace," Charles said in a dry tone, "that anyone could be Holmes's equal. He is, after all, a fiction, and does not work or live in the real world." Neither, he thought, did Marlborough.

"That's an excuse." The Duke pushed out his lower lip. "I

won't have excuses. I want action, I tell you. I want answers. I want Miss Deacon found." He raised a clenched fist, his face contorted, his voice at an hysterical pitch. "I want her *found,* do you hear? Now, go and do it. Immediately!"

Charles felt the anger rise within him. Most of the realm's peers seemed to him to demonstrate this same blind, unreasoning arrogance, this unconscionable idea that all men were theirs to command. They did not seem to understand that the center of political power was shifting—had indeed already shifted—and that a new, more democratic order had already replaced the authority of the traditional landed aristocracy. Inevitably, the power of the House of Lords would be broken, and the old nobility rendered irrelevant. Marlborough was a dinosaur. He was among the last of his kind, and was not wise enough to know it.

But Charles bit back the sharp retort that came to his tongue and said, in the mildest tone he could manage, "If His Grace will reflect, he may recall that I am not his servant, but his invited guest. Whatever I do to help him, I do of my own free will, rather than at his bidding." And with that, he turned on his heel and left Marlborough sputtering.

In the Saloon, the Duchess, Winston, and Kate—looking unusually beautiful, he thought, in mist-green chiffon— were gathered in front of the fireplace, just finishing their tea.

But the Duchess, dressed in an ivory-lace tea gown that emphasized her youthfulness and doll-like fragility, was also leaving. "I do hope you'll excuse me, Lord Sheridan," she said, coming toward him with a bright smile. "I am expected upstairs in the nursery, to read to my sons after they've had their tea. It is one of the greatest pleasures of my day, and I try never to miss it." She gestured to the footman standing behind the tea table. "Conrad, please see to Lord Sheridan's tea."

As the footman poured a cup of tea for him, Charles watched Consuelo out the door, thinking that she seemed too young and fragile to carry the responsibility of such a huge house on her shoulders, without (as far as he could tell) the support and assistance, or even the encouragement, of her husband.

But young as she was, she had already performed the Duchess of Marlborough's most important function: She had produced not just one male heir—the future Duke—but two, ensuring that Blenheim would remain in the hands of the immediate Churchill family. Charles knew many men who married only to beget an heir and carry on the name; that crucial obligation accomplished, they simply ignored their wives and turned elsewhere for their pleasures, as Marlborough seemed to have turned to Gladys Deacon. He wondered when the Duchess would begin to do as other women in her position usually did: take a lover for herself, if only to relieve the monotony of her life and reassure herself that she was desirable and desired.

Charles took his cup of tea and plate of pastry and walked over to Winston, who was sitting with Kate in front of the fireplace. "I wonder," he said quietly, "if you would mind dismissing the footman, Winston. I'd like a word with both of you, privately."

And while Winston was speaking to the footman, Charles bent over and kissed the back of Kate's neck with a greater tenderness than usual, wanting her to know that she was both desirable and desired. She reached for his hand, turned it over, and kissed the palm, an intimate gesture that touched him deeply. He was indeed a fortunate man to have this woman for his wife.

The footman having left the room, Winston came to stand in front of the fireplace. With a businesslike air, he said, "I spoke to Stevens just before tea, Charles. Your young man Lawrence seems to have made quite a favorable impression, in both appearance and manner. He is now in Alfred's care, being instructed in his duties. He will, however, be free to come to us when he is sent for."

"Very good," Charles said with some relief. "Very good, indeed." He sat beside Kate on the velvet settee, put his cup and saucer on the side table, and crossed his legs. At least that part of the business was underway, although it was too early to know whether the boy would meet with any success.

"Lawrence?" Kate asked curiously. "Who is that?"

"A young man of my acquaintance who has agreed to be our eyes and ears among the servants," Charles said. He smiled at Kate's questioning look and pressed her hand. "I'm afraid the story will have to wait, my dear. We have more urgent things to deal with, I think. Winston, what were you able to learn about Northcote in Woodstock?"

"Only that he took a room at The Bear very early this morning, and then caught the first train to Kidlington and points beyond," Winston replied, clasping his hands behind his back, under the skirts of his coat. "He's sent a telegram to the Duchess, begging her pardon for his sudden departure, which he blames on unexpected business. It arrived just before tea, she said."

"It was sent from—"

"From London," Winston replied.

"I take it that Miss Deacon was not with him when he left Woodstock," Charles said.

"That's correct. And the stationmaster does not recall seeing a young lady of her description at any point during the day."

"A young lady?" Kate put in eagerly. "What about a young man?" Winston looked confused, and Kate subsided. "Forgive me for interrupting," she said. "Please go on, Winston."

Winston nodded. "I sent a telegram to Cornwallis-West, asking him for whatever information he might be willing to send me. I expect to hear tomorrow or the next day, by post."

"Ah," Charles said. "And your visit to the Black Prince?"

Winston put on a nonchalant expression. "Drew a blank, I'm afraid. I met a fellow with a red beard, but he could tell me nothing about the missing housemaid." He went to the tea table, poured himself a cup of tea, and helped himself to a slice of cake. "More tea, Kate?" he asked, over his shoulder.

"Thank you, no," Kate said. She turned to Charles. "Missing housemaids? What are you up to, Charles?"

"Bear with me, Kate," Charles said. "First, I would like to hear what you found when you searched Miss Deacon's room."

Winston rejoined them, eyebrows lifted. "Kate searched Miss Deacon's room?" He sat down in the chair across from them, boyishly stretching out his legs.

"I thought it should be done," Charles replied, adding, with a hint of a smile, "It seemed more appropriate that it should be done by a lady, in case there was something that ought not be seen by male eyes."

"There was nothing in the room that should shock anyone," Kate replied. "And as it turned out, I was there twice. Once to find what was there, and once to find out what was missing."

"That," said Winston definitively, "has a whiff of intrigue."

Kate gave them a small smile. "Her room was exactly as might be expected. Several photographs of admirers, signed with effusive endearments. The usual hairpieces and cosmetics possessed by a young lady in Society. A locked diary, which I did not open." She reached down, picked up a tapestry bag, and took something out. "And this letter from Northcote." She handed it to Charles. "It was lying, unfolded, on her bedside table."

Charles opened and read it. When he had finished, without a word, he rose and handed it to Winston. Winston read it silently, pressing his lips together, until he reached nearly the end, and then began to read aloud.

" 'And if you refuse, why then I shall simply carry you off straightaway and the devil take he who tries to stop me—Marlborough or anyone else!' " With an indignant expression, he handed the letter back to Charles. "I guessed as much. Northcote is behind this whole affair. I don't know what he's done with her, but he's clearly no gentleman. No gentleman at all!"

"Perhaps one cannot blame him," Charles remarked, refolding the letter and putting it into the inside breast pocket of his jacket. "When he wrote this, he seems to have been laboring under the apprehension that Miss Deacon had accepted his offer of marriage, along with the family diamonds." He smiled. "Although perhaps their conversation in the garden last night disabused him of that notion."

"In the garden?" Kate asked in surprise. "But I thought Miss Deacon was there with the Duke."

"Marlborough says that the two of them had a disagreement and that he left her there before ten-thirty," Charles replied. "I rather imagine that Northcote was watching from an upstairs window, because he joined her shortly after. According to one of the footmen, who happened to witness the encounter, Northcote became rather heated. About twelve-thirty, the same footman saw him fleeing, bag in hand, from the house. He seems to have fetched up at The Bear, alone, and thence at the train."

Winston looked at Kate. "The diamond necklace Northcote gave her," he said tersely. "Did you find it in her room?"

"No necklace," Kate said, shaking her head. "Only the gems we've seen her wear—some of them quite fine—and a few others. Oh, and a pouch of odd-looking stones, trinkets, really. They were in the drawer with her diary, rather than in her jewelry box. I doubt that they have any particular value."

Not sure whether he was surprised or not, Charles turned to face her. "A pouch of stones?"

"Yes. A half-dozen or so, five, perhaps." She gave him a quizzical look. "They were individually wrapped in tissue."

"And what did they look like?"

"Like trinkets," Kate said. "One was a scarab beetle—the sort of thing you'd find in Egypt. The others were of different colors, cut in odd shapes, with carvings all over them." She frowned. "Are they important?"

Winston's eyes had darkened and he was leaning forward, urgently. "Charles, you don't imagine that—"

"Pound to a penny they're what's left of the Marlborough Gemstones," Charles said. "Did you have a look in the Red Drawing-Room?"

"No," Winston said, between his teeth, "although I certainly shall. But why would she—"

"Gemstones?" Kate leaned over and put a hand on Charles's arm. "Charles, you *must* tell me what you're talking about!"

Charles gave a deep sigh. He took no pleasure in the thought that his suspicions had been confirmed, for it only opened other, darker possibilities.

"I was reluctant to share this, but I see that I must. Friday last, a mysterious woman appeared at the Ashmolean. She brought a leather pouch containing five seal-stones, and asked the curator for an idea of their value. John Buttersworth, to whom she spoke, recognized the stones as similar to those in the Marlborough Gemstone collection, which was sold some thirty years ago. She apparently let it slip that she was an employee of the duchess—the Duchess of Marlborough, Buttersworth assumed." He paused, adding dryly, "The lady in question was veiled, but according to Buttersworth, who is a connoisseur of such things, she had a classical Grecian nose."

Winston's face wore a look of astonishment, and he whistled between his teeth. "I can see our Miss Deacon doing many strange things, but it's well nigh impossible to imagine her attempting to flog the Marlborough Gems. Whatever *for?* The lady certainly has funds enough of her own, or so she leads one to believe. Inherited a fortune from her father, I understand. And anyway, those stones, by themselves, aren't worth much—unless she thinks there are others." He pulled his brows together. "As well she might, if she hasn't heard of the auction."

"I can't speak to motive," Charles said, "but it's not difficult to test the hypothesis. If you'll have a look in the china box in the Red Drawing-Room, Winston, I'll see to Miss Deacon's room." He turned to Kate. "A locked diary as well, you said?"

Kate nodded. "I could have picked the lock easily, but I decided against it." She paused. "But there's more to tell you, Charles. I went back to her bedroom a second time, with the maid, and discovered that a suit of men's clothing is missing from the wardrobe—brown flannel trousers and jacket and brown boots. I also discovered that Miss Deacon took her small valise from the luggage room."

"Men's clothing?" Winston asked in astonishment. "And a valise? But what the devil—"

"A disguise," Charles said. He grinned, amused. "Perhaps our elusive Miss Deacon has done a moonlight flit with Botsy Northcote's diamonds." He raised his eyebrows. "Or perhaps she took the train this morning, after all—not in her gold evening gown, but in a man's brown suit."

"Oh, surely not," Winston said. "I can't believe—" He stopped. "But why a disguise?" He repeated it to himself, puzzled. "Why a disguise?"

The question, Charles thought, had no answer, at least at the moment. But Kate was going on.

"There are some other things I need to show you, Charles," she said. She reached into the tapestry bag once again and took out a gold leather evening slipper. "I found this in the boat house, in the bottom of the green rowboat. Not one of the Duke's boats," she added with a small smile, handing it to him. "A working boat, in the old boat house, according to Badger."

"Badger?" Winston raised an eyebrow. "He's Blenheim's fishery man. A bit of a character, and eccentric. But he knows the lake and the river better than anyone else." His glance darkened as he focused on the slipper Charles was turning over in his fingers, gazing at thoughtfully. "That slipper—it's not Miss Deacon's, is it?"

"I believe it is," Kate replied. "It is the color of her dress."

"Cinderella's slipper," Charles said, musing. "I wonder——" But again, there was no answer to the question, so he filed it away in his mind. "What other things have you there, Kate?"

Kate took a folded bit of paper out of her bag and opened it to reveal the butt of a cigarette. "I found this partially smoked cigarette in the boat as well, Charles. I doubt that it's Miss Deacon's, since she was wearing lip rouge, and there is none on the cigarette. I was hoping you might be able to take a fingerprint from it."

"I'm afraid not," Charles said, glancing at it. "But the boat house—of course, Kate! That tells us how she got to the other side of the lake, doesn't it? To Rosamund's Well, where you found the scrap of gold silk."

Winston was looking from one to the other of them, his ginger-colored brows furrowed in puzzlement. "Scrap of silk?"

"I was at Rosamund's Well this morning, sketching," Kate explained. "I noticed a scrap of gold silk, which I took to be torn from the dress Miss Deacon was wearing last night. It was snagged on a small bush, a bush that didn't seem quite sturdy enough to tear such heavy fabric." She glanced at Charles. "Were you able to get to the Well and see for yourself?"

"That's why I was late to tea," Charles said. "I had a look around." He hesitated. "I found several disquieting pieces of evidence, I'm afraid."

"Oh, dear," Kate said.

"Yes. There is a substantial smattering of blood on a paving stone beside the pool, and a bloody heelprint. I also found some marks in the dirt which suggest that something heavy was dragged toward the lake, perhaps to a waiting boat."

Winston leapt from his chair. "The devil you say!" he exclaimed. "Do you think Miss Deacon is dead? Northcote—that cad, that scoundrel! He took her to the Well, killed her, and dumped her body into the lake." He began striding back and forth, highly agitated. "What an appalling turn of affairs, simply appalling! And just think of the scandal, once this gets into the newspapers!"

"Well, that's a certainly a hypothesis," Charles replied, thinking that Winston's concern for the Churchill reputation seemed rather misplaced. "But I don't believe there's any concrete evidence to support it. We don't know whether Miss Deacon is dead or alive. And it's entirely possible that the blood is not human blood at all, but that of an animal. A deer, for instance, might have been killed on the spot and the carcass dragged to a boat."

Winston let out his breath in a gust of noisy relief. "Poachers!" he exclaimed, snapping his fingers. "Yes, of course! Why didn't I think of that? There have always been people who clip into the Park and help themselves to game every now and then. It's against the law, and Marlborough sees that they're punished as severely as possible, but that never stops them."

Charles did not point out that hungry people were not likely to be deterred by the fact that the deer belonged to the Duke. "And don't forget," he went on, "that another person, a servant, seems to have gone missing from this house."

"Oh, yes, of course," Kate said. "The housemaid you mentioned a few moments ago. What is her name?"

"Kitty," Charles said.

Now it was Kate's eyes that widened, and she dived back into her tapestry bag. "I found this note in the rowboat, as well, Charles." She smoothed out the crumpled paper and read it aloud: "Dearest Kitty, I need to talk to you, soon as ever possible. You know I love you dearest and long to hold you close." She looked up. "It's signed, 'Yours 'til death, Alfred.'"

"Alfred!" Winston exclaimed. "The cleverboots! So he and this housemaid—"

"Yes," Charles said. "Alfred and Kitty were together at Welbeck Abbey. After they left and before they came to take up positions here, they spent some time together in London." He paused. "It's time, Kate, that I tell you about this business with the servants. And it's entirely possible that Northcote and Miss Deacon are involved, as well."

"Botsy and Miss Deacon!" Winston cried. "In a ring of thieves? But that . . . that's impossible! It's absurd! Why, they are of our class! They—"

"Sit down and listen," Charles said quietly, thinking that Winston's noisy, unceasing bluster really did wear on one. "There is a thread here, as our friend Doyle is fond of saying, which may lead us through this tangle."

It took Charles several moments to lay out the entire story. First, there was the theft during a large houseparty at Welbeck Abbey, where Alfred and Kitty had been employed and Gladys Deacon and Botsy Northcote had been guests. Then there had been the theft from the Ashmolean of the Warrington Hoard, offered for sale to Mr. Dreighson by a mysterious, as-yet-unidentified lady. Then there was the apparent offer of five gemstones, resembling the Marlborough Gemstones, to the museum—again by a mysterious lady.

And finally, the appearance of Alfred, Kitty, Miss Deacon, and Botsy Northcote at Blenheim, with the Royal house-party only three weeks away.

"Perhaps you can see," Charles said to Kate when he had finished, "why I felt we needed a friendly pair of eyes and ears below-stairs."

"A spy, you mean," Kate said eagerly. "You've put in a *mole,* Charles."

"A mole?" Winston asked dubiously.

"An intelligence agent. I found the word in a shilling-shocker." Kate turned to Charles. "I can see why you think another theft might be afoot, Charles, given the fact that all four of these people are here. Or *were* here," she corrected herself, "since two of the four now seem to be missing, and Northcote appears to have gone back to London." She paused. "And perhaps a crime of passion, as well. There's certainly enough animosity in this matter."

"I'm afraid that's true," Charles said. "And if Miss Deacon, disguised or not, has met with foul play, the Duke, the Duchess, and Botsy Northcote must all be among the suspects, or so the police would think."

"Surely not the Duchess!" Kate objected, as Winston groaned.

"I'm not saying that I suspect her, Kate. I'm only pointing out the possibilities that the police would be required to consider, especially if the Yard becomes involved."

"As it no doubt would," Winston said gloomily. "This is not a situation that the local constabulary would be prepared to deal with."

Kate gave Charles a long look. "But perhaps Gladys didn't meet with foul play," she said. "Perhaps it *was* a deer that was killed at Rosamund's Well." She paused. "Or perhaps, well, there is a housemaid missing. Perhaps she's the one who met with foul play."

"But what of Gladys?" Winston cried. "Where the devil is she?"

It was not a question that any of them were prepared to answer.

CHAPTER TWENTY-SEVEN

The servants in this house are utter rascals, every one. They seem to plot among themselves to do as little as possible and get as much as they can, honestly or dishonestly. . . . I should like to hang a few and burn the rest at the stake.

Mary Fleeting, Lady Lindon, in a letter to her mother, 1902

Ned was a brash young man and not easily cowed, but even he could not help feeling abashed by the great palace within whose formidable walls he now found himself. Blenheim was so large and forbidding, so obviously the home of the great and powerful, that he could not help feeling very small and powerless—which might be exactly the reason, he thought to himself, why people built such grandiose houses for themselves: to make their authority seem even more immutably powerful to those beneath them, and to quash feelings of insurgency in any who dared to rise above their station. But once one knew this, he reminded himself resolutely, one had already begun to revoke the other's power. That thought—and the recollection that he was here as a *spy*, not a servant, gave him strength, and he hardened himself against his feelings of vulnerability.

After Ned had changed into his new clothing, Alfred supplied a green apron that extended below his knees and set him to cleaning and polishing the nursery boots. That chore done, he was sent off to tea with the scullery maids, kitchen maids, and odd man, and after that, was instructed to bring in a dozen buckets of coal and line them up in the lower hallway, where the footmen would carry them upstairs so that the maids could stoke the bedroom fires. All the while he did these chores, Ned was mulling over what Alfred had said to him about Bulls-eye and Kitty and the King, and wondering what Lord Sheridan would make of it all and how he would manage to get the information to his lordship.

He had just put down the last two buckets of coal when Alfred appeared. "You've been sent for," he said shortly. "Lord Sheridan's asked to see you, in the billiard room, right away." He wore a suspicious frown. "Didn't mention you was friendly with upstairs, now, did you?"

"Friendly, my hat," Ned replied, taking off his apron. "His lordship's an acquaintance of my father's." He made a face. "Haven't seen the guv for a while, and the nob prob'ly feels he has t' jaw me for it." The explanation sounded a little lame, to his ears, but Alfred didn't seem to notice.

"My guv went off to Australia when I was five," Alfred replied reminiscently. "Missed his lashings a fair treat, I did." He gave an ironic chuckle. "Well, come along, then. Hang up that apron and wash those hands and I'll show you the way. When you get back, it will be nearly time for dinner, and you can help Conrad and me bring the food from the kitchen to the dining room." He looked at Ned critically. "And don't forget to put on your gloves. Gloves is part o' the uniform. The blue bloods don't like to see our hands—reminds 'em that we're working and they're not."

The billiard room—a large oak-paneled room hung with trophy bucks, mounted game fish, and stuffed birds, with a large brown bear standing on its hind legs in the corner—was in the lowest level of the family quarters, next to the gun room. Lord Sheridan was not alone, Ned discovered when he was admitted. The gentleman with him, a brash-looking young man with red hair and a roundish, florid face, was introduced as Mr. Churchill, cousin to the Duke. The two men, both of whom wore evening dress, appeared to have just finished their game when he came in.

Lord Sheridan racked his cue. "Well, Ned," he said, taking out his handkerchief and wiping the chalk off his hands, "you certainly look like a page." He eyed Ned's costume approvingly. "White gloves, too. They've put you to work, I take it."

"Drudge work," Ned said, looking down at his hands in the unfamiliar gloves. "Blacking boots and hauling coal." Anxious not to be thought complaining, he added quickly, "I don't mind, of course, sir. It's all part of the job. I shan't muck it."

"I know you won't," his lordship said. "Have you managed to get a word with Alfred yet?"

Ned straightened his shoulders. "Oh, yes, I have, sir." He grinned. "He immediately leapt to the conclusion that I'm a messenger or go-between or something of the sort, sir. From a fellow named Bulls-eye, at the Black Prince in Woodstock."

"Bulls-eye!" Mr. Churchill exclaimed in dismay. "At the Prince!"

"Yes, sir," Ned said, wondering how this Churchill fellow came into it. But since Lord Sheridan had allowed him to stay, he supposed that the man could be trusted. "Alfred said he didn't like being alone here," he added, "and he was glad I'd come, if only for the company. He asked me about Kitty, and seems to've been . . . well, rather fond of her. He's awf'lly cut up about her leaving without telling him where she's going."

"Did he say anything about the Royal visit?" Lord Sheridan asked.

"Yes." Ned stopped, trying to pull out Alfred's exact words. He felt it important to report as accurately as he could.

"Well, get on with it," Churchill urged impatiently. "Don't keep us in suspense, young fellow!"

Lord Sheridan put his hand on Churchill's sleeve. "Give the lad a moment, Winston," he said quietly. "He's recalling details."

Ned threw his lordship a grateful glance. "About the King," he said. "Alfred is worried that the Royal party are coming in two weeks, and he doesn't know anything about the plan. 'Who's to do the work?' he was asking me. 'Who's to be the cracksman?'"

"The cracksman!" exclaimed Churchill, with relish. "You were right, Sheridan! There *is* a robbery plot afoot!" He dropped his voice, rubbing his forehead in a dramatic gesture. "And I had the ringleaders right in front of me, at the Prince. In my very grasp!"

"That was the pair you talked to, then?" Lord Sheridan asked.

"One of them was called Bulls-eye," Churchill replied. He gave an exaggerated moan. "Oh, what a dunce I am, to be taken in by that damned red-bearded rascal's hail-fellow-well-met! I'm a fool, a bloody blockhead!"

Ned had no idea what this was all about, and he privately thought that Mr. Churchill's histrionic mummery was foolish and self-centered. But he plowed on, addressing himself to Lord Sheridan.

"The thing is, you see, sir, that Alfred doesn't know anything about what's going on. He's had no word and he feels as if he's been cut off. 'Stuck in this place and forgotten,' was the way he put it. Whatever the plan is, he's not in on it."

"Interesting," Lord Sheridan remarked.

Churchill put on a frown. "Unlikely, seems to me. P'rhaps he suspects you, and he's trying to throw you off the scent. Make you think he doesn't know."

Ned shook his head. "Alfred isn't . . . well, he isn't that sort of person, at least as far as I can see. That is, he's not devious. He's . . . well, trusting, if you know what I mean. Maybe because he feels so desperate, and has nowhere else to turn. He asked me to find out from Bulls-eye what's going on, and tell him."

Behind his detached demeanor, Ned felt a twinge of guilt. Alfred was quite a decent fellow, and here he was, ratting on him, spilling his secrets. But that was part of his job, wasn't it? A spy couldn't have friends.

Churchill's frown deepened. "Sounds to me as if they've given it up," he said. "Pulled out. Having one of their people disappear—the woman, I mean—well, it must've made them think twice. If you ask me, she funked it and took herself off to London, or wherever she came from."

"Let's not grab at straws," Lord Sheridan said in a thoughtful tone. "They may have put someone else into the house."

"Another servant, you mean, sir?" Ned asked quickly. "Well, if that's the case, the new man hasn't got in touch with Alfred. He thinks I'm his new contact. I'll stake my life on that," he added, feeling that he ought to defend Alfred, who somehow struck him as a person who needed defending.

Lord Sheridan nodded. "You may very well be right, Ned. It sounds to me as if, for some reason or another, they've ceased to trust Alfred, so they're no longer communicating with him. However, he has already told us what we needed to know: the name of his contact and where he can be found." He turned to Churchill. "Winston, I wonder— would you be able to get a look at the estate's wage book for the past few months? Without giving a reason, of course."

"I suppose I might," Churchill said slowly, knitting his brows. "Both inside and outside staff?"

"No, just inside, I should think. The upstairs people— both male and female. We're looking for a lady's maid, perhaps, or a housemaid, rather than someone in the kitchen. Or an upper man servant. Has the Duke brought in a new valet recently?"

"No. Marlborough's man has been with him since he came into the dukedom." Churchill pursed his lips, giving him rather, Ned thought, the expression of a petulant bulldog. "About the household staff, I shall have to ask Stevens. He's the one who keeps the wage book, I'm sure."

"Oh, and while you're about it," Lord Sheridan added, "ask to have a look at their character references."

Ned cast an admiring look at Lord Sheridan. Character references would show what agency they came from. Really, for someone who spoke so modestly and unassumingly, the man was a first-class thinker.

But Churchill seemed puzzled. "Their characters? Whatever for?"

"Because it would be helpful to know which agency referred Alfred and Kitty," Lord Sheridan replied. "And any other recently hired staff."

"I'll do as you ask, of course," Churchill said, frowning. "But I'm not quite sure I see what you're getting at, Sheridan." He added, in a rather more apologetic tone. "Afraid all this sleuthing isn't exactly up my line. Now, if a gun were called for, I'd be glad to oblige. I've my Mauser, you know. Take it with me on general principles, though there's not much call for it in civilized society."

A gun! Ned thought, with a surge of barely repressed excitement. Would it come to that? Oh, topping, simply topping!

"I doubt that your Mauser will be needed," Lord Sheridan said matter-of-factly, and Ned felt disappointed. "However," he went on, "the evidence seems to suggest that this is all part of a larger plot. If that's so, it must involve substantial planning at various levels. We can quash a robbery here at Blenheim, but if we allow those who conceived the plan to get away, the same business will simply be repeated elsewhere." He paused, and added gravely. "As well-organized as this group seems to be, the chances are that it is engaged in other kinds of criminal activities as well. We need to get our hands on the ringleader."

"You must be looking for a man like Moriarty, sir," Ned said, now feeling thoroughly stirred up. Moriarty was the arch-villain who once went up against Sherlock Holmes. He grinned and recited, from memory and with dramatic emphasis: " 'A man with a criminal strain, increased and rendered infinitely more dangerous by his extraordinary powers.' "

"Ah, *that* man!" Churchill replied with an answering grin. He raised an eyebrow and declaimed theatrically,

" 'Fenced round with safeguards so cunningly devised that it seemed impossible to get evidence which would convict in a court of law.' "

"Oh, yes, sir!" Ned exclaimed. "The very one, sir! 'The greatest schemer of all time, the organizer of every deviltry, the controlling brain of the underworld—' "

" 'A brain which might have made or marred the destiny of nations—that's the man,' " Lord Sheridan concluded with a crooked smile. "The Napoleon of crime. A lot of pumped-up nonsense, of course, but somewhat apt to our case."

"Apt, indeed." Churchill clapped Ned on the back. "My word, young man, you do know your Doyle."

"Thank you, sir," Ned said, liking Mr. Churchill rather better now.

"However," Churchill went on in a cautionary tone, "I don't believe that we should overstate the case. I sincerely doubt that we are dealing with a villain as black as Moriarty."

"Perhaps not," Lord Sheridan agreed, "but the scope of the villainy is yet to be seen. For now, our immediate task is to discover whether other members of the theft ring are at work here at Blenheim, unbeknownst to Alfred. For that, we will rely on your investigation of the wage book and character references. And I think I shall have a look in the missing housemaid's trunk. It's still in her room, I've been told."

"And what about me?" Ned asked hopefully. "P'rhaps you'd like me to go to The Prince in Woodstock and see what I can find out about Bulls-eye." After all, he had told Alfred he'd be talking to Bulls-eye that night. He had been so easily successful in worming significant information out of Alfred that he was sure he could find out just as much, and perhaps even more, from Bulls-eye. A fellow could get to like this spying game.

But Lord Sheridan did not fall in with his suggestion. "You are *not* going to Woodstock, Ned," he said firmly. "It's far too dangerous. You are to go back downstairs to your work, and keep a close eye on Alfred. If anyone from the outside attempts to contact him, I want to know about it immediately."

"Yes, sir," Ned said glumly, trying to keep the disappointment out of his voice. He should like it if they could run into a little danger, and if Mr. Churchill had his gun, they would be all right. He hesitated, thinking of something else. "Sir? What about Alfred? He seems like a decent chap. Will he . . . well, will he get into trouble about this? All he wants to do, you know, is take Kitty and go off to Brighton."

"Brighton?" Churchill asked.

Ned nodded. "His brother wants him to buy into a pub there."

"A pub, eh?" Lord Sheridan shook his head ruefully. "I'm sorry, Ned, but it's too early to say what's going to happen to Alfred. We don't know how deeply involved he is. And until we learn the identity of the other person, if there is another person, that is, Alfred remains our only contact with the thieves." He frowned. "But this business about the missing housemaid concerns me. I wonder—"

From the floor above, Ned heard a loud, hollow gong. It sent a shudder down his spine. How could people abide being ordered about by a gong? If they were as powerful as they wanted everyone to believe, why didn't they just shut the damned thing up and do whatever they liked, when they liked?

"Time for dinner," Churchill said in a resigned voice, straightening his cuffs. "Gad, Sheridan, I'm not looking forward to it. Marlborough is nearly off his head about Gladys."

Lord Sheridan sighed. "Nor I." He put his hand on Ned's shoulder. "But you've done a fine job, Ned. I didn't imagine that you would make contact with our target and dig out this information quite so fast." A smile glinted in his brown eyes. "British Intelligence could make good use of a man like you."

"Intelligence?" Ned felt quite complimented. But of course, there were other things he wanted to do first. "I'm planning to become an archaeologist, you know. I want to do digs in Egypt and the Sudan, as you did. And on Crete, too," he added, thinking of the shipments being unpacked at the Ashmolean.

"Ah, yes," his lordship murmured. "Well, perhaps there's not much difference between digging artifacts out of the ground and digging information out of people who don't want you to have it. But we can talk about that later. Off with you, now, Ned. And keep close to Alfred, do you hear? That's your first order of duty."

"Oh, yes, m'lord," Ned promised earnestly. "I'll keep close to him. You can count on that."

At the time, he meant it.

CHAPTER TWENTY-EIGHT

Every man and woman in the kingdom, no matter how low-born, can, by self-discipline, hard work, and self-help, achieve wealth, prosperity, and social position. Remember, Heaven helps those who help themselves.

Self-Help, 1882
Samuel Smiles

Dinner had indeed been a wretched affair, Charles thought. The food had been cold, the Duke and Duchess had had nothing to say to each other or to anyone else, and even Kate's gaiety, usually so spontaneous, had seemed forced. Marlborough cut short the usual after-dinner port and cigars and retired, leaving Winston free to go off to confer with Stevens over the wage book, and Charles to go in search of the housekeeper.

Mrs. Raleigh did not know in which room of Housemaids' Heights Kitty had slept—did not know, it appeared, much at all about the housemaids' habits. She had seemed at a loss when Charles said he wanted to have a look in Kitty's trunk, and had rung the bell for Ruth, who had been Kitty's roommate. It was Ruth who, carrying a candle, showed him with alacrity up the steep stairs to the dark, chilly room in which she now slept alone, at the very top of the tower.

Ruth, a plain-faced young girl with thick brown hair, lit a second candle from the first and pointed to a trunk in the corner. "It's the blue wool I'd like, sir," she said eagerly. "The one with the blue and black braid. It's for my sister, y'see. She's gettin' married, sir, and she'll be ever so glad to have it."

Somewhat mystified, Charles said, "A dress, is it? You'll have to speak to Mrs. Raleigh about that, I'm afraid."

"Oh, sir," Ruth said, quite clearly disappointed. "I thought you was going to give me—"

"No," Charles said firmly, "Whatever it is, it's not mine to give. Thank you, Ruth. You can go back to your work now."

With a resigned curtsey, Ruth departed, taking one of the candles to light her way down the stairs. In the flickering light of the remaining candle, Charles surveyed the small, bare room, which was scarcely larger than a cubicle. It contained little furniture, only a broken chair, a small chest of drawers on which sat a badly chipped china pitcher and basin, and an iron cot covered with a thin straw mattress scarcely wide enough for one, let alone two. An uncurtained casement window was set into the stone outer wall, overlooking a landscape palely illuminated by a quarter moon. Streaks of occasional lightning split the night sky, and thunder rumbled not far away.

Charles placed the candle on the floor beside the cheap cardboard trunk, knelt down, and raised the lid. The inside smelt strongly of camphor. He took out a rolled-up cloak, a skirt and white blouse and some undergarments, and the blue wool dress that Ruth had wanted, carefully folded with camphor balls in tissue paper. There was also a pair of rough boots badly in need of new heels, a slim volume of *The Young Girl's*

Guide to Domestic Service and a copy of *Self-Help,* by Samuel
Smiles, its pages dog-eared and pencil-marked. Charles riffled
through it, noting that the sentence, "Heaven helps those
who help themselves," reoccured and was underlined in several places. As well, there was a small enamel box containing
an assortment of buttons and pins, a spool of white thread
with a needle stuck in it, a short length of narrow black velvet ribbon, a chipped ceramic dish bearing colored pictures of
the King and Queen, and a silver-colored hair ornament. A
worn leather purse contained two half-crowns and several
shillings. And that was all.

Charles frowned and picked up the candle, holding it so
that the light fell into the empty trunk. He ran the flat of
his hand across the inside of the lid and the bottom of the
trunk and on each of its four sides, inspecting the glued-on
wallpaper lining. On the left side, his fingers felt a ridge,
and on closer inspection, he saw that the paper lining had
been carefully pulled back at the top, creating a kind of
pocket into which an envelope had been slipped.

There was nothing written on the outside of the tan-
colored envelope, and it was unsealed. Inside, there were
three folded pieces of paper. One appeared to be a character
reference, signed by someone identified as the housekeeper
at Carleton House, Manchester, and bearing a date of ap-
proximately two years previous.

Another was a short article clipped from a newspaper,
headlined "Crime Mastermind at Work." A certain Richard
Turner, Scotland Yard detective, was quoted as saying that
several recent thefts appeared to have been carried out by the
same organization and masterminded by a man whose identity remained a mystery but whom the criminal element and

those who made their livings by breaking the law respect-fully (if somewhat jocularly) styled as "Mr. Napoleon."

The third was a small, smudged snapshot of a gentleman in a top hat and evening dress, emerging from a carriage. He had been caught by the camera in a full-face view, looking up, but the image was badly out of focus. On the back was penciled, in a labored script, the words *Jermyn Street*.

For a moment, Charles studied the photograph, follow-ing in his mind the sequence of events that might have brought it into Kitty's possession, imagining the uses she might have put it to, or intended to put it to. If this was what he thought it might be, it was a dangerous weapon—but perhaps more dangerous to the one who held it than to the one against whom it was meant to be used. Dangerous enough to spell death? he wondered. Yes, on balance, he thought so. Blackmail was not a game to be played by the un-tutored or the unwary.

He looked at the photograph again, feeling as if there were something familiar about the figure. But when he could not think what it was, he returned it to the envelope and slipped the envelope into his pocket. He then replaced the clothing and other belongings and got to his feet.

He stood for a moment over the open trunk, regarding its meager contents, feeling the pathos of this small, sad col-lection of items, mute testimony—perhaps the only testi-mony there would ever be—to its owner's personality, to her uniqueness and individuality. He had no evidence that the girl was dead, but he felt in his heart that she was. Whoever Kitty had been or hoped to be, it was all here in front of him, and there was woefully little of it.

Charles had closed the trunk and straightened up when

something else occurred to him. He set down the candle, lifted the trunk lid again, and took out the blue wool dress, still folded in tissue. He laid it carefully on Ruth's narrow cot, took a gold sovereign out of his pocket, and slipped it under a fold of the braid-trimmed bodice.

Then he descended the stair. He had one more search to make that evening: He was going to Gladys Deacon's room to have a look at her diary.

CHAPTER TWENTY-NINE

*How Grand is the Life of a Poacher. Yet it is more Grand to learn
the Habbits of Game . . . If I had been Born an idiot and unfit to
carry a gun—though with Plenty of Cash—they would have
called me a Grand Sportsman. Being Born Poor, I am called a
Poacher.*

A Victorian Poacher:
James Hawker's Journal
edited by Garth Christian

Badger had been on the Blenheim lake, man and boy, for
nearly seventy years. His father had maintained the
Blenheim Fishery before him, and his grandfather and his
great-grandfather before that, so that Blenheim's lake was
not only a family occupation, it ran in Badger's blood.

The great, sinuous lake, which occupied an area of some
hundred and fifty acres, had not always been there, of course.
Before there was a lake, there had been only the pretty little
river, the shallow, rippling River Glyme, meandering lazily
between steep, wooded banks through Rosamund's Meadow,
where sheep were put to graze under the frowning brow of
old Henry's stone castle on the brink above.

That had been a great many years ago, centuries, even, but a pen-and-ink drawing of the drowned river, its meadows and cliffs and the looming castle, hung on the wall in Badger's cottage. The drawing had been done in a rare moment of idleness by Badger's great-great-grandfather, who had an artist's eye and had left a yellowed portfolio of other sketches in mute and moving testimony to a forgotten past: the ancient buildings of Old Woodstock; a race meeting on the Four-Mile Course on the high ground north of the old king's palace; and the palace itself, where the great Queen Elizabeth, then a princess and a threat to her Popish sister Mary, had been imprisoned in the gate house, which had been reduced to a ruin of rubble-stones by the later bombardments of the Civil War.

Even as a child, Badger had loved his great-great-grandfather's drawings, and especially that of the river, for it was the only extant trace, it seemed to him, of a dim and ancient time, before powerful men laid their hands heavily upon the land, changing it and all of its creatures—a time before the Royal Park swallowed the village commons, before the Marlborough dukes and other large landowners did all they could to deprive free men of their freedoms, oppress the tenants, and strip the land of all that belonged of right to the people. Badger was no Radical, but he had heard that half of all England was owned by only a hundred and fifty families, and he agreed with Joseph Chamberlain, who described the gentry as an idle and parasitic class who toiled not, neither did they spin.

The green valley of the Glyme was gone now, and Rosamund's Meadow and the steep hills and even the old castle, for during the time of Badger's great-grandfather, the river had been dammed, submerging itself and its environs.

It was the celebrated landscape architect, Capability Brown, who had achieved this feat, having been commissioned by the fourth Duke of Marlborough. The Duke (the same duke who collected the famous Marlborough Gemstones) had charged him with transforming the stark Blenheim woods, streams, and meadows into something greater and more impressive than the sum of their disparate parts. Brown had dammed the river and created the lake, a spectacular feature that captured the attention and the admiration of all who saw it. That had taken place over a hundred years ago, and now only a few remembered all the smaller beauties that had been sacrificed to achieve the larger.

Badger's small stone cottage—the Fishery Cottage, where four generations of his family had lived—was located at the upper end of the lake. This area was called the Queen Pool, and being fairly shallow, with expanses of bullrush and bur-reed along the shores, was always busy with water birds: ducks and grebes and geese, as well as teal and wigeons and wintering cormorants. And of course, the dukes had always kept swans, which swam in elegant majesty the length and breadth of the lake.

But below the Grand Bridge, the water became much deeper, for the little Glyme had been edged there with tall cliffs. This was the part of the lake in which Badger was most interested—professionally interested, that is, for it was his duty to ensure a continued supply of fish by restocking, when he judged it necessary. It was also his duty, each day, to provide sufficient fresh fish for the Duke's table, which he did by setting nets and dead lines, and spending several pleasant hours a day with a fishing pole.

Depending on the time of year and Badger's luck, the Duke might dine on tench, rudd, roach, perch, or (His

Grace's favorite) pike. Badger, who was past seventy, had fished for five dukes: three Georges, a John, and this latter-day Charles—Sunny, to his family. All the dukes, to Badger's mind, had been bad 'uns, which he attributed to their living in that monstrous palace and having more money in their pockets than mortal man ought, so that they felt little compassion for the plight of ordin'ry folk. And while they might consider themselves grand sportsmen, they were not sportsmen at all, in Badger's scornful view, for they had no idea of the habits of fish, fowl, or game, and shot at (and often missed) only what was driven up before them.

But the present Duke, the ninth, was the worst, and Badger's animosity toward him had grown deeper and darker with each passing year. The man cared only for the palace and the Park, and took no thought for people. He was, Badger thought, a very cold fish. This was proved by the fact that the Fishery Cottage had seen not one bit of repair since the early days of the eighth Duke, and the cottages of the Farm's laborers were in an equally dilapidated state. And while the Duke's pheasants fed on bread and hard-boiled eggs and nested in clean, sweet-smelling straw, the cottagers lived with empty larders and leaking roofs. Moreover, the Duke was not friendly to the village, and kept the Duchess—the richest woman in the world, as everyone knew—from doing anything more than making the usual courtesy calls on the sick.

It was no wonder, then, that the entire countryside shared Badger's view that the ninth Duke was a hateful and mean-spirited man. And no wonder that this view fostered another: that, as the Duke treated them meanly, so meanly should he be treated in return.

And this explained why only some of the fish Badger

took found their way to the Duke's table, the remainder going instead to the tables of the poor in Woodstock, where the bread from the Blenheim kitchen also went. And why he had taken to fishing once or twice a week at night, and laying a half-dozen extra dead lines for pike in the deepest and coldest part of the lake, and setting another trammel net, some twenty yards long and six feet wide, not far from the sluicegate in the dam. All this required restocking the lake rather more frequently than one unaware of these activities might have supposed necessary, but the Duke didn't notice.

It was mostly at night that Badger tended the dead lines and net, especially when the moon was the palest sliver or was beclouded and gave a fitful light, when the quiet lake was a sheet of beaten silver and there was only the call of the owl and the night jar to break the silence, and the soft plashing of the lines as he took them up, unhooked his catch, rebaited with small live fish, and dropped them down again.

Tonight, Badger had taken his mackintosh with him, for the storm that had been gathering since late afternoon seemed about to break. It was past ten and gone full dark, and the freshening breeze brought with it the smell of rain. Honest folk were all abed, except, of course, for the Duke and his guests in the palace, where lights were showing in the windows of the east wing.

But then, Badger knew, they weren't honest, not a one of 'em above taking what didn't belong to them. Like the lady he had caught that morning prowling in his boathouse, obviously looking for whatever she could steal. Or the girl who rowed his yellow boat across the lake and let it go adrift, so that it fetched up against the dam, where he had to go and retrieve it. Or the other, who . . .

He grinned and lit one of the Duke's cigarettes. O'course, he'd been paid for that, and well enough to keep his mouth shut.

Other folk who, like Badger, were no more honest than they had to be, might also be abroad, for there was a brisk local trade in the Duke's hares and rabbits and squirrels and even an occasional deer, as well as the Duke's hen pheasants and their tasty eggs, in season. And while His Grace's keepers should have been out on armed patrol, preserving His Grace's peace, they generally preferred to stay (with the other honest folk) quietly in their beds and let those others own the night. Without the bounty of the Duke's Park, Woodstock's poor would have been much hungrier. There was an irony here that did not escape Badger.

The quarter moon, beset with moving clouds, was making a poor showing just over the trees, and the warm breeze carried a light pelting of rain. Hearing thunder rumbling somewhere in the distance, Badger put on his mackintosh. He had already brought up one large pike—twelve pounds, if it was an ounce—and his fingers were beginning to tingle the way they always did when he was about to bring up an even bigger one.

The great fierce pike—they could grow to nearly fifty pounds—inhabited the deepest part of the lake, its coldest, darkest waters. They sported a formidable set of jagged, knifelike teeth set in powerful, springlike jaws that could catch and hold the largest prey, alive or dead. The occasional guest who fished on the lake rarely caught one, for pike were shy and elusive, easily spooked by the shadow of a boat above them, or even by the moving track of clouds across the water. This was why dead lines were so effective, and while the Duke's gentlemen guests sneered at them as "unsporting," that was of no concern to Badger. His purpose was to catch these illicit fish, not just for the extra coins they put in his pocket but for the deep and rich satisfaction he felt in his soul when he reflected on the fact that His Grace's fish—indeed, the very best and the largest of his fish, the fish he most coveted for his table—were going to feed His Grace's poorest neighbors. *And that, sirs,* he thought to himself with pleasure, *is sport enough.*

But Badger's tingling fingers seemed to have misled him after all, for that first large pike was the only one yielded up by the lake. The hooks rebaited and the lines replaced, Badger took up the oars and, keeping to the tree-lined shore, rowed downstream toward the dam and the sluicegate, where the trammel net lay. If all else failed, the net, well hidden in the weeds, would certainly fill the basket in the bottom of his boat with tench and roach and perch, which would do as well among the poor as pike. And there was just time to clear it out before the storm broke. Already the rain was coming harder, and he was glad for the mackintosh.

In a few moments, he had reached the edge of the shallower, weed-filled stretch where the trammel net was staked. He shipped the oars, stood up in the boat, and took up the twelve-foot wooden pole that he used to propel the rowboat through the weeds. When he reached the net, which was held up by large flat corks, he laid the pole aside and began to haul it in.

But the net was extraordinarily heavy in his hands, either with the weight of a tremendous lot of fish, or having snagged something under the surface of the water, so that the more he pulled, the more difficult pulling became. Finally, he let it go and began to pole along the length of it, looking (as he now thought) for the snag and thinking that he should have to light the bull's-eye lantern he had brought along with him, to see how to work the net free, if he could without tearing it. And if he could not, he should have to come back tomorrow night, when the weather was more kindly.

A few yards along, he saw where the net was sagging, weighted by something beneath the water. Cursing under his breath, Badger took the net in both his hands and pulled up on it with great effort. At that moment, a jagged flash of lightning lit the sky, and he saw that the net was not snagged on something, but that something large and inert was caught *in* it—and not a fish, either, for the net was designed to hold fish alive and wriggling. It might be a submerged tree branch, except that the foresters kept the Park trees so neatly groomed that this did not seem likely. Bent double, breathing hard, Badger hauled, and stopped, and peered down into the water. And then hauled again, harder and faster and with a mounting panic, as he realized that the large, inert thing that was caught and held in the net was a human body.

There was another flash of lightning and a thudding, rolling rumble of thunder. As the horrible thing rose toward him out of the depths, the dead flesh gleaming whitely in the dark water like the bloated belly of a dead carp, the mass of long, loose reddish hair floating like trailing weed, Badger saw to his horror that it was a woman, and that she had not died by drowning. Her throat had been slashed from ear to ear, and the pike had been at her face.

At that moment, the heavens opened and the rain came crashing down.

CHAPTER THIRTY

"That's the way we all begin," said Tom Platt. "The boys they make believe all the time till they've cheated 'emselves into bein' men, an' so till they die—pretendin' and pretendin'."

Captains Courageous
Rudyard Kipling

After dinner upstairs was finished, Ned had helped Alfred load the last dishes on the carts and push them from the dining room back to the kitchen, a distance that seemed like a dozen miles. When people built such bloody great houses, they obviously didn't have the efficiency of their service in mind or the labor of their servants, and they couldn't much care about hot food, either. When Alfred said that the kitchen was so far away because aristocrats hated the smell of food cooking almost as much as the look of a bare working hand, Ned could only laugh and be at least temporarily glad that he was neither aristocrat nor servant.

In fact, Ned was something in between, for although his father was descended from the Irish aristocracy, the connection couldn't be claimed. Ned had discovered that his father—his real name was Thomas Chapman, not Thomas

Lawrence—was not married to his mother, Sarah Junner, whom he had met when she became a servant in the Chapman household. For Sarah's sake, Thomas had abandoned his wife and four young daughters in Ireland, removing himself, his mistress, and their sons to Wales, then to France, and finally to Oxford. There, Thomas and Sarah took the surname Lawrence and held themselves out as man and wife, concealing the illegitimacy of their five sons. Ned might be privately comforted by his aristocratic ancestry, but his birth disbarred him from assuming his rightful place as a gentleman. It was an uneasy knowledge that this current bit of work brought to the forefront of his mind.

Alfred had duty in the main hallway upstairs, where he would stay at his station until time to begin his locking-up rounds at midnight. He paused beside Ned in the hallway and bent close to his ear to say, with a passionate urgency, "Remember, lad, I'm hoping for some news of Kitty."

This remark took Ned aback briefly, until he remembered that he had told Alfred he would be meeting Bulls-eye that night—a suggestion that had been scotched by Lord Sheridan. He would have to come up with some story or another to satisfy Alfred. But short of a plan for the theft or word from the absent Kitty, he didn't know what that would be.

The other servants went off to their beds as soon as their evening work was done, but Ned was rather at loose ends. He could not go to bed in the room he shared with Alfred, since the footman thought he was meeting Bulls-eye in Woodstock; if Alfred should stop by his room and find Ned there, the truth would come to light. For the same reason, Ned did not dare to stay in the servants' hall, where coals still burned in the fireplace, or anywhere else Alfred might conceivably appear. On another night, he would have gone outdoors for a walk, but thunder was growling and lightning flashing, and a storm had been in progress for some time.

So Ned took himself off to the lamp-and-candle room, where the brass candlesticks were cleaned, the lamp chimneys polished, and all the lighting supplies and spare lamps stored. He shut and locked the door, lit several candles for good light, took a small book out of his jacket pocket, and sat on the floor with his back to the wall to finish reading Mr. Kipling's *Captains Courageous,* which he had brought with him from home.

Engrossed, he finished the book in an hour. He stood up and stretched, feeling restlessly that perhaps he was being a bit too cautious. After all, Alfred was on duty in the great hall upstairs, and it wasn't very likely that he would appear downstairs, was it? He could put the time to better use by exploring the labyrinth of hallways and corridors below-stairs. A real spy, he reminded himself, would undoubtedly use the opportunity to look around, reconnoiter, get the lay of the land. Anyway, he was hungry. And if memory served him correctly, he had seen one of the kitchen maids put a loaf of bread and some cheese into the corner cupboard.

So he took one of the candles and set off cautiously along the deserted back passage, making his way gingerly through the shadows cast by the flickering candle, feeling more and more like a spy. In the cavernous kitchen, the fire in the great iron range was banked for the night and the pans and dishes laid out in readiness for cooking breakfast. It took only a moment to ascertain that, indeed, the loaf and cheese were still in the corner cupboard and to cut off a sizable hunk of each, which he stowed in his jacket pocket.

Then he went down the corridor, past the empty servants' hall and the locked butler's pantry. Ahead of him, on the wall to his right, a variety of hats and umbrellas and

jumpers hung from pegs, and beyond, there was an outer
door. On the left, he noticed the large panel of electric bells
labeled with the names of upstairs bedrooms—the Green
Room, the Blue Room, the Yellow Room, all on the second
floor, east wing—and on the wall beside the bell panel, a
large, carefully drawn floor plan of the bedrooms and a roster listing the names of the guests in residence. He stopped
to scrutinize the floor plan. Mr. Churchill, he saw with some
interest, was in the Green Room, while Lord and Lady
Sheridan were in the Blue Room. A real spy, he thought,
would memorize the drawing, fixing all the points of interest in his mind so that when he had to creep about the house
at night without a light, he would not be lost.

Ned was still studying the floor plan when the outer door
opened and an old man stepped through, shaking himself
like a dog. The shoulders of his canvas jacket were wet, his
leather hat dripped rain, and his boots were muddy. His face
was pock-marked and leathery, and the red kerchief tied
loosely around his neck gave him the look of a gypsy.

"I'm here fer Alfred," he said in a low voice. "I been sent
to 'liver a message to 'im."

The skin on the back of Ned's neck prickled. Without a
second's hesitation, he said, "You've found him." He leaned
forward. "Bulls-eye sent you?"

The man took a step backward and eyed him up and down.
"Bulls-eye sez Alfred's a footman," he said with a genial snort.
He rubbed his knuckles, chuckling. "Ye're nor big 'nough t'
be a footman. Nor old 'nough, neither. Ye're jes' a boy."

Ned pulled himself up and put on a rakish grin, enjoying
the pretense. "P'rhaps the Duchess thinks I have other tal-
ents." He thrust his chin forward and, in a tone of threatening bravado, growled, "Bulls-eye won't be pleased if you

don't hand that message over. Want me to tell him that you kept me waiting?"

"Ye're a rough 'un, ye are, lad," the man said sarcastically, "'specially fer such a young chap, and not a very big 'un, neither." He sighed heavily, as if he were conscious of being terribly put upon. "Howbeit, it's here in me pocket, so I 'spose ye should have it, if ye're determined t' be Alfred. Save me the trouble o' looking fer 'im." He fished in the pocket of his jacket and took out a folded piece of paper. Still holding it in his hand, he tilted his head with an inquiring look. "Well?"

"If you didn't get your shillings from Bulls-eye, you're not going to get them from me," Ned retorted smartly. Then he grinned. "But if you'd like some bread and cheese to warm your belly on your way back to the Black Prince, you're in luck. It just happens I've got some here." He pulled the bread and cheese out of his pocket.

The man eyed the food. "Well, I reckon that'll serve," he said in a resigned tone. "But it do look dry. 'Ow 'bout a bot'le o' beer t' wash it down?

"Beer." Ned laughed in an ugly way. "Not bloody likely, old man."

"Ah, well," the man said regretfully. The paper and the bread and cheese changed hands, and the man touched his cap. "G'night, Alfred," he said with a broad wink, and went back out into the darkness.

Ned regarded the note. Pretending to be Alfred was one thing. But now what should he do? Take the note to Alfred, or—

He would read it first. He opened the note and held it up to the candle. It was rudely printed in pencil on unlined paper, and unsigned.

Alfred,

For word about Kitty and to hear the plan, come to Rosamund's Well. Midnight, no later.

Rosamund's Well was just across the lake from Blenheim Palace. Ned knew what it was and where it was, of course, for he had been there, with the other tourists. He could follow Alfred there, and hide in the bushes and listen to their conversation, or . . .

He stopped. Or he could go there himself, *instead of* Alfred. He could tell Bulls-eye that Alfred had been taken desperately ill, and had sent him in his place. He could pretend that he was anxious to join the gang and help with the robbery they were planning. That would put him in a position to learn much more than—

He stopped again. But Lord Sheridan had told him he couldn't meet Bulls-eye, and he hated to violate his lordship's direct order. He frowned, going back over the words in his mind. No, that wasn't what his lordship had said, exactly. He had forbidden Ned to go into Woodstock to the Black Prince, for he considered that too dangerous. Ned could understand that line of reasoning; Woodstock was rather like enemy territory. But Rosamund's Well was just on the other side of the lake, in Blenheim Park. Lord Sheridan hadn't forbidden him to go there. He could—

A loud crack of thunder and the sound of rushing rain recalled him to the immediate moment, and Ned frowned. He had no light and no rain gear, and if he went out into the storm, he would be thoroughly sodden in a matter of minutes—not that a real spy would be concerned about such a minor inconvenience, of course, but still, there it was.

And then, with a sudden thought, he looked up. Directly

in front of him, on one of the pegs beside the door, hung a mackintosh and hat. He stared at them for a moment, then he made up his mind. He took down the rain gear, bundled it under his arm, and went back to the lamp-and-candle room. Yes, there was an old-fashioned brass candle-lantern on a shelf, just as he had remembered. He made sure that there was a stub of candle in it, and pocketed matches and an extra candle. Best to be prepared.

Then he went back down the corridor to the room he shared with Ned. He changed from his page's costume into his own clothing, then hesitated, wondering if he should leave a note. He thought he ought to tell somebody where he was going, in the unlikely event that there was some sort of trouble. But he didn't like to tell Alfred, since he was under the impression that Ned had already gone out long ago, to meet Bulls-eye in Woodstock.

After some thought, he took a pencil, turned Bulls-eye's note over, and on the back wrote: *This came for Alfred. I'm going to R's Well to meet Bulls-eye and learn the plan.*

With a school-boy flourish, he signed the note "T.E.L." and put it in his pocket. Then he went back down the hall to the bell-panel and stood for a moment, studying the floor plan of the upstairs halls. Finally, sure that he knew what he was looking for, he opened the door to the service stairs and went to find Lord Sheridan's room.

A little later, having put the note under the door, Ned went back downstairs, put on the mackintosh and hat, and stepped out into the dark and blowing night.

If he had known what awful thing had been dragged up out of the lake and was at that very moment being laid out on the floor in the game larder, he might have thought better of what he was about to do.

CHAPTER THIRTY-ONE

Death cancels everything but truth.

Anonymous

Kate was beginning to wish that she and Beryl had chosen another subject for their book. After an awkward dinner, she and the Duchess had left the men to their port and cigars and gone to the family sitting room, where Consuelo played the piano and sang several pensive German lieder that seemed to reflect her melancholy. After a time, Winston joined them. He seemed distracted, though, as if his attention lay elsewhere, and a little later they bade each other goodnight and went off to their rooms.

Now, sitting at her dressing table, Kate began to brush her hair with a sense of positive relief, glad that the long evening was at last over. She had already found what she'd come to Bleheim for—good background and some strong ideas for her novel—and under other circumstances, she would be getting ready to return to Bishop's Keep, where life was a great deal more enjoyable. But Beryl wouldn't let her leave until the mystery of Gladys's disappearance was solved. And Charles wouldn't leave until he had unraveled the theft plot, if that's what it was, involving the servants.

Kate put down her hairbrush and lifted her heavy hair with her hands, letting it fall loosely again, down her back. She frowned, returning to what Charles had said that afternoon: that there had been a theft at Welbeck Abbey in which two servants, recently employed at Blenheim, were involved, and perhaps even Gladys and Northcote. But there was something else that was nibbling away at her, something odd that she had wondered about briefly and then forgotten. What was it?

It's Bess, Beryl said. *Her question about the crime at Welbeck.*

Ah, yes, Bess's question. And that sudden, wary look that had crossed her face. Why the question? Why the look? Surely, an unusual response to an idle musing.

And the keys, Beryl prompted. *She's not the housekeeper. So why is she carrying keys?*

Why, indeed? In a well-managed household, the house-maids wouldn't be allowed to have keys—that was a prerog-ative that Mrs. Raleigh would guard jealously. And Bess had been hired recently, Kate understood; surely she had not yet achieved enough seniority to be permitted to even use the keys without supervision. That way led to unautho-rized admission to the family and guest bedrooms, like those Kate and Charles occupied.

Kate glanced around the large, beautifully appointed room, which in spite of warmth of the night and the glow-ing splendor of its draperies, carpets, and wall hangings, still felt chilly. She and Charles shared adjoining rooms, the door left open between them, and slept in the same bed—breaking an established rule, Kate knew. When spouses were guests at a country house, they usually slept apart, the better to participate in the midnight revels. However, Kate and Charles had each found exactly what they wanted in the other; they preferred to sleep together when they were visiting, just as they slept together when they were at home, and Kate could not imagine it otherwise.

But why would Bess have keys to these rooms? Beryl asked impatiently. *Unless—*

There was a light tap at the hallway door and Charles came in. Pausing to drop a kiss on Kate's hair, he went to stand at the window, pulling the rose-colored damask draperies aside so that he could look out at the darkened landscape. A noisy thunderstorm had passed over an hour or so before, with flashes of lightning, claps of ferocious thunder, and a brief, gusty downpour. The storm had moved off to the east, but an occasional lightning flash still lit the night sky.

"That rain was fairly heavy," Charles said thoughtfully. "I'm glad I was able to photograph the heel print and collect the blood sample at Rosamund's Well. The evidence, if that's what it was, may have disappeared by now." He sighed and closed the draperies. "Of course, it might merely be evidence of a poacher's kill. Winston says there's plenty of that. And at this point, there's no way of knowing."

Kate turned from the mirror. She and Charles had not had a chance to talk privately since their conversation after tea, and there were things she needed to know. "You were going to have a look at Gladys Deacon's diary, Charles, and in the housemaid's trunk. What did you find?"

Charles turned back to the room. "The diary was a loss, Kate. Every page was completely blank. I suppose Miss Deacon had nothing of any importance to say." He grinned wryly. "Or perhaps she didn't want to write something down for fear it might be read and she would be held to account for it."

Kate sighed, feeling a sharp sense of disappointment. "I'm sorry. I was hoping you might find something that would give us some clue to her disappearance."

"I was disappointed, as well," Charles replied. "But I found that pouch of stones in her drawer, Kate. They're what's left of the Marlborough Gemstones, all right, without a doubt. I showed them to Winston a few minutes ago, and he identified them. Gladys Deacon must be the woman who talked to Buttersworth at the Ashmolean."

The Marlborough Gemstones? Kate got up from her dressing table and went to stand close to Charles, putting her arms around his waist and resting her cheek against his chest. "It seems so puzzling, Charles. So . . . well, almost silly, like a schoolgirl prank. What in the world could she have hoped to accomplish?"

"It is either very silly, or very serious," Charles said gravely. He lifted his hand to brush a lock of hair off her forehead. "Let's hope that the foolish girl has not got herself mixed up with the gang of thieves that seems to be operating here—and elsewhere, as well."

"You've confirmed that, then?" Charles's arms were around her and Kate leaned against him, feeling his familiar warmth, smelling the fragrance of pipe tobacco on his robe.

"Yes. Winston and I had a talk with Ned just before dinner. The lad's already made a good start. He's talked to the footman and learned that there is definitely a plan afoot. He's also found out the name of the contact at a Woodstock pub."

Kate tilted her head, looking up into Charles's face. "My gracious," she said, surprised. "That was fast work."

"Ned is an unusual young man," Charles replied wryly, "although he may be inclined to think rather too well of himself." He paused. "But it looks as if Alfred may have been excommunicated by the gang—perhaps because he became romantically involved with the housemaid who seems to have been his partner. Kitty, I mean. Of course," he added, "I'm only speculating. But there's that love note you found, and Ned reported that Alfred was very concerned about her. I heard as much myself, when I talked to him."

"But no clue to what's become of Kitty?" Kate asked urgently. "Did you find anything in her trunk that might explain her absence?"

Charles kissed her forehead and went to poke up the fire. "No explanation for her absence," he said, pulling up a chair. "But I found a newspaper clipping and a photograph that give me the idea that she might have come by some rather dangerous information, and tried to profit by it."

"Dangerous information?" Kate asked.

"I believe that what's going on here is only one part of a larger criminal enterprise, Kate." Charles sat down in the chair and put his feet on the fender. "Kitty may have discovered the identity of one of the ringleaders and tried to use it to extort money from the gang."

Extort money! Beryl exclaimed excitedly. *Now, there's an idea, Kate. What if—*

"More speculation, I admit," Charles said. "But if that's what happened, they may have decided that she knew too much and—"

"And disposed of her," Kate said aloud, finishing the sentence for him.

"Perhaps," Charles said. "I hate to think that's what might have happened, but it's a possibility."

Kate pulled her gown tighter around her. The whole thing was beginning to sound like one of Beryl's penny dreadfuls, the kind they used to write years before, filled with criminal intrigues and skulduggery.

"And Winston has come up with something that seems to support this line of reasoning," Charles went on. "He asked Stevens to show him the wage book, so he could see who's been hired in the past several weeks—since Alfred and Kitty arrived."

"And?" Kate pushed the other chair closer to the fire and sat down, pulling her bare feet under her. "What did he learn?"

Charles chuckled. "That servants come and go here with an amazing rapidity. In the last few weeks, they seem to have hired two new scullery maids, a laundry maid, a gardener, and a porter's assistant, as well as Ned Lawrence, of course. More to the point, the housekeeper hired a maid several weeks ago, from the same agency that sent Kitty and Alfred. And what's even more curious, when Winston took a look at the character references supplied by the applicants, he saw that all three had been written in the same hand, even though they were signed by different people."

Kate frowned. "In the same hand? I should have thought that the housekeeper or the butler would have caught that." It was widely known that many character references were forged, which was an important reason to hire only servants who came recommended by friends—although, of course, that was not always possible. Friends were not usually willing to part with servants they liked, if only because they didn't want their family secrets being carried off to another household. Even a trusted servant was likely to gossip.

"I gather," Charles said dryly, "that the situation below-stairs is chaotic. Mrs. Raleigh does not appear to be up to the task of managing the house, and Stevens is getting rather past it, too—at least, that's what Winston thinks. There's quite a rapid changeover in staff here."

"All of which," Kate said pensively, "would make it easier to arrange a burglary, I suppose—especially at a time when the house is full of visiting servants." She looked at Charles. "This third person, the one who comes from the same agency as Alfred and Kitty. Who is it?"

"Her name is Bess," Charles replied. "She's a housemaid. I'm planning to talk to her first thing tomorrow."

"Bess!" Kate said, sitting bolt upright, astonished. "Why, Charles, she's the maid who is looking after Miss Deacon! The one who told me about the missing trousers and jacket!"

The maid with the keys, Beryl said darkly. *The one who turned wary at the mention of a jewel theft at Welbeck Abbey.*

Charles's eyebrows went up. "You've talked to her, then," he said mildly. "What was your impression of her?"

Kate hesitated, analyzing exactly what she had felt. "That she's intelligent and observant. I think," she added, "that she may already have made free with Mrs. Raleigh's keys. She jingled as she walked."

"Jingled!" Charles chuckled. "How like you, Kate, to notice the jingle of keys."

Kate made a rueful face. "Perhaps. But I'm afraid I rather liked Bess, Charles. She seemed like the sort of person who could be given a great deal of responsibility, and she'd handle it very well."

"I imagine that she's all of those things," Charles said dryly. "She's probably been brought in to sort out the problems created by Kitty's absence." He frowned. "No, that can't be accurate; the timing is wrong. As I understand it, Kitty disappeared only last Friday night, while Bess has been here for longer than that. I wonder if—" He broke off, frowning. "There are too many tangled threads here, Kate."

"All we need is one," Kate said rather incoherently, thinking of the golden thread that Eleanor had followed that led her to the heart of the labyrinth. "If only—"

She was interrupted by a loud, excited rapping at the door, and Winston's booming voice, echoing in the corridor. "Sheridan! Sheridan, get up! You're needed, immediately."

With a muttered "What now?" Charles rose and went to the door. Kate heard a low-voiced exchange in the hallway and got up to see for herself what was going on.

As she reached the door, Charles came back into the room, a grave expression on his face. "I must go downstairs," he said. He put his hand to her cheek, then kissed her gently. "Your friend Badger has fished a body out of the lake, I'm sorry to say. A woman's body. She's been put in the game larder."

An image of Gladys Deacon, laughing and gay, rose unbidden into Kate's mind, and she put her hand to her mouth. "Charles! It's not—"

"The body has not yet been identified," Charles said quietly. "That's the next step, Kate. Now, go to bed."

Go to bed! Beryl exclaimed.

"But I'm coming with you," Kate protested. "I want to see her. I want—"

"No, you don't." Charles's voice was firm. "The fish have been at her, Winston says, and it's an ugly sight. You're to go to bed, Kate, and stay there. I'll tell you whatever I am able to learn—later."

Then he was gone. Kate went back to her chair, staring at the fire and thinking resentfully that sometimes it was very hard to be a woman.

And then she thought of the dead woman—drowned?—
who had been taken up out of the lake, and her resentment
dissolved into something else. Sadness, regret, pain . . . and
the thought of death, the end of all things.

Death, that cancels everything but truth.

CHAPTER THIRTY-TWO

Not a flower, not a flower sweet,
On my black coffin let there be strown;
Not a friend, not a friend greet
My poor corpse, where my bones shall be thrown.

Twelfth Night
William Shakespeare

The woman's body was laid out in the game larder, a small, stone-floored, stone-walled room off Blenheim's East Court, with wide slate shelves, several long rows of ceiling hooks for hanging game, and a huge zinc-lined ice box. The rain-washed air blew in through the pierced metal of fly-proof windows, which were designed to keep the room cool. There were no gas or electric lights in this part of the palace, and Stevens—in pajamas, robe, and slippers, as was Winston—had brought in a paraffin lamp.

"I trust your lordship will pardon me for sending Badger home," he said apologetically. "The poor man was wet through, and over-warm with the exertion of getting the body here. He trundled it up from the boathouse in a barrow."

"It's just as well," Charles said. "I'll speak with him to-morrow."

"Said he found her in a net down by the dam," Winston growled. "Didn't want to explain what he was doing out on the lake at this time of night, and in a storm, too. Poaching, no doubt."

"Don't be too harsh with him, Winston," Charles said. "Whatever he was up to, he's done us a great service. And a service to the poor soul he found." He knelt down beside the body, which lay flat on the cold stone floor. "Hold the lamp higher, please, Stevens."

"Yes, m'lord," the butler muttered. He did as he was bid, but turned his face away from the sight, and the lamp trembled in his hand.

Charles did not blame him. The woman had been murdered; that violent truth was told by the gaping slash across her jugular. But that and her sex—her hair was long and red-gold, she was heavy-breasted and dressed in a skirt and blouse—were the only truths immediately apparent. Her face was unspeakable, the features almost completely obliterated, and her hands had been chewed to the wrists.

"Pike," Winston growled. "Vicious things, teeth like bloody sawblades. They'll eat anything, alive or dead." He made a gagging sound, and he too turned away. "But it's not— I don't believe that's Gladys Deacon, Charles."

"I agree," Charles said gravely. "She has not the same figure. And the clothing is that of a servant." He glanced up at Stevens, whose face was still averted. "Stevens, were you acquainted with Kitty?"

"Saw her, of course, m'lord," Stevens said in a strangled voice. "When she was hired, and several times about the house. But I couldn't—" He swallowed, tried to speak, swallowed again. "I couldn't tell you if that . . . that *thing* is her."

"Who can?" Winston asked.

Wearily, Charles stood up. "Stevens," he said, "please be so good as to fetch Alfred." He paused. "But don't tell him why. I would prefer that he not know what to expect. And when you have brought him, you may go back to bed." He smiled a little. "I should recommend a large brandy."

"Yes, m'lord," Stevens said gratefully. He cast a last glance at the corpse that lay on the floor. "Alfred's doing the locking-up. It may take a while to find him."

But Stevens must have located the footman quickly, for he was back within minutes. "Here's Alfred, m'lord," he said thinly, and departed.

Alfred stepped through the door. He was still in full livery, and his costume—powdered hair, maroon jacket, white breeches, white stockings—looked oddly incongruous in the cold, stone-walled room. He was, Charles thought, very young.

"You wanted me, m'lord?" Alfred asked with a deferential courtesy. "What can I—" And then he saw what lay on the floor, and stopped. "Sweet Jesus," he whispered. He lifted his eyes, suddenly wild and staring, to Charles's face. "It isn't!" he cried, his voice going taut and shrill. "It's not her!"

"How do you know?" Charles asked gently. And then, when all that came out of Alfred was a kind of dying whimper, added, "Don't you think you owe it to Kitty to be sure?"

Alfred was shaking so hard that his teeth seemed to rattle in his head. "I . . . I can't," he wailed. "That thing . . . it don't look like her!"

Charles stepped forward and put his hand on the young man's shoulder, steadying him. "You were intimate with her," he said. "Do you recall whether she bore any marks on her body? Any moles? Birthmarks?"

Alfred had thrown his arm across his face, as a man does when he cannot bear to look on something terrible, something inhuman. He was sobbing now, the sobs coming from deep within him.

"Any moles, Alfred?" Charles persisted, more authoritatively. "Any birthmarks?"

Alfred choked. "On her . . . her left sh-shoulder," he managed. "A . . . a brown mark."

Charles knelt down again and pulled the woman's wet dress from her shoulder, far enough to see a dark brown birthmark about the size of a sixpence. He rearranged the dress, stood again, and spoke to Winston. "Kitty," he said, although he had not doubted it.

Alfred's sobs suddenly ceased, with a harsh, half-strangled sound. "She . . . she was murdered, wa'n't she?" he whispered. His voice was thin and reedy, the voice of a lost child. "Somebody slit her throat?"

"Yes," Charles said gravely, watching the emotions chase one another across the young man's face: disbelief, grief, rage, disbelief again. Such was death, and encounters with death. "Do you know who did it?"

The long silence was filled only with the audible rasp of Alfred's breathing. "No," he said at last. "O'course not. How should I know?"

Charles studied the pale face. "Perhaps you did it yourself," he remarked in a neutral tone.

Alfred's eyes flew wide open in unfeigned shock. "Me!"

he cried. "Me? No, never! I *loved* her! We was . . . we was going to Brighton and get married, we was!"

"That's what you *say*," Charles replied, more harshly now. "But perhaps Kitty wasn't as anxious to marry you as you to marry her. Perhaps the two of you fell into a lover's quarrel." He held up his hand, stemming Alfred's violent objection. "It's happened before, many times. A woman rejects her suitor, he turns on her, and—"

"Oh, never!" Alfred said brokenly. "Oh, I'd never do anything like that." He was sobbing again, his shoulders shaking. "Whatever else I've done, I'm no killer. And not Kitty. Never Kitty, I swear!"

"But someone did it," Charles said. "If not you, then who?"

"P'rhaps she had another lover," Winston put in helpfully. "One of the other servants. Or someone in Woodstock. A rival, Alfred."

"No!" Alfred howled. He dropped to his knees, raising his clenched fists as if in torment. "Kitty didn't have nobody else but me! We was going to be married, I tell you! We—"

"Well, then," Charles said, more soothingly, "perhaps it wasn't another servant. Perhaps it was someone who knew why she was here at Blenheim."

"Why the *two* of you were here," Winston added.

There was a sudden silence. "Why . . . why we was here?" Alfred managed at last. His glance, apprehensive, darted to Winston, then back to Charles. He looked cornered.

"Yes," Charles said. "Someone else who was in on the robbery scheme. Bulls-eye, perhaps. Could Bulls-eye have killed her?"

Alfred got clumsily to his feet. "Bulls-eye? How d'ye know about . . ." He stopped, sucking in his breath. His lips had turned blue and he was shivering violently. He wrapped his arms around himself in an effort to stop shaking. "I don't know what you're talking about. I don't know anybody named Bulls-eye."

"Of course you do, Alfred," Charles said, unmoved. "Bulls-eye, at the Black Prince. He knew that you and Kitty were here at Blenheim, and why, and how it was all to be done." He paused, adding thoughtfully, "Perhaps Bulls-eye was Kitty's lover. Perhaps—"

"No!" Alfred cried. "Bulls-eye don't care about Kitty, nor me, nor anybody. All he cares about is getting the job done." He stopped, swallowing, seeming to realize that he had confirmed what he had tried to deny. "D'you know Bulls-eye, then?"

"I'm afraid I haven't had that pleasure, but Mr. Churchill has," Charles replied. "We know who he is, and where he is, and what he plans. And I think it's possible that he killed Kitty, especially if he felt that she had become a danger to him, or a threat." Alfred was biting his lip and Charles paused, letting that sentence sink in, before he added: "Did she say anything to you that might suggest that she knew the identity of the gang's leader?"

Alfred was bewildered. "The . . . leader? She knew—?" He stopped, shaking his head back and forth, numbly. "How could she know? Nobody knows. How could—?"

"She didn't mention a photograph to you, then?" Charles interrupted. "Or that she planned to have a go at Bulls-eye?"

Alfred was still shaking his head, but the color was beginning to come back into his face. "I don't know anything about a picture. You . . . you think Bulls-eye killed her because she knew too much?"

"I believe it's entirely possible," Charles said. He narrowed his eyes at Alfred. "And I should think, if you truly loved Kitty, that you would want to do something about it."

"Do something?" Alfred cried, as if he were heartbroken. "But what can I do? What can anybody do?" He held out his hands in a gesture of despairing helplessness. "Nobody can bring her back to life!"

"But you can help us bring Bulls-eye to justice," Charles said. "If he killed her, you can see that he goes to the gallows for what he has done."

There was another silence. Winston broke it with a dismissive cough and an amused half-smile. "I doubt that he has the stomach for it, Sheridan. After all, there's some danger."

"Not the stomach?" Alfred said, between his teeth. "You'll see what stomach I have for danger, when it's Kitty we're talking about. You'll see!"

"Then you'll do it?" Charles asked.

Alfred looked down at the corpse on the floor. "I'll do it—for her," he said brokenly. "If it will get him, I'll do it."

"Perhaps we can begin," Charles said, "by finding out what you know of the situation here."

It took only a few moments for Alfred to tell what he knew, which turned out to be not a very great deal. Kitty had been the one who had the contacts with the gang, it seemed. She had recruited Alfred when they were both at Carleton House in Manchester, and she had obtained both their positions at Welbeck Abbey. When they were finished there, she'd got posts for them at Blenheim, working through a London agency. The two of them had been at the palace for a week or so when she told Alfred that a man named Bulls-eye was making the arrangements for the job, which would take place during the Royal visit. Alfred himself had met Bulls-eye only twice, once with Kitty, some weeks ago, and again more recently, at the Black Prince, when he had gone to ask about Kitty.

"I haven't heard anything more from him," he said, "until today, when——" He stopped.

Charles and Winston exchanged glances. "Yes?" Charles prompted. "What happened today?" Alfred was about to say that Ned had appeared, he thought, sent by Bulls-eye to make contact with him.

But Alfred appeared to have second thoughts about mentioning Ned. He shook his head. "I haven't heard anything from him at all," he said. "Don't know whether they're still planning the job. Nobody's told me anything."

Winston took a step forward. "Miss Deacon," he said in a low voice. "Is she a part of this?"

"Miss Deacon?" Alfred said, sounding puzzled. "I don't think so—but then, what do I know? As I said, nobody's told me anything." His eyes narrowed. "For aught I know, you two could be part of the gang. You could——"

There was a noise outside, and the door opened. Charles turned and to his surprise saw Kate in the doorway, still wrapped in her dressing gown. She was holding a lamp in one hand, its gleam shadowing half her face.

"I need to see you, Charles," she said urgently.

In one stride, Charles was at the door, blocking her view of what lay on the floor. He pushed her outside and closed the door behind them. "I told you to go to bed, Kate."

"I know," Kate said. She had dressed and flung a shawl around her shoulders, but she was visibly shivering in the damp chill. "I wouldn't have come looking for you, but I found this and thought you ought to see it right away." She thrust a folded paper into his hand. "I went into your bedroom to get another pillow from your bed and noticed this, lying on the floor. Someone must have pushed it under the door. Please—you need to read both sides."

Charles unfolded the paper and read it, as Kate held the lamp. Then he turned it over and read the note signed *T.E.L.* Ned's note, written in his boyish hand.

"Damn," he whispered. "I thought he was too smart to pull a grandstand stunt like this."

"You have to go after him," Kate said. "But please, dear, be careful."

Charles put his hand on her shoulder and kissed her quickly. "I will," he said. "Go back to bed."

"Be careful," Kate said again, and was gone.

CHAPTER THIRTY-THREE

❖━━❖

Human blood is heavy. The man who has shed it cannot run away.

Arabic proverb

The rain had stopped but the damp wind licked at the candle in the lantern so that it flickered tremulously, casting grotesque shadows across the path to Rosamund's Well. The darkness clung to Ned like a damp, suffocating shroud, a crowded darkness, dense with the darker bulk of ancient oaks, the lake filled with liquid ebony, the sky heavy with black, malefic powers. It was a noisy darkness, too, a babble of sly, secretive sounds: the joints of old trees creaking like old bones, the shrubby willows whispering treacherously, the black lake lapping greedily at the blacker shore, the faraway thunder rumbling in grim, deep-throated displeasure.

Ned was a town boy, and although he knew the lanes and hedgerows around Oxford by daylight, he had little experience of the countryside at night, for his mother insisted that all of her boys be at home before darkness fell. Now, it was dark, very dark, frighteningly dark, and Ned wished that he was safely back in Oxford, in his bedroom, surrounded by his books and rubbings and collections of medieval artifacts. But he loathed that wishing part of himself, that anxious, spineless, cowardly part, and he subdued it as well as he could, focusing his attention on the flickering circle of light cast by the candle-lantern, counting his footsteps to distract himself from the shifting shadows and whispering dark. One, two . . . fifty-six, fifty-seven, fifty-eight . . .

And then he was at the Well, and the sweet innocence of the burbling, bubbling spring was added to the cunning cacophony of night sounds. Ned held up the lantern, peering through the blackness around him.

"Is anyone here?" he whispered, and then, having barely heard his own voice, raised it, trying to make it strong, make it casual and cool. "Anyone here?"

There was no reply. No human reply, that is. From the hillside behind the Well came a quavering *Whooo?* Fright loosened Ned's knees, and he suddenly regretted his shabby trickery, regretted his agreement to Lord Sheridan's beguiling proposal, regretted the whole rotten, damned day, from bloody start to bloody finish.

Whooo?

There was a great rush of wings in the darkness, and after a moment of strained listening, Ned gave a short laugh of scornful bravado. *It's only an owl, you bloody coward,* he told himself. Next thing, he'd be blubbering like a baby. He set the candle-lantern on the ground. What sort of idiot was frightened by an owl? But there was no quieting the rapid trip-hammer pounding of his heart, which throbbed so loudly in his ears that it smothered the other night sounds.

But not all. Behind him, a branch snapped and he

whirled. "Who's there?" he demanded, his voice cracking.

"Who d'ye think?" came a low, wary growl out of the blackness.

Apprehensive, Ned sucked in his breath. "Bulls-eye?" he said tentatively.

There was a longish pause. Then the fierce demand: "Who the hell are you?"

Silently, Ned cursed himself. Instead of counting his steps, he should have been inventing an explanation for his appearance at the Well, some sort of fabrication that would win Bulls-eye's confidence and extract the information Lord Sheridan wanted. Aloud, and almost desperately, he said, "I'm . . . Foxy."

Another pause, then a chuckle, its bonhomie even fiercer than the demand. "Foxy, eh? That's a good 'un, that is. Well, then, Foxy—if that's yer name—what's yer game?"

Ned's apprehension grew, for while the voice coming out of the darkness was rather more genial now, it was also rather nearer, although he could not tell from which direction it came.

But he steadied himself and made a breezy reply. "Same as your game, Bulls-eye. Same as the game at Welbeck, and here, with the King's visit." He paused, listening. Hearing nothing, no snap of twig, no rustle of leaf, he went on. "Alfred's on late duty t'night and couldn't get away, so he sent me. Said to tell you he wants to know if there's any news of Kitty. And he wants to know the plan, too—what you said in your note."

"Oh, 'e does, does 'e?"

The voice, even more menacing, was even nearer. A great, sinister hush seemed to have fallen over the woods, although the lake seemed to lap even more greedily, licking up the shore. The candle-lantern flickering at Ned's feet cast wicked, twining shadows, like black ropes.

"That's right," Ned said, with a studied carelessness. "Alfred showed me your note. He said to tell you that he wants to know what—"

And then suddenly there was an arm around his neck, an iron arm in a rough woolen sleeve that smelt of tobacco and garlic and stale beer. The crushing grip flattened his larynx and cut off his air, at the same time that he felt a sharp, painful jab in the small of his back.

"Alfred wants t'know, does Alfred?" the gravelly voice demanded. "Well, I got somethin' I wants t'know, Foxy. Wot's the gull?" The evil mouth came close to Ned's ear. "Wot's the gull, I say!"

Ned's hands came up and he struggled to break the choking hold. But the knife—for it was a knife, he knew—was rammed more sharply into his back, and he forced himself to stop struggling. "Wot's the gull?" the voice said again, harsher now. "Who're you?"

"I . . . can't breathe," Ned managed. It felt as if his neck were being crushed. "Loosen up, will you?"

But Bulls-eye, himself in the grip of a fiery rage, didn't feel like loosening up. He felt like choking the kid until he was blue, if only because he wasn't Alfred. And because Alfred had been so stupid—or perhaps so tricky—as to give up the lay. What did he have up his sleeve, anyway, sending this boy—Foxy, by damn!—to do a grown man's business? Some sort of bloody gull, of course. But what sort of gull? And why? Had Alfred twigged to his scheme? Suspected that he was game for Bulls-eye's knife and sent the boy as bait?

Bait. Bulls-eye tightened his grip around the boy's neck. What lurked out there in the darkness, beyond the fluttering light? He hadn't thought that Alfred was smart enough to come up with a plan, but—

"Where is 'e?" he growled. "Where's Alfred?"

"He's . . . back at the palace," the boy choked out. "Couldn't come. Sent me to—"

"Aw, hell," Bulls-eye said disgustedly. He put his knife between his teeth, yanked the boy's hands behind his back, and pulling a length of stout twine out of his pocket, bound his wrists. Then he shoved him to the ground, hard, face-down, and lashed the long tails of twine around his ankles, pulling ankles to wrists, and taking another twist and a hard knot. Then he rolled his captive to one side and put a heavy foot on him.

"Cough it up," he commanded brusquely. "I want the tale, all of it, by damn. I want it fast. And straight. Lie and I'll kill ye."

Pinned down and lashed, the boy writhed. "I . . . can't talk," he gasped. "Can't . . . breathe."

Bulls-eye shifted his weight, but as he did so, he heard it: the muffled sound of an oar breaking the water. Alfred! It could only be Alfred.

He tensed, listening for the next stroke. Then he felt rather than heard the boy's sudden deep intake of breath, and faster than thought fell forward, clapping his hand over the mouth that had been open, ready to cry out. He whipped off his neckerchief and gagged the boy.

"Warn 'im, will ye?" he snarled. "I'll teach the both o' ye to try yer schoolboy tricks on old Bulls-eye. Aimed t' use ye fer bait, did 'e? Well, ye're bait, now, by damn."

And Bulls-eye stepped back out of the circle of dancing light, leaving the boy on the ground, trussed like a fat fowl for the roasting spit and ready for the knife.

Out on the lake, laying strongly to the oars and not caring who heard, Alfred glanced over his shoulder and saw the shadows writhing about the pin-prick of light. He steered toward them. Ned had to have taken a lantern when he went to meet Bulls-eye. And that must be his lantern, that flickering point of light, and the reeling, struggling shadows could only be Ned and Bulls-eye. Drops of water splashed his face as he dug in with his oars.

The night around him was damp and cool, chill, almost, but although Alfred was lightly clad in breeches and cotton shirt, he did not feel the cold. Within, he was a furnace, seething, burning, ablaze with rage, mad with grief and fury and fear, grief and fury for Kitty and the unspeakable death that Bulls-eye had done to her, and fear for young Ned and what Bulls-eye might do to him. No, *would* do to him, without a doubt, just as he had done to Kitty.

For in spite of Ned's duplicity and double-dealing, in spite of the fact that he had been well and truly deceived by the boy, Alfred felt responsible for him. More, he felt a warm liking for him—and for the first time in his life, fired by fury and fear, Alfred was moved to violence. Half-sobbing, he pulled with a strength past his own on the oars, and in a moment or two, felt the bow of the rowboat grate on the shore.

He leapt out, and heedless of the cold lake lapping around his calves and spoiling his satin breeches and patent leather shoes, dragged the boat onto the shore. Above him, close to Rosamund's Well, the light of Ned's lantern glimmered like a hostage firefly, and on the ground beside it—

He stopped. On the ground beside the lantern lay Ned, unmoving, and while Alfred could not be sure from this distance, he seemed to be bound, hand and foot. Bound? Or already slaughtered, his throat slashed ear to ear, his life bleeding into the dirt. With no more thought than he had given to the cold water, he scrambled up the bank.

"Ned!" he cried. "Ned!"

Reaching the boy, he knelt down and began to fumble at his lashings. No, Ned wasn't dead. He was shaking his head violently, as if to warn Alfred off, his eyes wide-staring and terrified.

Alfred stopped. Of course. Lord Sheridan had said as much, and in his furious rage, he had forgotten. Bulls-eye might try to use Ned as a decoy, to lure—

And then he felt the hand clamped powerfully on his shoulder, the arm pulling him to his feet, the knife-point thrust like a hot pocker into his back. He heard Bulls-eye's harsh, rasping voice.

"Trick me, will ye, Alfred? Dare t' diddle me, do ye? Well, I'll—"

Alfred whirled, breaking Bulls-eye's hold, stepping backward out of reach of the long-bladed knife that glinted wickedly in the light.

"I dare," he cried, with a flinty hatred. "You killed Kitty, you bloody murderer! You slit her throat and dumped her in the lake. And now I'll kill you!"

With a roar, Bulls-eye lunged at him. At the same instant, Alfred's heel caught on the raised edge of the paving around the square pool and he went down flat on his back. Bulls-eye was on top of him in an instant, knife-hand upraised to strike, the blade catching the candlelight with an awful gleam, the same blade that had carved all the life from Kitty. Alfred's thoughts whirled with monstrous, unforgettable images—Kitty's gaping throat and annihilated face, hands gnawed to the wrists—and he felt a cold, sick sweat breaking out on his brow as he waited helplessly for the blade to fall.

And then Bulls-eye was grinning down at him, a gap-toothed evil grin, and lowering the knife.

"Naw," he said. "That's too easy. Too quick. Some things I got t' know first." He stood, gathered Alfred's shirt in his fist, and yanked, pulling Alfred to his feet. "Why'd you blow the bloody lay, Alfred?" His face darkening, he gestured with his head at the trussed boy on the ground. "Who's yer friend 'ere? Why'd ye tell 'im the plan? And 'oo else 've ye told?"

"I . . . I didn't," Alfred gasped, pushed to defend himself. "Didn't tell him nothin'. And he's not my friend." He pulled in his breath on the lie, wishing he could call it back and hoping Ned hadn't heard. He covered it with a blustering question: "Why'd you kill Kitty, Bulls-eye? What'd she do to you?"

"Didn't tell 'im, eh?" Bulls-eye's growl was mocking, and he ignored Alfred's question. "Then 'ow'd 'e come t' know 'bout Welbeck, tell me that, Alfred!" And he gave Alfred a rough shove that sent him stumbling.

Alfred flailed his arms, gaining his balance. Welbeck? How had Ned— He pulled in his breath. But that wasn't the point. He went stubbornly back to his refrain.

"Why'd you kill Kitty, Bulls-eye? What'd she do to you?"

"Shut yer mouth!" Bulls-eye bellowed fiercely. He reached down and pulled a second knife out of his boot, a knife with a shorter but no less vicious blade. He held it up, his voice derisive.

"If ye told 'im nothin' and 'e's no friend o' yers, ye won't mind slittin' the boy's pretty throat, now, will ye, Alfred?" And with a swift, easy grace, he tossed the knife at Alfred, who, without willing it, reached up and caught it in mid flight.

"There, now," Bulls-eye said, his grin wider still, and more evil, as Alfred stared speechlessly at the knife in his hand. "It's yer turn, me fine-feathered friend. Ye want t' share in the winnings, ye'll 'ave t' share in the killings."

"No!" Alfred cried, hearing the raw edge of panic in his own voice. He turned to Ned, whose eyes were open and staring, following the two of them. "I can't. I *won't!*"

"Ye can an' ye will," Bulls-eye growled, advancing on him. A beefy hand seized his arm and shoved him forward, toward the bound boy. "Once 'tis done, ye'll 'ave blood on yer 'ands, Alfred. Ye'll 'ave earned the right t' be one of us." He put his face close to Alfred's. "And if it ain't done, yer dead, and then 'e's dead, and wot's the sense of that, I asks ye? Better 'im dead than you, ain't that right?"

Alfred sucked in his breath, grasping the knife, steadying himself, remembering why he was there. "He's no friend of mine," he said, very low. "I'll kill him, if that's what you want me to do." He raised his voice. "But first you have to tell me why you killed Kitty."

Bulls-eye's laugh was harsh and grating. "That's easy. I killed the drab 'cause she knew Mr. N's real name and threatened t' spill it."

"Mr. N?" Alfred felt his mouth drop open. "Kitty knew *that?*" he asked uncomprehendingly. Mr. N's real name was the most closely kept secret in the Empire. Not even the man's trusted aides knew who he was, and nobody even dared to wonder. That was the only way a gang like this one could work, Kitty had told him. Utter secrecy. And yet she had known, and kept the secret from *him.* For the first time, Alfred wondered about Kitty, and whether they could have—

Bulls-eye laughed again, bitingly. "Stupid dolly-mop. Thought she was goin' t' get 'er a great pot o' money, di'n't she?" He pushed Alfred forward. "Now, get to 't. Sooner it's done, the better fer both of us."

Holding the knife, Alfred knelt beside Ned, whose terrified eyes flashed at him. He raised his hand as if to strike, then lowered it.

"I . . . can't," he said brokenly. "Ned, I never meant to. I just had to hear him say he'd killed her, that's all."

"That's all, is it?" Bulls-eye grabbed a handful of Alfred's hair and yanked his head back, pressing the knife blade into his throat. "Kill 'im," he rasped. "Er ye're a dead man."

"Drop that knife, Bulls-eye!" the voice boomed out of the darkness. "Or *you're* the dead man."

Bulls-eye's head jerked up, but the knife remained poised to slash at Alfred's throat. " 'Oo's that?" he cried. " 'Oo's out there?"

"Drop that knife!" came the repeated command.

"The hell I will," cried Bulls-eye defiantly, pulling Alfred's head back farther, pressing the knife harder against his throat. "I'll kill both o' 'em. I'll—"

The night was shattered by a sharp report, and Bulls-eye pitched heavily backward in a spray of blood.

"Got 'im!" crowed Mr. Churchill exultantly, bounding out of the blackness.

"You weren't suppose to *kill* him," Lord Sheridan said severely.

"Did I?" Mr. Churchill said, in an innocent tone. "Let's see."

With trembling hands, Alfred cut Ned's bonds. "I wouldn't have done it, Ned," he whispered penitently. "I was playing along, to get him to confess to killing Kitty. I knew that Lord Sheridan and Mr. Churchill were out there in the dark somewhere. They had to hear him say he was the one that did it."

To tell the honest-to-God truth, of course, Alfred hadn't known for certain that the two men were out there in the dark. He *hoped* they were, because that's what they'd said, but he hadn't been sure he could trust them.

Ned sat up and pulled the gag out of his mouth. He had to take several gasping breaths before he could say, "I believe you, Alfred. You played it all perfectly." He grinned. "You had *me* quaking, I'll tell you." Up on his feet and rubbing at his wrists, he asked, "Is he dead?"

Mr. Churchill was bending over Bulls-eye's sprawled form. "Very nearly, I'm afraid," he said. "My aim must've been off. It's a little hard to get a clear shot when you can hardly make out the gun-sight in the dark."

Beside him, Lord Sheridan knelt down, lifted up the dying man, and spoke in an urgent tone. "Just one question, Bulls-eye. What about Gladys Deacon? Is she one of yours?"

Bulls-eyes eyelids fluttered. "Deacon?" he muttered thickly. "Deacon?" He managed a crooked grin.

"Wudn't ye like t' know," he said, and died.

CHAPTER THIRTY-FOUR

Friday, 17 July

And yet the motives of women are so inscrutable. . . . Their most trivial action may mean volumes, or their most extraordinary conduct may depend upon a hairpin or a curling tongs.

The Adventure of the Second Stain
Sir Arthur Conan Doyle

"And that's where we are at this point, at least as far as I know."

With those words, Kate finished her long tale—a convoluted chronicle of criminal schemes and espionage that even Beryl Bardwell would envy—and leaned back in the chair beside the fireplace in the Duchess's luxurious private sitting room.

Consuelo had sat unmoving during the whole of Kate's story. Now, she pushed up the sleeves of her blue silk morning dress and poured each of them a second cup of tea. "So our housemaid's body has been found, and the man who killed her is dead," she repeated incredulously. "You said that Winston actually *shot* him?"

"I'm afraid so," Kate said ruefully. "It wasn't meant to happen that way, Charles said, but Winston misjudged, or so he said. The two of them are going to Woodstock to see the constable and the coroner and explain the whole story, from beginning to end. Given the circumstances, they thought it best not to ask the Duke to accompany them. They are counting on Scotland Yard to support their claim that this is part of a larger investigation which should not be pursued locally, thereby forestalling an investigation and curtailing the inquest."

"They're right, I'm sure," Consuelo said, adding sugar to her tea and stirring it. "I hope—oh, I *hope*—that it can be kept out of the newspapers, since it's such a frightful embarrassment. People are likely to think that Blenheim's staff is disorganized and security terribly lax." She sighed heavily. "As I suppose it is. I try very hard, but the servants take advantage, and there seems to be very little I can do to stop it. Or to keep them here, either. Bess left this morning, Mrs. Raleigh said." She sipped her tea and added, in a worried tone, "Marlborough has been informed about the shooting, I suppose."

"I believe so. Charles said he was going to tell him at breakfast, so I assume it's been done."

Charles had returned to their bedroom at a very late hour last night, or more accurately, very early this morning. He'd been tired and cross, and more than a little angry at Winston, who (it seemed) had blundered badly by killing the man—Bulls-eye, his name was. Hoping to take him alive so they could pry information out of him about the gang of thieves, Charles had intended that Winston's gun be used only to capture and control Bulls-eye. But now he was dead, and Kitty was dead, poor thing, and all they had to go on, Charles said, was the blurred photograph he had found in Kitty's trunk, with *Jermyn Street* written on the back. And when he and Winston had gone to apprehend Bess, they found that she had packed a bag and fled, although it wasn't clear how she had known that the conspiracy had been found out. So even though they seemed to have checked the plan to stage a robbery at Blenheim Palace while the Royals were visiting, the theft ring itself—and its criminal ring-leaders—remained untouched.

Consuelo sighed again, even more heavily. "I don't suppose it will ease Marlborough's mind much. Oh, he'll be glad to know that the man who killed that poor girl has been taken care of, and he'll be grateful that Charles and Winston have ensured a safe visit for the King and Queen."

Kate raised her eyebrows. Charles hadn't been quite so confident about the Royal visit. The fact that Bulls-eye had been killed did not guarantee, he had told her, that the theft would be called off. She said nothing, however, not wanting to trouble the Duchess about something she could do nothing about.

"But none of this answers the question that weighs most on Marlborough's mind," Consuelo continued sadly.

"I suppose you're thinking of Gladys?" Kate said warily. She had not told Consuelo that Miss Deacon's visit to Welbeck Abbey at the time of the theft there had made her a suspect, or that Charles viewed Bulls-eye's final words as a refusal to exonerate her from suspicion. Again, she had not wanted to trouble the Duchess, when there seemed to be no ready solution to the mystery of Gladys's inexplicable disappearance.

"Yes, of Gladys," Consuelo said, putting down her cup with a weary air. "Marlborough is terribly in love with her, you know. Irretrievably so, I'm afraid. It's wrecked our marriage beyond all hope of repair. If it were possible, I would gladly seek a divorce, but since it isn't, separation seems the only answer, although I suppose I shall have to wait until the boys have been sent to school."

"It's probably for the best," Kate said regretfully. The marriage—based not on love or even a friendly affection, but on simple greed—had been so obviously a mistake from the very beginning. To find any happiness in herself, to discover her real strengths and powers, Consuelo would have to abandon it and begin a life of her own. "I believe," she added, "that you will find it in yourself to be glad, when you have moved past the most painful parts and can see a brighter future."

"Do you?" Consuelo asked, arching her dark brows. "To say that, Kate, I think you must understand me better than I understand myself."

Kate summoned some of her own hard-won wisdom. "We can't always know who we are, especially when things are darkest."

"Yes, I suppose so." Consuelo looked away, out the window. "I feel I know Gladys rather better, Kate, and I have changed my mind, just in the past day or so. I thought she was only a careless, playful child. Or perhaps it was that I only wanted to think this, that I was deceiving myself so that I wouldn't have to deal with the truth and its consequences. But now I believe—"

She stopped as if to steady herself and gather her strength, as if she had come to a crucial turning point and needed to acknowledge its importance. She turned to Kate, her large dark eyes full of pain, her lips trembling. But her voice held firm and her words were emphatic as she said: "Now, I believe that Gladys does what she does deliberately and with malice, to betray those who care for her. I don't understand her design or her motives, but I know that it's so.

Perhaps she tells herself that she's only pulling a prank, but much of what she does is meant to embarrass, or hurt, or even wound deeply."

"Like that business with the gemstones?" Kate asked quietly.

"Yes, exactly." Consuelo frowned. "But I still don't understand her object—for taking them to the Ashmolean Museum, I mean. She knew they belonged to Marlborough, and that they were important to him. Did she actually intend to sell them? Or perhaps she meant simply to embarrass me, by pretending—or implying, at any rate—that she was my employee."

Or, Kate thought, it was as Charles suspected: that Gladys Deacon was a member of the ring of thieves, practicing the same modus operandi that had been successful in other burglaries.

"I wish we could ask her," Kate said aloud. "If only we could know where she is!"

Consuelo put down her teacup. Her lips had thinned and her face had grown paler, but her voice was still steady. "I've been giving this a great deal of thought since we talked yesterday, Kate. I think it's entirely possible that Gladys has simply gone away—that she planned to disappear and stay away for a while."

"But why?" Kate asked, although she thought she knew the answer. When Consuelo replied, it appeared that they had come to the same conclusion.

"To make Marlborough realize how much he cares for her." Her tone was despondent and her mouth curved downward.

Beryl Bardwell was almost jumping up and down with excitement. *Planned to disappear!* she exclaimed. *Of course, Kate! Remember that business about the missing trousers and*

*jacket, and the valise Gladys took from the luggage room? Maybe
she cached the clothing somewhere, at Rosamund's Well, say, and
left a trail of clues.*

Kate considered. Beryl often flew off on wild tangents,
but this certainly seemed plausible. Gladys's gold evening
slipper in the rowboat, the scrap of gold cloth on the bush at
the Well. Clues pointing to something—

Something nefarious, Beryl interrupted in a conspiratorial
tone. *Maybe she wanted to make it appear that she had been abducted, although in that case, you'd think she would've sent some
kind of ransom note.*

"Marlborough's heard nothing at all from her, I suppose," Kate said. She glanced at Consuelo, trying to gauge
how much she knew, or guessed.

"If he has, he hasn't said anything to me—and I think he
would, if only to let me know she hasn't simply deserted
him." Consuelo shook her head despairingly. "I don't love
him, Kate, but I'm sorry to see him in such torment. He's
simply out of his mind with fear for her safety. I think he'd
do anything, pay any amount of money, if only it would
bring her back."

Pay any amount of money? Beryl asked meaningfully. *There
it is, Kate! That's the answer!*

Kate frowned to herself. The answer to what? Really,
sometimes Beryl took things much too far. Aloud, she said,
"If Gladys went away, Consuelo, where would she go?"

Consuelo sat for a long moment, saying nothing. Then,
as if she had suddenly made up her mind, she stood.

"Come, Kate," she said. "I have an idea."

Kate stood, too. "I'll get my jacket and hat." She said.

CHAPTER THIRTY-FIVE

A difference of taste in jokes is a great strain on the affections.

Daniel Deronda
George Eliot

Charles had been up and about since very early that morning. He had gone to the railway depot to send a telegram to Leander Norwood, Chief of the Burglary Division at the Yard. Then he had returned to photograph the two bodies that were now in the game larder at Blenheim and write an affidavit briefly describing the circumstances surrounding the murder of Kitty Drake and the shooting death of Bulls-eye, whose surname was still a mystery—but not quite all of the circumstances. He omitted, for instance, the business about the planned burglary during the Royal visit, feeling that it was more the concern of the Yard than that of the local constabulary. And he did not explain why Bulls-eye, Ned, and Alfred had been at Rosamund's Well, or how it happened that he and Winston had been there, too.

Charles had just finished the affidavit when the telegram arrived from Chief Norwood, saying that he would be arriving by the afternoon train. Charles breathed a sigh of relief, glad to know that the larger investigation would be taken out of his hands.

He took his watch from his pocket and noted the time with satisfaction. The first train should have left Woodstock with the two boys aboard: Ned on the short trip back to Oxford, Alfred to a less certain future in Brighton. There had been no point in detaining Alfred, for there was no proof of his role in previous robberies, and he had earned his release by his valuable service the night before. Ned had vigorously protested his own banishment, arguing that his services might still be required, but Charles had assured him that nothing remained but some rather boring administrative details. It was his objective, of course, to keep both the young men clear of any investigation that might follow. Also, Charles could not be certain that, even at this point, the gang would abandon their plan. He blamed himself for having exposed Ned to far more danger than he had anticipated. If Marlborough could not be persuaded to cancel the house party, a small army of Pinkertons would be wanted to provide even the most minimal security.

Charles slipped the watch back into his pocket. Then, with the telegram and the affidavit, he and Winston drove the Panhard to Woodstock, to the police station, and presented themselves to Constable Grant.

The constable was a man of few words. He read Charles's affidavit, and then read the Chief's telegram, and then put both down on the desk in front of him. "Bodies?" he grunted.

"In the game larder, at the palace," Charles replied.

The constable looked at Winston, who was standing uncomfortably, holding his hat in his hand. "Didn't mean t' kill 'im, eh?" he said, skeptical. "Fired to wound, did ye?"

Winston cleared his throat. "That's right, Constable. But it was very dark, y'see, and he was holding a knife to the footman's throat, and my aim was not as true as it should've been." He cleared his throat again. "It seemed to us—to Lord Sheridan and myself, that is—that since these deaths occurred on the estate of the Duke of Marlborough, it would be better if the investigation were turned over to the Yard, rather than handled as a local matter. We hope you agree."

"And wot would it earn me if I didn't?" the constable replied darkly. "You lot at Blenheim are going t' do wot you please, wotever I say."

Winston reddened. "Now, Constable, that's no way to—"

"Thank you, Constable Grant," Charles said, taking Winston's arm. "You can reach us at the palace if there are any other questions. I'm sure that Chief Norwood will be glad to keep you posted on the progress of the investigation."

The constable growled something unintelligible, and they left. A few minutes later, they pulled up in front of the Fishery Cottage, got out, and went around the back.

An old man looked up from the task of cleaning a large pike on a plank table under a willow tree, a collie dog lying at his feet. Charles introduced himself and Winston and explained that they had come to hear the circumstances of his discovery of the body, and to ask a few general questions.

The man—Badger—put down his knife, wiped his hand on his tunic, lit a cigarette and told his story. He'd been busy all day—on Fisheries business, of course—and hadn't had been able to check the net by the dam. Thinking he should do it before the storm, he rowed directly there and found the body of the woman entangled in the net. With great difficulty, he had hauled the foul thing into the boat, rowed it to shore, and trucked it up to the palace forthwith, where, not wanting to make a stir and commotion, he had quietly knocked up the butler and the two of them determined that the corpse should be stowed in the game larder.

"And quite right, too," Winston said, having been instructed by Charles not to mention the word poaching. "His Grace is grateful for your discretion."

"Thank'ee, sir," Badger said solemnly. "The Duke c'n count on me, sir." He wiped the other hand on his tunic and Winston, taking the hint, took a five-pound note out of his wallet and gave it to the old man.

"One or two other questions, if you don't mind," Charles said quietly, when the note had been folded and safely stowed in Badger's pocket. "I wonder whether you have noticed any unauthorized use of your boats in the past week or so."

"Unauth'rized, ye say?" Badger squinted. "Well, at the last weekend, I found the yellow rowboat adrift, if that's wot ye mean, sir."

"That would've been Saturday or Sunday?" Charles asked. The housemaid had gone missing on Friday night. She might have gone over to Rosamund's Well, where Bulls-eye had slashed her throat and dragged her to the rowboat, and then rowed her out to the middle of the lake.

"Satiddy, sir," Badger said. "Reckoned it was one o' the servants, though they're s'posed t' know better."

Charles nodded. "And any other use?" he asked in a casual tone. "Someone, perhaps, who paid you to row her across the lake—say, on Wednesday night, rather late?"

Badger's eyes opened very wide in an expression of injured innocence. "Paid *me?* Why, m'lord, I—"

"A lady dressed in a gold evening gown and wearing a diamond necklace. Who gave you some of the Duke's cigarettes." Charles hardened his voice. "Come, now, Badger. I'll have the truth."

Badger squirmed, coughed, and said, at last, in a sulky tone: "Well, since ye know. Yes, she paid me t' row 'er."

Charles heard Winston's quick intake of breath, and shot him a warning glance. To Badger, he said, "When did she first speak to you about it?"

"Monday or Tuesday," Badger said.

Charles considered. So Gladys had made the arrangement for her disappearance well in advance. It had all been part of a scheme, arranged, perhaps, to give everyone—especially the Duke—a scare. "Did she tell you why she was doing such a thing?" he asked.

Badger shook his head. "Only that it was a joke she was playin'," he said glumly.

Some joke, Charles thought. He was only surprised that the Duke had not yet received a ransom note.

CHAPTER THIRTY-SIX

We are only falsehood, duplicity, contradiction; we both conceal and disguise ourselves from ourselves.

Pascal
Pensées, 1670

Gladys Deacon put down her pencil and stared, frowning, at her third attempt at writing a note. The handwriting sloped crookedly across the page, she had misspelled two of the words, and the bottom of the paper was smeared with something that seemed to be blood but was really only the juice of a ripe strawberry. It certainly looked convincing, but was it? Would Marlborough be taken in by it? Did he care enough to pay the ransom? How *much* did he care?

If you want to see Miss Deecon alive, you'll pay. Five thousand quid, for a start. And not a word to the coppers, or give her up for a goner.

Gladys got up, went to the shelf where she'd put her small supply of food, and took down a loaf of bread, a pot of butter, a slab of cheese, a knife, and an earthenware plate.

She could have purchased anything the Woodstock shops had on offer, of course, or she could have gone to one of the local pubs for a meal. Dressed as she was in trousers and a jacket, her hair pinned up firmly under a cap, she was in no danger of being recognized. But it suited her, while she was staying in this rustic woodsman's cottage at the very edge of the Blenheim estate, to eat like a woodsman: plain, solid, nourishing food, no frills, no fancies. She had found a rabbit snare in a shed—why, she might even set it and trap a rabbit to roast on the spit in the fireplace.

But she wouldn't be staying here long, Gladys reminded herself with a brief smile. Tonight, she'd give a village lad a shilling to deliver the note, and then—

She stopped, frowning. Where should she tell Marlborough to leave the money? And in what form? Coins were too bulky. Bank notes were better—a thousand five-pound notes would easily fit into a valise.

But where should he be instructed to put it? A busy place, where there was a great deal of commotion, and where she could watch from a distance to find out whether he cared enough to pay the money to insure her release from the appalling criminals who had abducted her. But where?

And then she thought of it, and smiled at the amusing irony. Fair Rosamund, the name of the locomotive that pulled the railway train to Kennington. Marlborough could put a satchel containing the bank notes on the train—of course, she'd add that instruction to the note. No doubt he would employ several private inquiry agents to ride the train and pounce on whoever picked it up. If some hapless person were so unfortunate as to look inside the bag, there would be a great commotion and he would be hauled off to jail.

She sighed. Unfortunately, she wouldn't be there to see

all the fuss, for she wouldn't be riding the train. She didn't give a fig for the money, of course; she only cared that Marlborough loved her enough to pay for her release. In the safety of her disguise, she would enjoy watching him put it on the train, and after that, it was no business of hers. After that, she would hide herself away in France for a week or so, selling Botsy's grandmother's diamond necklace to fund her stay, then reappear at Blenheim just as the Royal entourage descended on the palace. Marlborough would tell her how deliriously happy he was that she was safe, and she would tell him what a narrow escape she had had. And it would be immediately clear to everyone, including the King and Queen, exactly what her position was with the Duke.

Gladys's smile grew wider, and she sat down to her simple meal with a genuine enthusiasm. Her position with the Duke, indeed! She had been only fourteen when Marlborough had engaged himself to Consuelo, in October of 1895. She had read the stories in the newspapers—really, the entire world had been full of the news!—and it had so entirely captured her imagination that it came to obsess her. Unable to think of anything else, she had written to her mother,

I suppose you have read about the engagement of the Duke of Marlborough. O dear me if I was only a little older I might catch him yet! But alas I am too young though mature in the arts of woman's witchcraft and what is the use of one without the other? I suppose I will have to give up all chance to ever get Marlborough.

Remembering her childish letter, she laughed aloud, for she had never given up the chance to get Marlborough, and when she understood that his marriage to Consuelo was no bar, she had done exactly as she'd intended: She had *got* him. And she had him still, she told herself triumphantly, for even though Consuelo had given him an heir, she could not give him what he wanted most, love and adoration and—

At the sound of wheels crunching in the gravel outside the door, Gladys felt suddenly alarmed. She pushed her plate aside and stood up. The cottage was abandoned, Consuelo had told her, when they had passed it on one of their drives in the electric motor car; no one had lived here for some years, nor was expected to, since the fields to which it was attached had been sold. So who—

The door opened without a knock and Consuelo came in, followed by Lady Sheridan.

"Hello, Gladys," Consuelo said calmly enough, although the two red spots high on her cheeks betrayed her feeling. "I thought we might find you here." She smiled slightly. "What a charming costume, my dear. Men's clothing suits you, I must say."

"Hel . . . hello, dear Connie," Gladys said, forcing herself to smile. "I . . . I didn't expect—"

She reached for the unfinished ransom note on the table, but she wasn't quite quick enough.

Lady Sheridan had it, read it at a glance, and handed it to the Duchess, who read it and folded it carefully, tucking it into her sleeve. "I think I had best keep this," she said. "I daresay you won't be wanting to use it, after all."

Gladys tossed off a light laugh. "It's just a harmless little joke, you know, dear Connie. Only a prank. You know how I love jokes. Of course, I wouldn't have taken the money. You and Marlborough would have gotten it back, and we'd all have had a good laugh together—"

"No doubt," the Duchess said, holding herself in a regal

posture, looking at Gladys with distaste as if she were an errant child—no, worse, someone for whom she had no use and no liking. "No doubt we would have laughed ourselves into hysterics at this shabby little bit of trickery, Gladys. And when we were quiet and calm again, I'm sure you would have thought of something else to liven things up."

"Oh, yes," Gladys said quickly. "I love Blenheim, you know, but it *is* awfully dull at times."

"I know exactly how you must feel," said the Duchess, her voice full of significance. "That's why I think it's time that you went back to Paris, my dear. Or Rome, if that's your pleasure." She glanced down at the watch pinned to her lapel. "In fact, I believe there's just time to get you to the station so that you can catch the one o'clock train." She looked up at Lady Sheridan. "Don't you agree, Kate?"

Gravely, Lady Sheridan nodded.

"Oh," cried Gladys, "but I have no suits or gowns or—"

"No matter," Consuelo said, smiling gaily. "You can travel as you are—you make quite a handsome young man. I'll have your wardrobe packed and sent to you. It will be there almost as soon as you are."

"But . . . but I want to say goodbye to Marlborough," Gladys cried, knowing that although the Duke might be angry at her for deceiving him, he wouldn't stay angry for long. He would—

"I don't think that's wise," Lady Sheridan said firmly. "You see, there has been quite an upset while you were gone. A housemaid has been found dead, a man has been shot, and a ring of jewel thieves has been discovered." She cleared her throat delicately. "And there is some suggestion, I'm afraid, that you might have been involved in it. The Duchess and I are sure that it's a mistake, but you do see the difficulty, don't you? Poor Lord Northcote's diamond necklace is gone, which makes it seem that you might be one of the thieves."

"Oh, but that's absurd!" Gladys exclaimed. "Totally, entirely absurd!"

"Oh, I'm *sure*," the Duchess replied. "However, it might be a good idea if I returned Lord Northcote's jewels to him. He really is quite concerned."

Gladys flushed. She had not intended to return the necklace, but now it seemed that she had no choice. And no choice but to get on the train, either. As she went to get the necklace, she cast a hard look at Lady Sheridan. *She* was the one who had turned the Duchess against her, and the Duke, too. It was all her fault.

"Here you are," Gladys said, putting the necklace into the Duchess's hands. She gave her a hard look. "This will change things, you know, Consuelo. Between us, I mean. You and me. It will be open warfare now. And in the end, I will get him."

"Of course you will," the Duchess said gently. She smiled, and there was a genuine compassion in her voice. "I am very sorry for you, Gladys. He will not make you happy."

"P'rhaps not," Gladys said, stung. "But there is always Blenheim."

"Indeed," said the Duchess. "There is *always* Blenheim."

AUTHORS' AFTERWORD

*A strange thing happens when you write about people in the
public domain. After a while you feel that you created them and
that nobody else has any rights over them whatsoever. What
you invent and what you remember become the same in your
mind. This might have worried me had I been writing a history
piece, but I wasn't. . . . To an historian this may sound like
heresy, but even the strictest biographies are, by definition, sub-
jective and in the end, we all guess.*

Introduction to *Mrs. Brown: A Screenplay*
Jeremy Brock

Susan Albert writes about two of the people in *Death at
Blenheim Palace*:

When Bill and I first began this book, I knew nothing
about Gladys Deacon, who in 1921 became the thirteenth
Duchess of Marlborough. Sometime in the 1990s, I had
read about the Marlborough marriage in *In a Gilded Cage*, a
chronicle of the lives of five American "dollar duchesses."
This book led me to Consuelo's autobiography, *The Glitter
and the Gold*, which gave me the Duchess's own sad report of
her marriage and her life at Blenheim. I immediately felt

that Bill and I ought to use the story as the centerpiece of a book about Blenheim Palace. It was quite by accident, however, that I stumbled across Gladys Deacon—specifically, Hugo Vickers's *Gladys, Duchess of Marlborough*—and realized that any story about Consuelo and the Duke would also have to include the Duke's mistress.

The Marlborough marriage, engineered by Alva Vanderbilt, was doomed from the moment of the fabled wedding. The shy teen-aged bride was completely unfit for her job as mistress of Blenheim; the aloof, unfriendly groom seems to have cared for nothing but the continuance of the Marlborough line and the rescue of his beloved estate; and neither had any genuine feeling for the other. The unhappy marriage was ended by stages: a legal separation in 1906, a legal divorce in 1921, and a Catholic annulment in 1926.

Given the strictures of British law and the social horrors of divorce, however, the Marlboroughs might have remained married (at least for a longer time), if it had not been for Gladys Deacon. The story that Bill and I tell in this book is essentially true, if bizarre. At fourteen, Gladys declared in a letter to her mother that her heart was set on the Duke of Marlborough. At sixteen, she arranged to meet him at a London dinner party; at eighteen, she was romantically involved with him; and at forty, she married him. Gladys's wedding veil had been a gift from the Emperor Napoleon to Josephine—not, perhaps, an augury of future felicitude. The Duke, when asked about the motorcar he gave his bride as a wedding present, remarked glumly, "We are both awfully poor." Poor or not, Gladys had finally achieved her life's ambitions: She had become Duchess of Marlborough and mistress of Blenheim Palace. She should have been happy.

But she wasn't, of course. Gladys was no more prepared than Consuelo to take on the management of the Blenheim household, and the servants made her life miserable. The local folk had been fond of Consuelo and ignored the new Duchess. The Royals eventually received her, but their tepid acceptance did not result in the social recognition she expected. She suffered a miscarriage and fell into a deep depression, not least because her early attempts at facial reconstruction had ravaged her beauty. Consuelo's sons did not like her, and within two years, she was voicing the same complaint that Consuelo herself had made about Marlborough's rudeness, both in private and in public. Ten years after their marriage, the Duke fell in love with a Canadian actress named Bunny and left Gladys to console herself with her King Charles spaniels, to whom she gave the run of the palace, to the great detriment of the Vanderbilt-financed rugs and furnishings. Not long after, she was turned out of Blenheim, then out of the Marlboroughs' London house. Within four years, the Duke was dead of cancer and Gladys, as her biographer put it, "seemed to the world to have disappeared into smoke." She died in 1977, at the age of ninety-five, alone and friendless. But not entirely penniless: Her possessions were auctioned at Christie's for seven hundred and eighty-four thousand pounds.

Consuelo fared rather better. After her legal separation from Marlborough in 1906, she became active in social work and philanthropy, setting up lodging houses for poor women and working girls, creating an insurance society for women domestic servants, establishing a school to teach mothering skills to women of the London slums. For her interest in children's welfare, the newspapers dubbed her the "Baby Duchess." Initially too shy to speak in public, she asked

Winston to coach her, and became a first-class speech-maker. In 1909, she wrote a long piece on the rights of women, remarking that life does not end with marriage, "as fairy tales would make us believe," and that a woman is robbed of power, strength, and influence when she "adjusts herself to man, to be judged by his individual standard and to conform her whole personality to his ways of thinking."

When the divorce was granted in 1921, Consuelo married her long-time friend, Frenchman Jacques Balsan. Happy in this marriage, she continued her philanthropic interests and returned to Blenheim frequently after Marlborough's death to visit her son, the tenth Duke, and her grandchildren. She died in 1964, at the age of eighty-seven. At her request, she was buried beside her son Igor in Bladon Churchyard, within sight of Blenheim Palace.

Bill Albert writes about the plot of *Death at Blenheim Palace*:

One of the most rewarding things about a writing collaboration is the opportunity to discuss the project with someone who has a vested interest in it. In the environment of the writing industry as it exists these days, such discussions seldom happen between a writer and his readers, his fellow authors, his agent, or even his editor. As collaborators, Susan and I have endless conversations about the writing process, discussing subtle shades of word meaning, quirks in human motivation and personality, and possible directions for developing the plot. To me, our most fascinating discussions involve postmortems on how it was that a particular book turned out as it did.

As you may have guessed, given the complexity of numerous subplots and multiple points of view that we include in these books, story development is not a particularly linear process. The analogy of a jigsaw puzzle may be trite, but it's still a useful way of describing the process. We start with certain key pieces—hard facts about historical characters and the settings associated with them—and then begin to build outward in all directions. For us, research is essentially a search-and-fit process: We search through boxes of pieces (some of which don't even seem to belong to our puzzle), picking up apparently unconnected historical facts and bits of information about people and events, and trying to fit them (often with a little reorientation) into our puzzle.

In *Death at Blenheim Palace,* Susan wanted to use Consuelo Vanderbilt as a main character. Initially, I had my doubts, for the twelfth Duchess was little more to me than a marble bust that I had glimpsed on one of the palace tours. I have long had a great affinity for Blenheim, however. I visited it with my parents when they were living in England in the 1960s, and again in 1985 when I was visiting my brother, who was studying at Oxford. There had been a rather heavy snow that week. I remember trudging down what seemed to be a back street in Woodstock, through the ancient wooden gates in a low stone arch and suddenly being confronted with the "finest view in all England," as Jennie Churchill put it: the lake, the bridge, and the palace beyond, set in a blanket of white. If Susan wanted to include Consuelo in the story, that was fine, as long as I could have Blenheim.

But there were other pieces to our puzzle. Blenheim was always important to Winston Churchill (it was his birthplace), and when we learned that he was in residence at the time of our story, writing his father's biography, we decided that he would play a major role in the plot. In his earlier accounts of his wartime exploits in India and the Sudan, Winston boasted that he had killed a number of men in combat; given these claims, his action at the end of the book does not seem to us out of character—although shooting Bullseye was not something he would want to see in print. (Endings always present us with a special problem: If a historical character were involved in a murder, how did this fact escape history's notice?)

The Ashmolean Museum, in Oxford, offered us another piece of the puzzle. We had long considered the possibility of including T. E. (Ned) Lawrence in one of our books, but were stymied by his youth: He was born in 1888. However, when we read *The Golden Warrior* and learned that Ned was living and attending high school in Oxford at the time of our book, that he had developed a passion for brass rubbing and a keen interest in archaeology, that he enjoyed reading police reports, and that he had a significant relation with the Ashmolean somewhat later in his life, it was obvious that young Lawrence was also going to join the cast. While there is no evidence that he and Winston Churchill met before the Great War, their casual friendship rapidly developed into a firm regard and affection, fired by mutual admiration. There is a marvelous photograph of the two of them, with Gertrude Bell, all three mounted on camels, taken just outside of Cairo at the time when the country of Iraq was being created from three Ottoman provinces. Winston, writing after Lawrence's early death, described him as "a man who held himself ready for a new call." Our knowledge of their later friendship gave a special poignancy to the scenes in which Ned and Winston are together.

We felt we had a powerful setting and a strong cast of characters, but the plot didn't begin to emerge until we put together three unrelated pieces of the puzzle. The first was a brief description (which we encountered in Marian Fowler's *Blenheim: Biography of a Palace*) of the Marlborough Gemstones, collected with great effort by the fourth Duke and flogged for a pittance by the seventh. The second was a charming anecdote I recalled from the BBC-TV production "Treasure Houses of England," which related how the current occupants of a stately home were having a look round the house and came across a statue of two wrestling boys which was used as a doorstop. Upon investigation, the doorstop turned out to be a rare Japanese porcelain that was listed on a household inventory more than three hundred years before— and "lost" thereafter. These two bits spoke volumes about the careless treatment of inherited works of art by certain members of the British upper class. Finally, Susan happened on Ben Mcintyre's biography of master thief Adam Worth, the prototype for Doyle's "Napoleon of Crime," an American who posed as an English gentleman and operated a successful and well-organized crime ring in London shortly before our period, staging jewel thefts, bank holdups, and postal robberies. When we coupled this casual view of inherited wealth with a daring and cunning (and quite secret) antagonist, we knew we had found a key piece that would tie the mystery together—and a character who will undoubtedly play a major role in future mysteries.

REFERENCES

Here are a few books that we found helpful in creating *Death at Blenheim Palace.* If you have comments or questions, you may write to Bill and Susan Albert, PO Box 1616, Bertram, TX 78605, or e-mail us at china@tstar.net. You may also wish to visit our Web site, www.mysterypartners.com, where you will find Reading Group Guides and other resource material.

Blenheim Palace, Norwich: Jarrold Publishing, 1999.

Balsan, Consuelo Vanderbilt. *The Glitter and the Gold,* New York: Harper & Brothers, 1952.

Bond, James. *Around Woodstock in Old Photographs,* Phoenix Mill: Alan Sutton Publishing Ltd., 1991.

Fowler, Marian. *Blenheim: Biography of a Palace,* London: Penguin Books, 1989.

————. *In a Gilded Cage: From Heiress to Duchess,* Toronto: Vintage Books, 1993.

James, Lawrence. *The Golden Warrior: The Life and Legend of Lawrence of Arabia,* London: Weidenfeld & Nicolson, 1990.

MacColl, Gail and Wallace, Carol. *To Marry an English Lord,* New York: Workman Publishing, 1989.

MacGregor, Arthur. *The Ashmolean Museum: A Brief History of the Institution and its Collections,* London: Jonathan Horne Publications, 2001.

Macintyre, Ben. *The Napoleon of Crime: The Life and Times of Adam Worth, Master Thief,* New York: Farrar, Straus & Giroux, 1997.

Morgan, Ted. *Churchill: Young Man in a Hurry 1874–1915,* New York: Simon and Schuster, 1982.

Rowse, A. L. *The Later Churchills,* London: Macmillan & Co. Ltd., 1958.

Shelmerdine, J. M. *Introduction to Woodstock,* Woodstock: The Samson Press, 1951.

Vanderbilt, Arthur T, II. *Fortune's Children: The Fall of the House of Vanderbilt,* New York: William Morrow & Co. Inc, 1989.

Vickers, Hugo. *Gladys: Duchess of Marlborough,* New York: Holt, Rinehart and Wilson, 1979.